RISEN SHADOWS

A FANTASY THRILLER

FAE FILES BOOK SIX

CECILIA DOMINIC

This book is dedicated to my fellow mental health professionals. Over the past few years, we've had to pivot how we practice, help our clients through unheard of distress, and basically all become grief therapists regardless of specialty. We did all this while dealing with our own challenge and sacrificing our own needs. I see you and your sacrifices, and I'm grateful for your support as colleagues and friends.

COPYRIGHT

Risen Shadows
© 2023 Cecilia Dominic

gated by the FBI and is punishable by up to 5 years in prison and a fine of $250,000.

Ebook ISBN: 978-1-945074-72-1

Paperback ISBN: 978-1-945074-74-5

Editorial services provided by Evil Eye Editing

Cover design by Best Page Forward

1

REINE

The dumbest thing I ever did was to make a Fae bargain with my mother.

The second dumbest thing was to make one with myself.

I'm not sure what instinct made me agree to spend my sentence in the asylum in the dark Fae capital of Cruaidh. While I didn't regret agreeing to a self-imposed exile in exchange for the lives of my lover and friends, I almost immediately questioned my judgment as to where. But that's what had gotten me in that situation—bad judgment, even though it was for a good cause.

After the trial, I rose and faced Basil. Two burly guards stood on either side of me. One's angular face reflected stoic regret, the other's, rounder and almost boyish, a kind of cruel glee that reminded me of the joy some Fae took in torturing humans in certain fairy tales.

Fairy tales or part of our history? It was hard to tell anymore. Before I'd left Faerie, I'd thought I knew our history, my history. Now I questioned everything I'd been told, taught, or remembered.

The one who looked like he'd rather be doing anything but that said, "Come along with us, Your Highness. Your transport is ready."

Basil regarded me with sorrow and something else, that thing in his expression I chose not to see. "Good luck, Your Highness. I'll continue to work on your case."

I nodded and said, "Thank you. I trust you'll do your best."

"I always do for you."

He'd come a long way from the mischievous Troubadour to the serious Fae researcher who was part of my Council of Three. Perhaps he'd gone too far in the other direction. Another regret to add to my list. One thing hadn't changed, though... When I glanced back at him, I found him gazing after me with longing and sadness. I suspected he'd find an opportunity to visit me shortly.

The two guards led me toward a doorway at the side of the courtroom, the one that condemned prisoners left through. Before we got there, a male voice said, "A moment, if you please."

The youngest member of the Fae Council, Roshal, approached. I recalled he had been in the palace when I was growing up, but as children of the Crown Princess Maeve, Rhys and I hadn't been encouraged to play with the other Fae kids. Or rather, we had, but only the ones my mother wanted to ally with. We were wielded as weapons, and my heart went out to my younger self. How would my life have been different if I'd learned to make allies earlier?

Maeve doesn't teach her daughters to say no, Ellerin had told me once. It was true, at least when it came to her. And she'd forced me into another difficult yes.

Roshal walked up to me and bowed. His nut-brown hair curled around his ears, and when he rose, his amber eyes had gone dark with grief. "Your Highness, I wanted to express my sympathy." He glared at the two guards, and they moved back, although I was sure they could still hear us. Roshal touched my wrist and said in secret conversation, *"I don't believe for a moment that you are guilty or that you made this plea bargain willingly."*

"Thank you," I responded, *"but I don't know what there is to be done for it at this moment."*

"I'll work with your counsel, but I can only do so behind the scenes. I fear that your mother will soon have an iron grip on us all."

With that, he scurried away.

Maeve had left the courtroom after the fall of the gavel sealed my sentence. Hopefully she wouldn't find out about Roshal's and my interaction, but I also suspected that the gleeful guard's loyalties lay with her. I hoped Roshal hadn't put me in the position to make another difficult bargain.

I turned to the guards and mustered my best royal attitude. "All right, gentlemen, let's go."

The hallway off the courtroom held the chill of centuries of despair, and not even the glowing Fae lights in intervals along the sandstone wall did anything to dispel the thick gloom. The guards brought me down a set of spiral stairs, and instead of turning right to the prison, we went left, which brought us to a courtyard I had never seen. It, too, held a sense of lingering sadness and hopelessness. With a shiver, I surmised this was where the extremely unlucky—or evil—had been executed.

A black coach and four waited for me. The horses' eyes shone with the black light purple of the dark Fae.

The driver climbed down from the perch and removed his flat driver's hat. He bowed minimally at the waist. "Queen Lilith sends her regrets that this is the best she could send at such short notice."

"I'm sure it will be fine."

He held the door open, and I climbed in. The vehicle had plush purple velvet chairs, a small refreshment center that held a few nibbles—mostly fresh fruit, cheese, and bread—and crystal decanters of red wine and water.

The door closed. The click of a lock being engaged from the outside reminded me that although the accommodations might be nice, I was still a prisoner.

The coach vibrated when the driver resumed his seat, and then it lurched forward. I fixed and devoured a snack. I hadn't eaten in I didn't know how long. All my time-hopping made the determination of the last time I'd done normal bodily things difficult to pin down. Like the last time I'd slept.

It clearly had been a while because the jolt of leaving the lands of the light Fae woke me from a slumber I hadn't noticed I'd slipped into. The coach and four didn't slow their pace for their journey through the lands of the gray Fae, which had been created to separate those of the light and dark Fae...and to contain beings that neither wanted to face. I gazed out of the window, but the fog hid everything more than ten feet from the path. Every so often I thought I could see something move, but it could have also been the swirling mists creating the illusion of movement within them.

I'd become so accustomed to the horses' pace that when it sped into an erratic, panicked rhythm, I caught the change immediately.

"What's happening?" I shot the thought to the driver, whose mind swirled with panic.

"Revenants! Hang on tight. I've called for help."

I wanted to ask how and if they would be there soon, but he needed his concentration for keeping the horses on the path. Them bolting off it would spell doom for all of us. The revenants, reincarnated Fae souls, would devour any living creature they encountered until they grew flesh again, and they'd be harder to evade in the deep woods.

I found a handhold and opened the curtains wider. The

shapes' swirling had increased in pace and timing to resemble a silent hurricane. Glowing wisps whipped around the carriage, and I forced myself to breathe, especially when they darted closer and leered in at me. Occasionally a purple flash of light would drive them back, but not for long.

I attempted a repulsion spell, which gave us a few minutes' reprieve, but they closed in again. In spite of supposedly being mindless, ravaging ghost-like creatures, they appeared to be toying with us, and I had the sense that I was about to find out what a good chocolate dessert felt like when I pounced on it.

Would I ever eat chocolate again? The thought made anger explode in my gut. I refused to lose my freedom *and* my life on the same day, and I rubbed my hands together to prepare a banishment spell. Let them languish in one of the empty orthogonal dimensions.

But the thought came to me—*These were once Fae, and they will be again.* As a Queen of Faerie, I couldn't destroy them. How had they been handled in the past? Another answer lost to mystery.

Other hoofbeats came at us from the other direction, and I borrowed the trees' perspective to see a black-hooded rider on a black horse approach. The trees, less cooperative than those in Scotland, kicked me out, so I couldn't see the rider's face. They rode the horse with the grace one would expect of a High Fae.

They rode by my window and brandished an ebony wand tipped with amethyst. The stone glowed, and the revenants fell back with shrieks and cries. I could feel the Fae's magic, but I couldn't identify it. No, I knew it, but I didn't recognize it, so it must have been someone from my distant past, pre-exile. First exile.

The rider continued to conduct the revenant storm and bought us enough time to cross the border out of the Gray Zone. At least the revenants stayed in that area, which had been created to contain them, although I questioned for how long. If they were becoming smarter before turning into Fae, then they would figure out how to leave the Gray Zone like the ones that had attacked us near Aoine's castle on my last trip.

I slammed my fist on the chair beside me. The cushion kept the action from hurting, but I didn't need the extra pain. What were the rules the revenants followed? Could they only escape on the nights when their guardians, the owl-like gwenhwyfar spirits, flew?

Well, I supposed I'd have time to research the question, assuming I could access a library. No internet in Faerie.

The black rider galloped ahead, and I sent my appreciation after them. The horses had resumed their easy pace.

Crossing the lands of the dark Fae felt like a sigh of relief filled with an inhale of sulfur. A sense of repulsion filled me. Not disgust, but more akin to the sensation of trying to push two magnets together at their same pole ends. If this was how I felt here, how did Basil manage in my lands? Or was it because I was the queen of the light Fae? I hadn't had a similar sensation the last time I'd traveled to Cruaidh.

Soon the obsidian walls of the city itself loomed in front of us. Again, the pace of the horses didn't slow, and we passed into a tunnel that reflected the glowing purple of their eyes.

THE COACHMAN TOOK a back way to the asylum. Or perhaps an alternate way. I'd only been to Cruaidh the once with Kestrel Graves and the man she'd believed to be her father, John. Not that that journey had ended up well for them or for Lawrence, who had joined us later. Lawrence had almost been killed, John actually had, and Kestrel had attempted to use a dangerous facet of her power to save the man she'd known as her father and had never forgiven me for stopping her.

Lawrence... Not ready to touch the grief of never seeing him again, I'd managed to keep him from my mind, but memories flooded back. Lawrence flying in his gargoyle form to help us over the lake when the water wolves attacked. The first time we'd made love...and then had to escape from Aoine's castle. His helping me to rescue our little group and evade the revenants in the woods. I'd ended up using my own dangerous power, that of folding the distance between us and our destination, but it had worked out and had further given me an inkling that the Gray Fae Ellerin was my father since that was a journeying talent.

There would be no folding space or sneaking anywhere here. When the carriage passed under the iron gates of the asylum, I found an entire retinue waiting for us. The last time I'd been there had been as a visitor with Ellerin, who had wanted to show me what my old nurse had been forced to become. He had gradually widened my vision of my past so I could see past the unwavering loyalty I'd had to my grandmother. I'd idealized her, but I'd come to find out she'd done a lot of ruthless Fae things in her long rule, the likes of which I'd sworn I wouldn't.

But then I'd gotten myself locked away, once again going too far in the other direction.

I laid my forehead against the side of the carriage, and sorrow for my people flooded through me in a wave of regret and grief. What had I done? I'd agreed to this imprisonment to save Lawrence but hadn't thought more than a step ahead to what would happen to the light Fae with their queen locked up. Maeve couldn't rule, could she? The queen spell hadn't left me to land on her. I would have felt if it had, wouldn't I?

Again, my long exile in the Earth realm made me wish I could go back and access more of my memories from before, but so much had happened they'd been covered over like the markings of a gravestone under layers of dirt, moss, and lichens. Except in my case, the coverings had been composed of grief, resentment...and love.

The carriage rolled to a stop, and the driver opened the door. I stepped out and blinked at the watery sunlight. I knew intellectually that the same sun shone over Lorien, the capital of the light Fae, and Cruaidh, that of the dark Fae, but it appeared different here. Colder. Dimmer. Or maybe that was me.

The ear-splitting whine of real iron had joined the underlying repulsion of the dark Fae lands. I rubbed my arms to force myself to attend to a different sensation.

"Welcome to the Asylum, Your Highness." Healer Wilfrin, the blue, gnome-like Fae who ran the asylum, bowed. "Your room is right this way."

I closed my eyes at the words I'd been dreading to hear. I'd dreaded them the last time I'd been there, as well.

"Thank you. Who are all these Fae?" At least a dozen of them, most of them wearing the black and gray livery of the dark Fae queen Lilith, stood arrayed like a goth version of Downton Abbey.

"The queen sent them to attend to you and make sure you're comfortable."

I saw right through that one. Every effort from Queen Lilith would make for an obligation to me.

"Send them away. I don't need special treatment."

He nodded. "I was hoping you'd say that." He motioned for them to be gone, but they didn't move. "Ah, you may have to command them yourself."

I turned to the group. "Thank you all for coming. Please convey my gratitude to your queen, but I do not need extra attendants. I managed on my own in the Earth realm for centuries without servants. I can do so here."

They all bowed their heads, then filed out. Each one flinched when they walked through the iron gate. Wilfrin and I watched them go, and when the last of them had left, he turned to me.

"I'm happy you're here, Your Highness. I could use another healer on staff."

"I'm not here to be staff, Healer Wilfrin. I've had my own series of traumatic experiences and need to heal for a while."

He cocked his head. "Spoken like someone who's spent a lot of time in the Earth realm. And yet I sense you're not acknowledging them to yourself. If you're going to heal, you need to deal."

I snorted. "Is that one of your catchphrases? Or did you pick that one up from a pop psychology podcast?"

"Pod..." He shook his head. "No, it's the truth. You may change your mind about not joining the staff when you see your room."

Intrigued, I followed him through the route that led to to Olred's room. Instead of turning down her hall, he took me down a wing that ran along the back.

"This is our VIP wing. It was designed to house those of royal blood." He opened a door and gestured for me to precede him.

I walked into a circular room with stone walls, windows on three sides, and a canopy bed with pink lace-edged curtains and linens in the center. A dressing table along the back wall held a familiar wood-handled brush and comb set. Even the same paintings and tapestries, those of knights on horses and dreamy ocean scenes, hung on the walls. The only differences? There were no pins or ribbons on the dressing table, and instead of the tops of the buildings of Lorien, the views through the window showed the asylum grounds.

When I'd wished to access my memories from before my exile, I hadn't meant this. Not only was I trapped in the asylum. They'd sent me right back to my past. I could almost feel the Fae I'd become in the Earth realm sloughing off me. But how?

This place couldn't change my identity, could it? I had too much of the new Reine I didn't want to lose.

"No, no, no, no, no... I can't stay here." I tried to back out, but Wilfrin placed a firm hand on my back and pushed me in with strength that belied his small stature. The door closed behind us, and the thunk jolted through my entire body.

My throat tried to tighten into a scream, but I choked out, "What is the meaning of this? How could you have decorated it so quickly?"

"There was no decorating spell needed, Your Highness. Even if we had needed to do so, we couldn't have because, as you'll find soon, magic is muted in this place for everyone's protection."

"How is that protection for those of us who aren't crazy? And how in Hades is this supposed to be therapeutic?"

He didn't answer either question. He only shrugged and said, "I'll leave you to get settled in."

"No! You can't leave me here. You don't understand."

"I'm sorry, but this is how it must be."

"You're saying that this room has been like this..."

"Since your grandmother cooperated with Queen Lilith to create the asylum. I don't know what she was thinking, but she must have anticipated you coming here."

I walked to the bed and ran my hand over the fluffy pink comforter. The silver threads sparkled in the light, and small crystals at the apex of each little stitched diamond made rainbows dance on the underside of the canopy. Just like my bed in the palace in Lorien, where I'd slept for months, since I didn't feel right moving into my grandmother's suite.

"Every last detail, Wilfrin. What does it mean?"

"I don't know, but it seems you'll have plenty of time to find out."

With that comment, he turned the key in the lock. Once again a true prisoner, I folded my arms and turned in a circle.

What cruel joke was this? Between the sense of repulsion vibrating in my brain and throat and the memories that attempted to flood into my mind, I suspected that I wouldn't be the healer Wilfrin hoped for.

No, I feared I'd become as mad as Olred.

2

——————

LAWRENCE

I walked into Barton Lucia's office with my mother by my side. He stood and inclined his head to each of us in turn.

"Doctor Gordon, Mayor Gordon, it's good to see both of you."

I tried to read his expression, but it remained his usual medical neutral. His computer monitor sat at such an angle that only he could see it, and my fingers twitched with the desire to turn it and reveal my fate.

"Please have a seat." He motioned to the two chairs in front of his desk. He'd replaced the plastic ones with wooden ones with maroon cushions.

I lowered myself into one of them, and my mother took the other. We exchanged a worried glance.

Barton directed his dark attention to each of us, then broke into a smile. "The therapy appears to be working. Better than I'd hoped, actually." He turned the monitor, and it showed two pictures of my lungs. Spiderweb-like scarring marred the lobes in the image on the left. In the one on the right, wisps of the scars remained, but most had cleared.

I released the breath I'd held and took what felt like my first full one in weeks.

My mother squeezed my hand. "That's amazing news, Doctor Lucia." She blinked, and her eyes released two tears, the only indication of how worried she'd been. The stoic Agnes Gordon didn't show vulnerability, at least not where anyone could see her. "Does this mean he'll recover fully?"

Now Barton's expression snapped back to doctor neutral. "I don't know. It's possible he could always have some damage, and we'll have to do regular scans to make sure what scarring remains doesn't turn into something more nefarious. I've heard of Fae fire scarring becoming cancerous, but that was also a case where the lesions were much thicker than these appear to be."

"What's my final prognosis?" I tried to keep the urgency out of my voice.

He wouldn't meet my eyes, and I suspected what he was thinking, but I refused to give in to the disappointment before he uttered a word.

"It's possible you'll return to full functionality." He held up a finger. "Slowly. You're still deconditioned from your long stay here in the hospital."

"I've been flying regularly and building up my strength." Granted, they were short flights, but they were still flights requiring full changes and wing strength. I recalled how embracing my inner gargoyle had healed me the last time, and so I let him out more often now in hopes that would help. Although we were integrated, I still felt the urges the primitive creature part of me expressed as somewhat separate.

"We still don't know yet. Remember, cases of Fae fire poisoning are rare, and prolonged exposures to the toxic atmosphere of Faerie are unheard of." His eyebrows lifted a centimeter, giving him a sympathetic expression. "The truth is, I don't know. We have to take it one day at a time."

I'd said similar words to pet owners, and I liked hearing "one day at a time" as much as they had—which was to say, not at all. The chances of him medically clearing me to go back into Faerie had gone from slim to nonexistent. My fists clenched for a second before I forced them to relax. My mother didn't know of my plans to rescue Reine from the Fae asylum, and I didn't want to give anything away.

Reine... The scan didn't show the hole in my heart where our connection had throbbed until she'd been locked away behind iron bars in the dark Fae capital of Cruaidh. Now I felt our bond anchor's absence almost more keenly than I'd sensed its constant presence. The space where it had been ached with an emptiness alternately filled with the leaden heaviness of grief and sharp stab of despair.

No, I'd figure out some way to go to her, to be with her again. I'd steal her away and bring her back to the Earth realm where the Fae authorities, whoever they were, couldn't find her.

I just needed to be clever about it. Thankfully *clever* was my middle name. Well, it wasn't, but I held on to the sentiment.

My mother's phone rang, and we all jumped.

"I'm sorry." Her cheeks reddened, and she pulled her phone from her Southern lady-sized purse. "The only calls that should be coming through are from the emergency line." When she saw the incoming number, her color went from pink to pale. "Stones." She placed the phone to her ear. "Hello?" She dashed from the room.

"Well?" I asked Barton. I didn't worry too much about the call. My mother had allowed the city officials of The Aerie to depend on her too much, and she'd gotten these "emergency" calls before.

"Aren't you concerned about...?" He nodded to where my mother had exited.

"No, I'm surprised Sheriff Jones doesn't call her for permission to take a dump."

He smirked. "I see. As for you..." He leaned closer. "Now that your mother has left, I can tell you... Desmond is working on a breathing device for you. Don't worry, we haven't given up all hope."

"Thank you." It wasn't the best solution, not by a long shot, but at least it was something. A thousand questions piled up behind my tongue, but I decided to hold them until I saw whatever contraption he proposed.

Mother walked in and held out her phone. "Lawrence, did you see anything like this while you were in Faerie?"

I took the device and pinched the picture out so I could see the details of the strange insect. It looked like a firefly and a wasp had birthed a baby that had gone bug-goth with its violet butt light and nasty sting.

"I haven't seen one, but Reine talked about them. It's a black lightning bug. Where did this come from?"

"Outside." She took her phone back, and the corners of her mouth tightened. "They're attacking The Aerie."

BARTON DROVE us from the hospital, which sat outside of The Aerie on a bluff, to the edge of town. A glittering purple swarm hovered over the bridge that spanned the river between us and downtown. I spotted my twin siblings Micah and Minerva on the other side. They held what looked like flamethrowers, but I could tell the implements hadn't proven effective. Fire, being a primarily destructive element, wouldn't hurt dark Fae creatures on its own.

Barton stopped his car about twenty feet back from the lilac cloud. The insects didn't seem to be doing much besides hanging out midair. Occasionally one would fly forward, sting someone, and return to its swarm.

"I need to get over there," Barton grumbled. "But they've got the bridge blocked, and it will be too long for us to get out and go around by the trail."

"What do they want? Where did they come from? " Mother practically hissed. Then she narrowed her eyes. "Well, we know where, but why?"

I searched my memory for what Reine had told me about them. They'd been summoned to greet her upon her return to Faerie, and she'd banished them with her Fae powers back to whoever had summoned them, which had turned out to be her mother.

"Have you heard much from Maeve lately?" I asked.

Mother's surprised expression appeared genuine. "No. I told her to leave me alone after she almost killed you. In fact..." She placed a palm on her forehead. "I told her to bug off."

"Looks like she took you literally."

"You're the one Reine is mate-bonded with," Barton pointed out. "Can you use that connection to do something?"

"I'm no spellcaster."

"No, but I am." Astrid the former river nymph emerged from the woods. She wore nothing on her feet, and a gauzy green gown almost floated around her.

"Astrid! What are you doing here?"

"I come back to check on my river periodically, and I'm not thrilled it's under attack by those things." One of the bugs swirled out of the swarm and approached her, but she flicked ice at it. It flew back to its brethren with a little squeal. "Apparently my former possessor left me some of her talents."

"Can you use them to help us?" Barton asked.

Astrid inclined her head. "I can try. But it's up to the prince and the Regent. They're the ones with the command."

"Do what you need," Mother said before I could reply that I didn't have any authority here. But then everyone turned to me.

A plan formed in my head. I proposed it to Astrid, who

nodded but qualified, "Only if you can lend me some of your water elemental strength."

I then sent a couple of quick texts to Micah and Minerva and waited for them to check their smart watches, then nod to me from across the river. They spoke to the police who had gathered around them, including Buck Jones, the useless sheriff. Well, he was useless from my perspective, and I could tell the feeling was mutual from the scowl he sent me. But he retreated with the others.

Micah and Minerva changed into gargoyle forms with a speed they would never have managed even a few months before, and my pride in them kicked off my own change. My clothing tore, but there wasn't any help for that. At least I'd worn stretchy boxers so nothing indecent would hang out. Micah and Minerva also wore sports undergarments. That was another improvement—all the gargoyles had learned to wear underwear that would stretch with our changes. We weren't as concerned about scandalizing anyone as we were with uncomfortable dangling during complicated midair maneuvers and leaving vulnerable bits uncovered.

"May I?" I asked and held out a hand to Astrid. She nodded and allowed me to pick her up by the waist. We all took off at once to surprise the swarm, and indeed, it sparkled with the insects turning this way and that trying to assess the threat.

"Now," I texted Micah and Minerva. They turned their phone flashlights on and set them to strobe, then tossed them to the middle of the bridge. The bugs swooped down to investigate, coalescing the swarm.

"Now," I told Astrid, who raised her hands. Twin waves of water rose over the side of the bridge and flanked the bugs. Half of the swarm split off to attack us directly, half toward my siblings. Micah and Minerva deployed their flamethrowers, and Astrid her ice until the two streams met in the middle and melted the ice into water, which washed the insects onto the bridge and into the river.

A few flew off and then disappeared, presumably to return to Maeve and give her a report. I hoped they told her we were too clever to be messed with, but I also suspected this wouldn't be the last we'd see of her influence.

I returned Astrid to the ground, and we convened in the middle of the bridge. Barton rushed past to attend to those who had been stung, and Sheriff Jones swaggered over. He'd let go of his denial of the existence of magical creatures, but he'd held on to his ego and belief that humans were superior. I didn't know why Mother kept him around.

"Nicely done, Prince."

"Doctor Gordon is fine." In my gargoyle form, the correction came out as a growl.

"Well, Doctor Gordon, what do you think those critters wanted?"

I squinted into the sky, but the rest of them had disappeared. "They could have really hurt some people and done some damage if they'd wanted." I exchanged glances with my mother. "I'm afraid they were a warning."

"Of what?" Minerva asked. Her partner Karen, a petite blonde gargoyle in human form, practically tackled her in a hug.

"I was so worried!"

Minerva kissed her on top of the head. "I'm fine. Lawrence figured out a plan to get rid of them. Maybe we should call him The Exterminator."

Micah smirked, but he hadn't taken his eyes off Astrid. Could he have actual feelings for her beyond what the witch had manipulated in him? That would be another interesting complication.

"Please don't call me The Exterminator." I glared at my

sister. "Besides, I don't know that I'll have such an easy time next time."

"What do you mean, 'next time?'" Mother asked.

"I think that was a warning for us to stay out of Faerie."

"But you weren't planning to go back there, were you? It almost killed you last time."

As much as I hated the distress on the faces of my family around me, I couldn't lie to them. "If I can rescue Reine, then I'm going back. I can't let her stay trapped in that asylum forever."

"Nor should you." A dark cloaked figure strode out of the woods wielding his wooden staff with the clear crystal atop it. A shadowy figure darted around his legs and then came to rub against mine.

I picked up the purring Sir Raleigh. "Ellerin."

"Prince Gordon. Nicely done, by the way. Maeve will have a true bee in her bonnet after that. Probably several."

My closet didn't hold child-sized apparel, thank goodness. In it, I found several dresses of striped satin, all in relatively plain colors. I supposed that was asylum uniform for patients, but a more upscale version. With a sigh, I closed the door. I'd keep my jeans, T-shirt, and faux leather jacket on as long as possible.

After I'd been in the asylum for a day, it became clear that I'd be forced to change my clothes. First, they needed to be washed after having traveled to at least three different times and a place out of time, where I'd had to sit in the garden. Second, while Fae didn't sweat and stink like humans, we did lose a certain amount of freshness.

I hesitantly removed my garments in the en-suite bathroom, which thankfully had more modern accoutrements than my childhood privy room. The shower felt fantastic, and I could almost—almost—pretend I'd gone back to the Earth realm. But that sense of repulsion remained. A strong spell kept the asylum buffered from magical forces, so my own power, strong as it was, had become muted, as had the repulsion. But both hovered just out of conscious awareness and made me soul-itchy from wanting to reach for my own magic and get away from the other.

I would be lucky if I didn't go mad before my sentence was up.

When I reached for my clothing after my shower, it disappeared. I bit my tongue before I cried out lest I alert one of the orderlies—or worse, Healer Wilfrin—to my distress. That was the irony of the asylum. It was supposed to be a place of healing and peace, but only if the patients played along. I'd seen on my last visit what happened when someone got too emotional.

Wrapped in a thin, scratchy bath sheet with my hair in a sorry excuse for a hair towel, I approached my bed to see that plain underwear and one of the dresses from the closet had been laid out. I dressed with a sigh and pulled the sage green one-piece garment over my head. At least it was fitted —no belts for the inmates—and somewhat flattering, but I would have preferred trousers and a blouse or knit shirt. Dresses made me remember the times I'd danced with Lawrence.

Tears threatened to come, so I focused on drying my hair. I thought about leaving it loose and curly, but I didn't want to appear to be a stereotypical wild woman, so I braided it and wound it into a bun at the back of my head. The dressing table lacked pins, so I tucked the end in as best I could.

After I finished, a knock heralded the arrival of a visitor. I'd only had one so far—the dark-haired Fae who had been bringing my meals. I bade her to come in, and she entered, but not with food.

"You have a guest, Your Highness. Oh, you're already dressed."

"Do you know what happened to my clothing? I'd like it washed and returned to me, especially my jacket."

She bit her lip. "I don't know. The spell that runs this place takes the guests' personal items and tucks them away some-where. We haven't found where yet."

"Great." I rubbed my eyes and resolved to research the spell to see how I could get around it. "Who's the visitor?"

"Your patron, Queen Lilith of the dark Fae!" The way she announced it made me think they didn't get many celebrities here, unsurprisingly.

"Thank you. Where will I receive her?"

"She will receive you in the parlor room. We have one in this wing for special guests."

"You don't have to keep calling me a guest. I know what I am."

She shot a coy look over her shoulder. "Do you?"

With that strange question, she led me from the room and down the hallway. I had to pick up the train of my dress so it wouldn't trail on the floor, which somehow remained clean without any evidence of mopping or sweeping. Did the asylum have self-cleaning capabilities? The thought made me shiver more than it charmed me. Could it be alive on some level?

I trailed my hand along the smooth stone wall, but I didn't sense any spark of sentience or hint of underlying intelligence. I added the question of what, exactly, the asylum could be to my growing list. Perhaps they'd let me send a letter to Basil to see what he could scare up in the light Fae archives.

We descended the corner staircase and emerged in a sunnier hallway with a large, multi-paned stained-glass window at the end. The squares shed crimson, gold, forest green, cobalt, and indigo shadows on the floor. The orderly stopped by a large wooden door and knocked.

A soft "enter" increased the sense of dark Fae repulsion, and I steeled myself to encounter the queen whom I'd only heard about as a warning.

~

WHEN THE ORDERLY opened the door for me, I walked into a room that could have been a queen's receiving room in any palace in Faerie or the Earth realm. Walls with pastel blue damask wallpaper framed white-painted windows. The furniture all had curves and swirls. Not a sharp corner anywhere. A Chopin nocturne played itself on the white piano in the corner.

Queen Lilith stood like a nightmare in the middle of a child's nursery. All angles and red-black patterned clothing, she gazed at me through eyes too dark to be blue and too light to be brown, but not hazel. No, she had the mythical purple-irised eyes I'd heard some of the dark Fae royalty had been bequeathed by an ancestor with a strange genetic mutation. Or a curse, as it had been known back in the day. She wore her hair swept back from her face, and dark curls cascaded from the crown of her skull down her back. No circlet, tiara, or crown graced her head, but the way she held herself left no doubt as to who she was.

I resisted the urge to curtsy. We were equals, even if she had me at a disadvantage. I was acutely aware of both facts plus the one that her very presence repelled me.

I pushed that awareness to the back of my mental cabinet, which threatened to burst with all the things I'd shoved into its depths in the last few days.

"Queen Lilith, it is an honor to meet you."

She inclined her head. "And you, Queen Reine."

"I wish it could have been under better circumstances." I cast through my memory—had the light and dark Fae queens ever visited or met? I couldn't think of a time. Since the Great Treaty, each had kept to herself.

"Yes. Please accept my condolences on the loss of your grandmother and my congratulations on the acquisition of the Queen Spell. I'm sure I wasn't the only one not surprised it skipped Maeve."

With a one-shoulder shrug, I declined her invitation to vent about my mother and sat on the pink-cushioned chair farthest from her. She didn't appear to take insult and settled on the loveseat. The orderly wheeled in a tea cart and served each of us. She offered me a plate of dainty powdered sugar-covered cookies and white petit-fours. I chose one of the latter.

Part of me wanted to scream. What was this farce? But I inhaled the strong tea and smiled. "Thank you for allowing me to spend time in your lands. I appreciate your graciousness, particularly as I didn't consult you before I agreed to take my sentence here."

She sipped her own bitter brew and smiled with blood red lips that I was pretty sure didn't have any color added to them. "You've always been a clever girl, Reine. I look forward to seeing how this plays out. I heard you traded your freedom for the life of a gargoyle?"

Of course, I couldn't lie, and I didn't feel like trying to dance around the truth, so I gave her the complete answer with a blunt, "Yes, and a wizard and a lycanthrope."

"Quite the combination. They must be very special to you. Had you not thought to guard them?"

I shrugged. "No. I owed them for their kindness to me during my exile." All right, I'd dance around the truth somewhat. I didn't want to give *her* reason to go after Lawrence, Max, or Gabriel and use them to manipulate me. They'd had their lives upended enough by the Fae.

"Ah, yes, reciprocity. It can be tricky, can it not?"

"Yes."

She placed her teacup on the saucer and set it on the coffee table. "You see, you've put me in a bind. Your grandmother and I had an equitable arrangement. I allowed her to build the asylum here in exchange for her staffing it with my citizens. It gives them a purpose, you see."

I didn't, so I sipped my tea.

She continued, "And you being here disrupts that balance.

The conditions of the bargain you made with your mother dictate that you reside here. However, you are here because I allow it, and your support comes out of my treasury."

I raised my eyebrows. "I thought it would be paid for by the light Fae coffers." I pressed my lips together before I added, *"We certainly have enough."* I'd looked at the balance sheets the previous week.

"Ah, yes, perhaps that's an issue you need to take up with my nephew Basil. How is he doing?"

"Well, the last time I saw him." I didn't tell her he was royally pissed at me for getting myself in such an awkward situation.

"Good. I'm glad you found something to occupy him. I grew weary of that Troubadour act he put on. Really, he's five and a quarter hundred years old. It was high time for him to grow up." She tapped one long shiny black fingernail against her lips. "Your kindness to him does reduce your debt to me somewhat. In fact, at this point you have a credit. But how long will your sentence be?"

"Thirty years."

"Ah, yes. The credit isn't that large, I fear." She leaned forward, and I braced myself. I knew on some level she was about to ask me for a big favor in return for her largesse and support.

Would she insist I promise to marry Basil? She didn't know that I couldn't because I was mate-bonded to Lawrence. Or if I did unite with Basil, it would just be for show. But then, wasn't that most Fae relationships?

Instead, she surprised me. "I do have a way for us to even the score between us."

"How so?"

"As you know, my granddaughter Liliana has been missing for a hundred years."

"Yes, the lost dark Fae princess. Whispers of that situation reached me in the Earth realm." I couldn't help my curiosity. "Was she kidnapped?"

Lilith shook her head, and for a moment, the raven's feet at the corners of her eyes deepened to the point I could see them. "No, she ran away. She had no desire for Fae life, especially not life at court. She told her mother that she found all our deception and trickery to be unethical, and she wished for a more straightforward existence."

I couldn't blame her, but I also couldn't say so...or that I sensed more to the story. "That's hard. You must miss her."

"I do. And her mother..." She shook her head. "Those are my problems, and I only want to share one aspect of them with you. Desdemona is my difficulty." She hit me with the full force of her indigo gaze. "Did you at any time in your exile hear anything of my granddaughter? Even a whisper or a rumor?"

Her pain came through in her voice and poked my heart. Lilith had a reputation as relatively heartless and seeing her upset over her granddaughter upturned all my assumptions. Well, most of them.

"I'm sorry, but no. I never heard anything, but I mostly kept to myself."

She sighed. "I was afraid of that. Lily—that's what she calls herself—was always good at hiding in plain sight. I understand you have contacts in the Earth realm still. If you hear anything about my granddaughter and her whereabouts, your letting me know would even the score between us. Even the tiniest bit of information would cancel your debt, which will be considerable after thirty years."

I thought through the potential ramifications of agreeing to her bargain. I did still have contacts, although I had no way to get in touch with them, and what were the chances I'd hear anything of Lily? And did I want to put her in danger? Even if I did, I could warn her before I told her grandmother.

"I agree to your terms."

"Good. If you hadn't, I was going to insist you promise to marry Basil upon your release. He needs someone to settle him down, and he seems quite fond of you."

I straightened. "I wasn't aware he was communicating with his home court beyond official dispatches about the revenants."

She shuddered. "Dreadful things. Thankfully the threat seems to be exaggerated. But no, I can tell by how he writes about you."

"Oh."

She stood, as did I. "Thank you for receiving me. Please consider this place your palace. I shall not come again without invitation."

Wait... Did that mean she wanted to be invited? Or did she mean she'd wait until I heard something about Lily?

"Thank you for your visit and your patronage."

"It's all in service of maintaining peace in the realm. We don't need another Great War."

"No, nor another Great Rising." I wanted to ask her what she knew about the revenants and the asylum, but I recognized we stood at an uneasy place of reciprocity and truce. Perhaps another time.

She turned just before she reached the door. "I'm so glad you didn't turn out like your mother, even if it meant you're of mixed blood. But then, who could resist Ellerin?"

And with that parting shot, she left. I sank to the chair, my head spinning. Had Ellerin canoodled with the dark Fae queen or princesses as well? If so, how many half-siblings were out there?

"Hades, Ellerin," I whispered. "I don't need any more complications."

4

LAWRENCE

Ellerin and I walked through town toward my mother's house. I continued to watch for errant insects, but my strategy seemed to have worked. I only saw insects of the normal, mundane variety.

Ellerin seemed deep in thought, and even Sir Raleigh maintained a sedate pace with us. Instead of coming from a victory over a magical foe, we appeared to be marching away from the site of a great defeat. And perhaps we were.

When we crossed the bridge to the residential area, Ellerin said, "I'm sorry."

I stopped. The only Fae I'd known to apologize was Reine. "Excuse me?"

He turned, and for the first time, the depth of the lines on his face hinted at his ancient age. "I'm sorry. If I'd known Reine was going to do what she did..." He rubbed a hand over his face. "I don't doubt she acted according to some instinct, but it's going to make all this damn hard to untangle."

"Basil told me she bargained for my life as well as those of Doctor Fortuna and Mister McCord." I started walking again, and he fell into step beside me. "If I'd known, I would have died before allowing her to take that fate."

"I know. That's why you're one of the few people, creatures, whatever I trust to have her best interests at heart."

The admission surprised me. "What about Basil?"

Ellerin snorted. "He's a Fae. He has his own interests at heart most of all. Never forget that. We're not to be trusted."

"Not even you?"

Sir Raleigh glared over his shoulder at Ellerin, the first time I'd seen the grimalkin unhappy with his summoner.

"Not anymore. Not after I let her go to that courtroom and seal her fate. I should've been there to counsel her, to protect her. I would have helped her figure something else out. And still saved you," he added too quickly.

I didn't trust Ellerin with my well-being, but he was Reine's father, and the males of the species appeared to have more nurturing instincts than the females. Except for Reine. I'm sure she missed Sir Raleigh as much as he missed her. My veterinarian's eye could tell he looked off, although the changes were subtle. His coat appeared less lustrous, and he moved with less energy. I resisted the urge to check his teeth.

"What are you proposing?" I asked Ellerin. We turned on to my mother's street. She wouldn't be home yet, but I found myself tired from the day's activities. I tried to tell myself it was due to all the excitement and the change and the battle, but in truth, I knew I still hadn't recovered my stamina. Plus, Astrid had channeled some of my water elemental energy.

"Basil said he's working on her case, but I fear that the wheels of Fae justice may turn too slowly for the good of the realm. There are those who deny it, but the revenants are increasing in number and power. I can't pass through the Gray Zone safely anymore, which forces me to take cross-realm paths that pose their own threats."

"And Faerie needs its queens at full strength."

"Yes, and able to command their armies."

"Maeve can't do that? Having a Fae army at her command seems like something she'd enjoy."

He smirked. "You don't know the half of it. But no, since the Queen Spell didn't land on her, she can't control the army."

"What are you hoping to get from me, then?" We'd reached the front walk, and weariness pressed down on me like a hand trying to grind me into the concrete sidewalk.

"I don't know how it can possibly happen, but Faerie needs its defenders. It needs its gargoyles."

"But we'll die. We can't breathe there, remember?"

"Yes, but weren't you working on that?"

I sat on the front wall. "I was, but I was informed that if we were to manage to change the atmosphere, it could result in the deaths of entire species that had evolved since it changed."

"And if you don't help defend Faerie, they may die as food for the revenants anyway. Think about that for a moment."

I shuddered. "But if Reine made the bargain, can she be released from it for an emergency?"

Ellerin's lips curled into a half-smile. "No, but there are always loopholes. I don't suppose you were there when she made the bargain, were you?"

"I was, but I was semi-conscious, so I don't remember any details." Only a sense of doom falling over me, then the pang of her being taken away and the place where our bond connected in my chest going numb. Not painful, just numb and achy with the absence of something that had been there, like a deep puncture wound that had healed as a divot.

"All right, then. Think about it. Faerie needs its crown prince of gargoyles, and today you proved yourself more than worthy of taking your rightful place."

"Aw, shucks, I bet you talk to all the handsome gargoyles like that."

He didn't look amused.

"Look, I'm sorry, but I don't know what you want me to do. Until I can get the breathing thing straightened out, I'm stuck here hoping she can figure a way out." I could have told him about my and Barton's plans, but I decided to heed Ellerin's warning about not trusting him. I'd wait for Ellerin to prove himself before I did.

"I understand. Can I leave Sir Raleigh with you for a while? I need a break from his glaring and sighing."

I looked down at the grimalkin, who gazed back up at me. With a light hop, he landed on the wall beside me and pushed his head under my hand.

"I don't think that will be a problem." I might have temporarily gained a feline-like grimalkin, but I still sensed that I'd ended up with a net loss.

THE NEXT MORNING, I got a text from Barton: *The device is ready. Come to the hospital when you can.*

An electric thrill shot through me, leaving fear in its wake. What if they disappointed me? What if the device worked but wasn't practical?

What if, in spite of my efforts, I still couldn't rescue Reine from the fate she'd agreed to?

Yes, said the little voice of doubt that had plagued me during those years when I'd searched for my father's killer. *What if you're not good enough? What if you're not the one worthy of this task?*

Then at least I'll know I did everything I could to save her.

And then what?

The doubt voice wasn't known for giving up easily.

I'll figure it out when I get there. Wherever *there* was. Continued solitude? I hadn't felt lonely until Reine had barreled into and then vanished from my life.

Sir Raleigh pushed his head under my hand, and I rubbed the soft places behind his ears. He settled on my chest and purred, and the rumbling chased away most of the tension my inner argument had evoked.

"What is it?"

He didn't answer me, which comforted me. He only spoke to me when something dire had occurred, so at least I knew we remained in situation normal. He slow-blinked, and tears pricked my eyes.

"You're right. I'm not alone anymore, am I? You're here, and I don't think you'll leave me until it's time."

He lifted his head, and his ears perked. His bright green eyes—the same color as Reine's and Ellerin's—took on that far-away feline look. Then he stood and padded out of the room.

"Or until it's breakfast time," I mumbled, but amusement lifted the corners of my lips.

I walked down the stairs and nodded to Micah, who sat in the living room. He wore his city uniform and drank a cup of coffee while he read the paper. He raised a hand in greeting but didn't look up from the article.

"What is it?" I walked around the armchair to look over his shoulder.

"You're a minor celebrity—'Crown Prince saves Aerie.'"

I groaned. "They can't be calling me that."

He smirked. "Oh, they can, and they are. Good. If you don't do it, they'll be looking to me and Min, and neither of us want the job of herding these particular cats."

I supposed I should have been glad he didn't want to take over Mother's position as Regent when she was ready to step down. It would keep us from going into old gargoyle patterns of challenge and battle, as our history said had happened between the heir to the throne and those who wanted to be. I'd recently met my siblings and didn't want to be in conflict with them. We'd already had a tough start, which I was grateful for since it had brought us together.

"Speaking of cats, did you see Sir Raleigh?"

"That giant gray thing? Yes, he dashed through here when Mum opened the bacon package. Check the kitchen."

"Thanks."

"No worries, CP. I'll come in and give you the official summary of the article once it's done."

"I'm sure you will." With a sigh, I walked back into the kitchen. Mother had a chef who came in and prepared dinners as well as lunches for the working gargoyles of the house—just Mom and Micah since Minerva had moved in with her girl-friend—but she liked to cook breakfast for "us kids," as she called us. I didn't argue with her. I suspected we felt the same—that we would have loved to have had the chance to have a normal mother-child life, whatever "normal" was.

Sure enough, I found Mom at the stainless-steel stove and Sir Raleigh at her feet looking up at her hopefully. I pecked her cheek and picked up the grimalkin. He craned his neck to watch her, and his nose twitched.

"Your cat is a little beggar."

"He's not mine, he's Reine's." Sir Raleigh chirped and dug his claws into my arm, so I put him down. "He's ours, I guess."

"I'm glad he likes you. It would be hard if he'd been a one-person cat."

I resisted the urge to correct her and remind her he wasn't a cat. If he wanted to look and act like a cat, that was up to him.

"He may decide he likes you if you share some bacon with him."

"I already did." She shot an indulgent glance at Sir Raleigh, who bathed himself in a sunbeam. "He was trying to fool you that I didn't. If you want to share with him, that's up to you. What does that kind of cat usually eat?"

"I don't know. Grimalkins are pretty mysterious. He seems to find his own sustenance."

She grinned. "Self-cleaning *and* self-feeding? And he doesn't use a litter box or poop in the yard? That's my kind of pet."

Sir Raleigh paused to glare at her, and I laughed.

She didn't allow his annoyed expression to stop her. "It's a good thing the twins didn't know about those. They would never have let me alone about getting one."

Sir Raleigh turned his back to us and continued his bath. Mother and I smiled at each other, but I caught the hint of sadness in her eyes. She probably saw the same in mine. She'd buried two husbands, and I didn't dare ask her if she wanted to be married a third time even though she had plenty of her long gargoyle life left. I doubted I would ever get over Reine, both because of the mate bond that persisted and because I couldn't imagine falling in love again.

I almost asked Mother how she had managed to survive the heartbreak of losing my father, and then Micah and Minerva's dad, but Micah strode in and helped himself to more coffee. Mother put eggs, three strips of bacon, and a biscuit on a plate and handed it to me, then did the same for Micah.

"Thanks, Mum." Micah pecked her on the cheek. "This looks and smells amazing. Did the cat quality test the bacon?"

"Yes. Don't give him any more unless Lawrence says it's okay."

"I wouldn't dare risk the ire of the 'Crown Prince of the Aerie.'"

Mother rolled her eyes. "Have they started up with that again? Lawrence, we may have to do a press conference to remind them that you have your life in Atlanta."

I sat at the table and opened my mouth to agree, but no sound came out. What had Ellerin told me? That these times called for a crown prince, not a veterinarian. But did I trust him to guide me? He'd admitted to his mistake.

Both Mother and Micah shot surprised looks at me.

"Lawrence?" Mother asked. "Has something changed?"

"I... I don't know yet. All I'm sure of is that I don't know."

She nodded, and turned, but not before I saw the flash of hope in her expression. I almost groaned.

"Take your time," she said and then echoed my earlier thought. "Gargoyles live long lives, which gives us many paths."

I turned to Micah, expecting to meet his usual smirk. Instead, he nodded and gave me a thumbs-up.

Stones, I really wanted to talk to Reine about all of this, but I couldn't.

All I knew is that I now had empathy as well as sympathy for her conflict between being with me and being the Queen of Faerie.

Hades.

$$5$$

REINE

Soon after Lilith visited, I had another meeting in the receiving parlor.

"Basil!" I hugged him and noted how he didn't repel me like Lilith had.

He squeezed back, then held me at arm's length and frowned. "Reine, how are you settling in? You look...subdued."

I'd again braided my hair, and this time I wore a dusty blue gown. "It's standard dress for royal guests here, I've come to find. My clothes disappeared after I took them off, and no one can tell me where they went."

A blush bloomed and faded on his cheeks, and he cleared his throat. "Well, ah, that's no good. I'll see if I can get some regular clothing brought to you."

I rubbed my eyes. "No, no, that's all right. I'm trying to make this experience as frictionless as possible, at least for now." I sat on the couch, and he took the cushion beside mine. "I honestly don't have the energy in me to fight."

His blond brows drew together. "What's wrong? Are you ill?"

I couldn't help the sigh that escaped. "Yes and no." I rubbed my chest. "The bond to Lawrence is so muted I can't feel it, and something about this place repels me. It's like a constant scream in my ear that I need to leave. I don't belong here."

"If you'd told me your plan before you agreed to it with Maeve, I would have counseled you against it. Our queens aren't meant to spend long amounts of time in each other's lands. It keeps them from getting ideas of conquering them. A negative association, if you will."

"Ugh." I buried my face in my hands, and he rubbed my shoulder. I dropped my hands back to my lap and asked, "Please tell me you're here with good news? Did you find Gerald Brigadine so he can testify that most of the things I was blamed for were actually his fault?"

"No, alas. You won't be surprised to find out Maeve killed him."

"What? No!"

"Yes, with an ash spell. She accelerated his aging and decay until he became loam in the border forest."

"How long ago?"

"Twelve days."

I drummed my fingers on the cushion. "We may still be able to raise his spirit. Or you could. Get that Aria medium from the Earth realm. She's the only one I know who's powerful enough to do it."

The gentle weight of his hand stilled mine. "I'm afraid we can't. We don't have the exact location, and that forest is too big."

"But there could be a search. Or Aoine may be able to communicate with the forest. Those are her lands."

His full lips twisted. "For that you'd need to have Aoine's cooperation. And you didn't exactly part on good terms."

My shoulders slumped around the hollowness of defeat in my chest. "And then the bitch testified against me at my trial. No, you're right, you'll have to keep looking for his letters."

"I'm working on it, I promise."

I attempted a smile, but I couldn't manage. Sorrow and despair froze my lower face. "Where did you hear about Gerald?"

"Lawrence told me."

The smile broke through. "Lawrence? You talked to him? I didn't know you'd visited the Earth realm."

Disappointment flashed over his face with a down-tilt of his brows and a purse of his lips, but he resumed his typical jovial expression. "Yes, I needed to question him about how he ended up in that prison and find out if Maeve had said anything that could be useful to us in figuring out where Brigadine's letters—the actual ones, not the altered ones Maeve's counsel gave us—have been hidden. But there's more bad news."

"What?" I almost said I couldn't handle any more bad news, but he'd told me that Lawrence lived. I could handle almost anything.

"Lawrence said that Maeve called on Rhys to shoot the dart that tranquilized him."

Anything but that. "Rhys? He betrayed us again?"

Basil squeezed my hand. "Maeve called on Rhys. A Rhys. Maybe not our Rhys. It's possible another one was born, and she's using that one."

"What does Rhys say about this?" I wished I could question my little brother myself. Or shake some sense into him.

"Well, ah, he's still missing, so I can't ask."

"Argh!" I slumped back into the cushions behind me. "Why does this all have to be so complicated?"

He scooted and slid his arm behind me. I allowed him to guide me into a hug. "Don't worry. Just do what you need to here to convince them you're a good, compliant patient—"

"Prisoner."

"Right, prisoner. That will satisfy the terms of your bargain and not allow Maeve or anyone else to say you intended to do otherwise. I'll keep working on my end."

I sat straight. "Thank you. I don't know what I'd do without you."

He didn't respond. Instead, he reached behind him and pulled out a plush toy. The two-foot-long gray cat had one white paw and twinkling green eyes. "I know you miss Sir Raleigh. This is a poor substitute, but at least it's something. Give him lots of squishy hugs."

"I never thought I'd hear you say the word 'squishy.'" I took the cat and held him to me. It didn't purr, but again, it was something. "Thank you."

"You're welcome. All right, now I have some business to attend to at the palace."

"The dark Fae palace?"

"Yes. Auntie Lilith has summoned me."

"Probably to talk about the terms of her patronage. Please see if you can get some funds released to pay for my stay here so I'm not totally in debt to her when I'm released."

"I'll see what I can do, and again, I promise I'll do everything in my power to figure out how to get you out of here."

We both stood, and he bowed over my right hand and kissed it. Then he left me with the question of how far I'd end up being in debt to *him* when all this was over.

I squished the fake Sir Raleigh to my chest and felt something hard inside.

6

——————

LAWRENCE

I opted to walk the few miles to the hospital, both as part of my rehabilitation and to give myself time to think through things. Sir Raleigh accompanied me and trotted alongside me until we reached the path along the river. The residents of The Aerie had built it after Reine defeated the witch that had held the town—and the river nymph—by a magical stranglehold. The path also helped me to avoid the townspeople, who likely had more questions than I had answers to after the previous day's events and the morning's article. What was the fascination people had with royalty, anyway? It wasn't like I could help being the son of the Regent.

It didn't surprise me to round the bend under the main bridge into town and find Astrid sitting and gazing into the water.

She turned and smiled. "Well met, Crown Prince."

"Oh, no, not you as well."

Astrid's laugh resembled the burble of water trickling over rocks in pure mountain stream. I found myself chuckling with her.

"Your laugh reminds me of an avalanche," she said with a coy glance. "Strong, powerful...determined."

Her words sobered me. What was I doing laughing with her when I had serious business to attend to?

"Determined, yes. I'm on an important errand."

"I'll walk with you." She didn't leave room for argument, and I accepted her company. Maybe she'd keep me out of my head.

Sir Raleigh sniffed at her blue skirt hem, then dismissed her with a lift of his tail. He scampered ahead of us after a fallen leaf, and we followed.

Astrid shot him an indulgent glance. "Creatures of Faerie aren't so different from here, are they?"

"No. One has to wonder how both realms developed in parallel. Why not together?"

She cocked her head. "Perhaps they were originally one, but then something happened to separate them. Some say that belief creates its own reality. If certain creatures weren't believed in, maybe their reality would separate from that of the nonbelievers."

We ascended the stairs to the bridge in the woods, and I touched Uncle Augie's stone shoulder. The statue didn't react, and I again questioned who had put him there and why. I didn't believe he'd stayed in gargoyle form so long he'd turned to stone, but that was the legend. What deeper truth could it be hiding?

The shadows of the trees caressed us with cool shade. I cast one more glance at the statue before our steps took us out of view. Yes, that day I felt like he was watching me rather than the other way around. I returned to a more comfortable topic. "What of the species that are still being discovered? Are you saying that they come from a different dimension?"

"Not necessarily. Perhaps they've been so isolated that lack of knowledge protected them."

"What about you? You were a water nymph before the ice

witch possessed you. But no one's believed in those in centuries."

She shuddered, and I cringed.

"I'm sorry," I said quickly. "I shouldn't have brought that up. You've lost a lot."

"Yes, and that's why I believe as I do. If more had believed in me and accepted the presence of a water nymph, it would have been harder for Grylja to possess and control me as she did. I thought I was protected."

"By what?" She reminded me that although The Aerie belonged to the gargoyles, I knew little of it.

"By the fact that this place is not entirely of the Earth realm. You can't tell, but I can feel it. That's why it's easy for me and Ellerin to come here from Faerie."

"And why Maeve could send the black lightning bugs."

"Yes. Someone must have told her about it."

We passed into particularly deep part of the woods, where the canopy blocked the sky entirely. She shivered, and I resisted the urge to put my arm around her. I didn't want her to be cold, but I also feared giving her the wrong idea. I had no interest in the former water nymph beyond friendship.

And that made me recall when we'd parted two months previously...

"You accompanied Rhys back to Faerie. I'm sorry if this is another difficult subject, but I have to know—what happened to him?"

She crossed her arms and rubbed her triceps through the sheer blue fabric. "I don't know. I thought things were going well with us, but one day he came to the gardens, where I awaited him for us to go on a walk, as we typically did in the mornings."

Oh. Had she and Rhys developed more than a friendly relationship? The Fae prince certainly had that rugged look women tended to admire, even without the scar.

She seemed to sense my curiosity. "I don't think he returned my interest. Rhys isn't one to be happy in a single place with a single person. I think he chafed at his responsibility of being part of the Council of Three, especially once Ellerin went on his mission."

"That tracks. What did he tell you in the garden?"

"He said he had his own mission. Like Ellerin, he couldn't say where he was going or how long he'd be gone, but it was urgent that he leave."

"Interesting. You're perceptive. Did you get any sense of what he was hiding?"

And I needed to remind myself of how, like water itself, Astrid both reflected and carried what she saw and who spent time with her. She had pure elemental qualities, unlike we gargoyles, who carried a balance of both earth and water with a little air.

"No. Only that he felt the same way you do today —determined."

The trees thinned out. The trail inclined upward, and the gray bulk of the hospital blocked out the sky.

"I'll say goodbye here." Astrid didn't give me a chance to respond before she turned and retreated into the gloom.

"Huh," I said to Sir Raleigh, who blinked at me in what I interpreted as the feline version of a shrug.

A raven landed at the edge of the asphalt. Black smoke swirled around it, and it expanded into the shape of Desmond Eath, the dark-skinned hospital coroner. Like most shifters, he seemed comfortable in his nakedness.

"We've been expecting you."

I laughed. "Could you make that any more creepy?"

His mouth split into a white-toothed grin. "I've been practicing. Barton says I need to work on my delivery."

"Seemed perfect to me." He paused by a dark blue Altima

and opened the rear driver's side door. He reached down and unzipped a duffel bag. I looked away while he dressed.

"All right," he told me after a minute. "We can go in."

"Were you and Barton afraid I wouldn't show up?" We crossed the parking lot and entered through a door marked, "Employees Only."

"No, but we expected you earlier."

"Yeah... I had to take the long way through the river path so I wouldn't get waylaid. At least, I feared I would be." I sagged with some relief when we took a back stairway to the basement floor. No one would ask me uncomfortable questions down there. I hoped.

"Oh, the crown prince thing?"

"Yes." Something about him made me want to confide in him. I sensed his perspective combined the wisdom gleaned from his long life as a shifter and the fact he dealt with death every day. "The problem is that, prior to yesterday, I hadn't taken the idea seriously."

He studied me with obsidian eyes. "What changed your mind?"

"Someone confronted me with the necessity for a prince."

He didn't ask further, for which I was grateful. "You have a deep sense of duty. Is it possible that now that you've solved your father's murder and you're relatively helpless to save your bond-mate, you're looking for a new purpose?"

I winced, although I should have expected him to put the issue bluntly. Desmond had a reputation for not mincing words. "It's possible."

Sir Raleigh craned his neck to look up at me, and I couldn't read his expression.

"Your friend here says that like his mistress, you haven't yet found the entirety of what's possible in yourself."

"You can understand him?"

"Only when he chooses to speak to me." He paused his

strong strides and reached down to pet the grimalkin. "I am honored he did."

Sir Raleigh consented to one caress, then trotted ahead.

"And he is eager to see what you've come here for."

"He told you that, too?"

A low chuckle. "No, but I can tell."

We entered the morgue. The door plate said, "Morgue, D. Eath, M.D., Coroner." What would Desmond have been had his first initial and last name not spelled, "Death?" Had they doomed him to life dealing with the worst possible outcome of hospital stays, or had he chosen that path on his own due to his abilities as a raven/vulture shifter? I doubted he would have been a pediatrician. Perhaps he had come to The Aerie to hide from the curious since dual shifter abilities tended to be rare and therefore the object of magical curiosity and suspicion. I'd only heard of a few others in my previous life.

Although I'd encountered plenty of animal corpses in my training as a vet and then creature corpses in my work with the CPDC, I exhaled with relief to find the room empty of deceased patients.

"Slow week, huh?"

"Slow for me. Good for the doctors, nurses, and patients. And you, since I had time to work on the device. We'll get started when Barton arrives."

A knock on the door preceded it opening, and Barton poked his head around. "Ah, good, you're here." He crossed the room in a few long steps, but the set of his shoulders and the plod in his stride betrayed his exhaustion to those of us who knew what to look for.

Desmond patted Barton on the shoulder. "Slow week for me, but a busy one for you, huh?"

Barton rubbed his eyes. "Yeah, one of my pediatricians is out with some sort of respiratory thing. Came down with it yesterday after being bitten by one of those bug things. I've pulled a two-day shift."

"Stones." I hadn't thought the bugs would cause lasting damage. "Any other reports of illness?"

"No. I suspect that one was an allergic reaction to the venom. She has an epi pen and has promised to call or have her husband call if she gets worse."

"Good."

"But we're not here to talk about weird bug attacks thwarted by our crown prince." I groaned, and Barton smirked. "Let's talk about how to keep you safe in Faerie."

Desmond led us to a workbench in the back. He pulled a sheet back to reveal a backpack with tubes leading to and from a modified oxygen mask.

"Go ahead and try this on."

I did so, and I found the backpack to be heavy and bulky. The mask fit, and I asked through it, "How does it work? And what are these hoses made of?" They looked like clear rubber, but they didn't have as much give.

Desmond went into lecture mode, and his enjoyment of the science came through in his animated hand motions and bright expression. "It filters the air through a substance that will neutralize the poison in Faerie's air. We analyzed your exhalations, which we trapped in the respirator. As it turns out, the substance that caused the breathing problems is similar to white phosphate, but with a different atomic signature."

I removed the mask. "How could you look at the atomic makeup?"

Barton looked anywhere but at me. "Trade secret."

"Meaning Truth Seeker technology." I hoped that meant I wouldn't owe them anything. Merlin's organization wasn't known for generosity in sharing their secrets. Or perhaps they had a matter witch on board who came to consult.

Barton confirmed my suspicion with, "Something like that."

"What's the substance in the backpack?"

"Copper sulfate. Luckily it works the same."

"How long will this thing last?"

"That's the problem," Desmond said with a sigh. "It's got enough for twelve hours, and you'll have to stop every hour and dump the spent material, or it will contaminate the rest. The other problem, as you noticed, is the hoses. The Fae Fire atom ate through rubber, so we had to use a different material that's currently under development and is something like glass, but bendier."

"And as fragile?"

Desmond nodded. "Yes. Don't pinch the hoses too hard."

I removed the pack. "So what you're telling me is that the time is limited, I risk leaving a trail by having to dump the spent copper sulfate, and it will be useless in a battle because all someone would have to do is grab a hose, and it's game over for me." My anger came through with each word, but I couldn't help it. "And I don't see how I could shift while wearing the thing because there's not enough room for my wings."

A strangely familiar sensation came over me then, of a power that moved through me. "Do better, Desmond. I deputize you in the name of the Regent to work out the bugs and problems with this device so I can do what I need to do in Faerie."

"Fuuuuck." Barton stepped back, his brown eyes wide. "You are the crown prince!"

Whatever it was passed through and left me leaning against the table. I pressed fingers to my eyeballs to give myself a sensation to anchor to. "What do you mean?"

"Has anything like that happened before?" Desmond asked. He sounded shaken as well. "I don't know what you did to me, but I can't not help you now. The compulsion is in me stronger than the one I have to shift, which is a constant battle." He sighed. "I supposed I should thank you."

I echoed his sigh. "Once. When I deputized a dimension-walker to help me rescue Reine from the time loop she'd gotten trapped in. I thought it was a fluke."

Barton shook his head. "No fluke. That was the power of the Crown Prince of the Gargoyle Court."

"What is that? Why haven't I heard of it before?"

"It's something that's been lost in the archives of history, but there have been rumors. It's a leftover from the era of the gargoyles protecting the Fae. If the Fae queen was in trouble, her primary consort, often the gargoyle prince, would have the power to compel help from the creatures around him. It's not something that can be used lightly, like if she wants a pizza. It's only if she's in mortal danger."

"So the power showing up now means she's in mortal danger if she stays in her situation?'

Barton shrugged. "I don't know. It's possible, but we don't know enough. And I don't know that I can access our historian for this considering this is gargoyle-Fae business, not something that will interfere with the human realm."

"But if Maeve keeps control of Faerie and allows the revenants take over, there may be an impact. A vet colleague told me that she's been seeing more injuries of animals who have been frightened into panic mode. What if that's from revenants appearing in the Earth realm?"

"Can you get more information?"

"Yes. I need to visit home anyway. I have a ward I need to check on."

"Kestrel?" Barton asked. "How is she doing?"

"I wish I knew." That made for another problem—Kestrel had become almost uncommunicative since my ill-fated last foray into Faerie. I suspected I was losing her like I had her parents, but I didn't know how to stop the process. All I could do was keep trying.

I politely thanked Desmond and Barton, then quietly stormed out. Well, to me it was a storm. It probably looked like a firm walk to them. Sir Raleigh darted around me and led the way.

But how could they think that their contraption was acceptable? Didn't they know that traveling to Faerie always had its risks?

All right, then. My normal planning mode was kicking in. And since it looked like my breathing apparatus was still under development, I'd have a brief chance to examine the other angles of the problem.

The question was, how long did I truly have?

7

———

REINE

I woke with the sun pouring through the windows of my childhood room. The only thing that had changed was the size of the bed, which still had its four posts and a canopy of living vines with pink and yellow flowers, the ideal colors for a small Fae princess. I rolled to my side, wishing to wake from the nightmare that had become my life. Not the kind of nightmare with monsters. Oh, no, I could face those down.

No, this nightmare was of the monotonous kind, with days that melt into each other like chocolates left too long in a bag on a hot backseat until they barely resembled what they once were.

My life in no way resembled what it once had been, not even before my exile.

A knock on my door made me squeeze my eyes shut and scrunch my face and scoot further under the blankets.

"Please be Olred, please be Olred." I wished for my old nurse to wake me as she had when I'd been a child. She would come into my room and chuckle when she saw my form under the blankets. Then she'd pretend she didn't see me and ask in a singsong voice, "Where's the princess? Oh, no, we've lost Princess Reine."

And then no matter how hard I tried not to, even to the point of one time biting my lips together so hard they bled, I'd giggle.

"Oh, what's that? Was that a bird?'

And I'd giggle harder until I was laughing, and then she'd come and whip the blankets away, and we'd both collapse into laughter.

And then we'd have to stop, and I'd get dressed and pressed and braided, and I'd have to be the perfect little princess until Rhys came along. After he began to toddle about, he'd become my primary responsibility, and I would go with Olred to wake him. He didn't play "lost prince." No, he had always been "grumpy prince," chafing at the restrictions of being a royal child. The scar had suited his demeanor.

Another knock dragged me out of my memories and away from that old resentment, which I couldn't help but poke at, like a mouth ulcer or the wounds inside a pair of bitten-too-hard lips.

"Your Highness, your breakfast is here."

I emerged from under the blankets. The last of the fog of dream-heavy sleep disappeared, and the sounds and smells of the world outside intruded. Sometimes there were screams and cries, sometimes moans. And always the faint odor of hospital-grade cleaning products that still didn't mask the underlying bitterness of the iron that kept us all imprisoned. I kept a glass of water with lime by my bed so when I woke, I could chase the taste from the back of my throat.

And the constant repulsion, a whine in the depth of my very soul. I had habituated somewhat, but it took every chance to reinstated itself into my awareness.

The orderly didn't knock again. A key turned in the lock from the outside, and she strode in with a wheeled cart with a silver-domed tray under which lay the breakfast for, oh, what day of the week was it? I couldn't remember, nor did I try to. It helped to have at least a little surprise, even if that surprise came in the form of lingonberry rather than blueberry pancakes or ham and eggs instead of a *croque monsieur*.

At least they didn't feed me hospital food. At least not yet. I knew the level of my perks would ebb and flow with the largesse and patience of Queen Lilith, who as of now treated me as a guest in her capital city. Like the room I slept in, it was a painful reminder of what I'd once been. Who I'd once been.

"Thank you," I mumbled and moved to the chair in the corner, from where I could see the grounds and the pond that lay under the dingy sky like an old, foggy mirror. I had yet to see into the pond, so opaque were its waters. Nothing appeared to live in it, as nothing marred its pristine surface. I'd avoided getting too close after that first look when I'd just arrived and had gotten the "tour," as Healer Wilfrin had called it. Mirrors and I didn't get along these days.

I ate my breakfast, which might have been French toast with strawberries. Perhaps it was Tuesday, then. Or did they mess with me by changing the rotation? It didn't matter.

The only utensil they gave me was a spoon with a dull edge, so I picked up my food and ate it by hand. The orderly waited for me to finish, then gathered everything up.

I stood back, having learned that they got nervous when I approached before they said I could do so.

"It's a lovely day to draw by the pond, Your Highness." Her pointed ears stood out against her dark hair under her little nurse's cap, and she smiled the wan grin of the overly patient and underly paid.

I didn't want to go draw by the pond, but I knew better than to argue. Her hint wasn't so much a suggestion as a command.

"That sounds lovely. I'll be ready in an hour." We could all pretend.

"Very well." She nodded, then unlocked the door again and wheeled the cart out. I tried to plug my ears against the sound of the key turning in the lock again, but I knew I'd still feel it even if I succeeded in not hearing it, which I never did.

I looked down at the little gray plush cat, which Basil had bleached so it had one white paw.

"Well, fake Sir Raleigh, what do you think? Shall I try to draw?"

It gazed up at me with unblinking green glass eyes, and I picked it up and cuddled it to my chest. It made for a poor substitute for my clever companion, but the asylum didn't allow pets, even if you were the queen of the Light Fae. I hadn't had the heart to tear the stitching to see what had been hidden inside. It felt rude to eviscerate my friend, although I knew I'd have to eventually.

I gave fake Sir Raleigh another hug and placed him on the ground by the bed, which I made. I didn't have to, but it gave me some satisfaction to have at least a little order in the room of my own making. Then I walked to the wall opposite the window and checked my reflection.

"You can't hide who you are here," Ellerin had told me the first time I'd come to the asylum as a somewhat unwilling visitor.

My eyes shone with as much depth as fake Sir Raleigh's, and I looked ever more the insane Fae I'd doomed myself to be. Or my mother and grandmother had.

Nope, couldn't go in that direction. If I wallowed in my resentment, I truly would go insane, and I wanted to avoid Wilfrin's favorite sedation method as long as possible.

I brushed out my curls, then braided them and twisted them into a long strand around my head, making them into the only crown I wore these days. I chose a simple long-sleeved satin gown. None of the dresses had metal fixtures, so I did the best I could to close the cloth-covered buttons up the back of the tan and blue striped dress. Hades, I missed wearing pants. How had I missed that the dress code for this place was mid-Victorian? I should've gotten the clue from it being an asylum, for Fae's sake.

The orderly, whose name might have been Jane or Joan or something else plain and human-sounding, unlocked the door. After she looked me over to make sure I hadn't done anything crazy to my appearance, she motioned for me to turn around. She closed the buttons in the middle of my back, which I hadn't been able to reach.

"There, now you look lovely. Shoes?"

I slipped my feet into the leather slippers that lived by the door and followed her out.

I had the entire back wing to myself. It supposedly had the biggest rooms to hold the VIP patients. Who had my grandmother anticipated imprisoning here? Besides me, which I could no longer deny.

The room had been ready and waiting for me in a place that didn't allow magic to be practiced in it, at least not strong magic.

No. Again, I'd put myself here. And I couldn't ponder beyond the day because then I'd truly go mad.

ALTHOUGH CRUAIDH WAS in its dreary season, I could tell myself that the gray sky only made the green of the grass and the yellows and reds of the leaves on the trees surrounding the lawn all the more vivid. As Jane-Jean had promised, I found my easel and pastels waiting for me near the pond, but not too close. They knew how I felt about it. The buildings of the city should have risen above the lawn like around Central Park in New York, but only blank sky stretched beyond the treetops. A clever illusion, I was sure, to make us feel as though we were in the countryside. Not that Faerie had much true countryside, at least not in the lands of the dark Fae. We had some in the light Fae lands, but no matter where one went, danger always lurked. It was just prettier in some places than in others.

I hadn't brought fake Sir Raleigh with me, and even if I had, I doubted he would make me miss the real one less. I recalled him chasing bugs in a field when Law—when my lover and I had gone for a picnic before I'd returned to Scotland.

No, I wouldn't allow myself to think my lover's name or even his species. I could only shove my heartbreak and grief into a little ball in the middle of my chest that felt like wistful longing near where our bond had gone numb.

"You'll eventually go mad if you keep doing that." Healer Wilfrin's voice behind me startled me, and I bent to pick up the green pastel I'd dropped.

"Keep doing what?"

"Stuffing your emotions." He walked around and stood by the easel. The top of his head barely reached the bottom of the pad of paper on it, and his facial wrinkles between his large ears arranged themselves into an expression that was probably supposed to be of sympathy. Instead, I'd come to name that particular moue "constipated Yoda."

"Everyone needs a hobby." I drew the contour of the ground.

"Just because you're stuck here doesn't mean you belong here. You don't need to drive yourself to madness to fit in."

A wisp of memory floated through my brain. *It's okay to not fit in. Different can be good, Princess. But sometimes you need to pretend. You can do that, can't you?*

The charcoal-colored pastel I'd grabbed to outline the cat wobbled in my grasp, so I lowered my hand and tried to speak without the tremor coming through my voice. "Do you need something, Healer Wilfrin?"

"I'm only doing my job, Your Highness. It wouldn't hurt for you to express your emotions, even if in private."

My lips tucked into a twist of distaste. "How do you know I'm not?"

He cupped his hands and pressed them together. "Because I sense them in you, like a balloon ready to pop if you blow any more air into it. You're a powerful Fae." His ears drooped, and he shook his head. "I dread to know what will happen if you do get to that point."

I shrugged. "Magic is muted here, so probably not much." And if I did have a good cry, I wasn't going to let him see it.

"One never knows." He bowed. "I'll leave you to your drawing."

I closed my eyes and willed my tear ducts not to overflow by picturing them as medical textbook illustrations and visualizing them as dry. After a few deep breaths, the pressure subsided, and I blinked the blurriness from my vision. I was a queen. I would act like one no matter where I was. I wouldn't give them any excuses to keep me in that place a second longer than my sentence.

My stupid, shortsighted, voluntary sentence.

But I'd done it to save the gar—the lover I couldn't let die. I wouldn't give Maeve the satisfaction of having hurt me that much. So I'd broken my own heart before she could.

Different for a Fae, indeed.

I wished the real Sir Raleigh was there. Although I'd never been much of an artist, I gave free rein to my emotions and allowed some of the pent-up frustration and sorrow to wash through my fingertips, which flew from pastel tray to paper and back in an almost blur. Like magic, the image of Sir Raleigh chasing bugs in the field appeared against the summer haze-blue of the sky and the green of the grass in Piedmont Park. I did put in the silhouettes of the downtown Atlanta buildings in the background, and I almost held my breath when the image of the grimalkin's impish expression began to form. I clenched my teeth so I wouldn't sob when the details filled in, and I tried to stop myself, but I couldn't. Finally, I loosened my control and allowed my memory to flow on to the page. My heart ached for any comfort, and if that was what it needed, who was I to stop it?

My fingertips tingled when I put the last pastel back in the tray. Half of the oily chalks had been used to bare nubs, but the magical tray restored them for their next use. The toys of the insane were self-perpetuating. I would normally have preferred pencils, but those were too sharp to be allowed.

I glanced down at my fingers and found my right hand sported several colors, the ones in the drawing. I pressed a handprint to the top right corner of the page, a sort of signature more personal than a single-word name. Besides, my name meant "queen," so my handprint gave the piece more specificity. I suppose I could have signed it with the name I used in the Earth realm, Renee River, but she was as inaccessible to me as Law—my lover.

My hand and head ached, so I went inside and left the painting on the lawn. I'd have Jane-Jean bring it to me later. Perhaps I'd even ask them to frame it and hang it in my room.

I cleaned up and napped until lunch, which I ate at the high table in the dining hall. Only a few other residents—the only other ones in the asylum—ate in there as well. We all had the same soup and bread and ate with the same dull spoons and smeared softened butter on the bread with our fingertips.

When I walked back out to the lawn to find my picture, the memory of which had caused me the first smile I'd had since I'd arrived, I found the easel toppled and the pad of paper lying in the grass.

"No!" I knelt beside it and gingerly picked it up like it was the fallen body of a friend. When I turned the picture over, I found a large, dark smudge in the middle where Sir Raleigh had been. The dew had ruined it.

"*No!*" I screamed, and the part of me in which I held all the emotions cracked open. Rage, frustration, sorrow, fear, and hatred poured from me in a lava-hot eruption of throat-searing shouts, sobs, and sighs. I beat my fists against the ground to punish *something* for my state and place and stuckness. I yelled. I screamed. I raged. I took the entire setup—easel, pad, paper, and pastels—and threw them in the pond.

The roiling of the water startled me out of my fit just before two orderlies grabbed me by the arms and dragged me back into the asylum.

8

LAWRENCE

I had plenty of opportunities to follow up on Barton's request to know more about potential revenant activity. Over the next week, I drove to Atlanta to grab clothes and make sure my house still stood. I also needed time to myself in a house without other gargoyles in it. My mother and Micah exchanged knowing glances whenever I did or said anything particularly authoritative, and I had to take breaks from their hope and my resistance. At least in Atlanta I could pretend to be the old me, Lawrence Gordon the veterinarian, but I found my old life didn't fit like it had. My best friends were gone. Kestrel had moved to an apartment in Athens, and the semester would start in a few weeks. I thought about reaching out to Professor Grand-Pied to see if he wanted to meet up for beers, but I left him alone. No telling what the Normals would do if they found he was hanging out with another paranormal creature. Probably try to get him to recruit me.

My only company came from two sources, my fellow scientist Latonya Francis and my fellow veterinarian Elise MacNamara, both of whom supplied me with information.

Latonya, a dark-skinned Black woman, and I met for coffee

or tea in a little cafe in Norcross, one of the northern suburbs of Atlanta far enough away from the CPDC for us to not be observed. Plus, she knew the owners, who gave us a private room in which to meet. On this particular Wednesday, I arrived first and ordered our usuals—an oat milk latte for her and a skim latte for me—then took them into the room, which had been marked as "Reserved—Article Club." I set down the drinks and the oversized chocolate chip cookie I figured we'd split at one end of the long table and reviewed my notes.

Barton had given me ideas of questions to ask and things for Latonya to search for to make it easier to gather information about the Order of the Silver Arrow. If we were going to find the letters to exonerate Reine, we needed to know about the secret society that held them. I'd heard of them as a young gargoyle, mostly as a warning to stay away from them and anyone wearing a silver arrow pin because they wanted to destroy all shifters. They had more of an obsession with purity than most Fae I knew.

Not that I knew that many.

Latonya entered through the back door, and her stern expression softened when she saw the drink and cookie. "You know how to brighten a girl's day."

Her arms were full with her bag, which she supported on the bottom with one hand and held the flap closed with the other, so I pulled out the chair at the head of the table. She set the bag on the chair and scooted out the one across the table. I could almost hear my mother scolding, *You should have helped the lady with the heavy bag, not the chair.*

Yes, I had definitely been spending too much time in The Aerie. Or had let my mother get too much in my head. Or both.

"Looks like you've got a good haul." I at least waited to sit until she had.

"Yes, we had some info on the OSA from several decades ago, when there was a threat that they'd use some sort of chemical attack to contribute to the chaos in Ireland. Apparently, they have a thing against leprechauns as well as shifters."

"I guess leprechauns are a kind of shifter. I've never met one."

She smirked. "Some can take different forms, but only a few have that talent."

Had she dated a leprechaun? No, I couldn't ask that, not even for scientific reasons.

"You look tired," I said instead, partially because I knew that was something concerned friends said to each other and also, she did.

"Long nights. Not doing anything interesting." Her shoulders slumped. "Cimex being in charge of the CPDC should feel familiar, but it's just wrong with John and Beverly gone. Oh, how's Kestrel?"

"Doing okay as far as I can tell. She texts me occasionally. I try to leave her alone while letting her know I care about her and am here for her."

"It's a tricky balance." She sipped her latte. "Perfect, thanks. Also, may I?" She gestured to the plate with the cookie on it. "I skipped lunch."

"Go ahead. Have all you want. What's going on?"

"You'd told me that Cimex was taking orders from the impostor queen of the light Fae, and I didn't believe it, until..." She shook her head. "I can't believe I'm telling you this, but it's horrible. Someone has been working on a way to make Fae, specifically high Fae, immune to iron. They've made progress, but it's stalled. Cimex has been trying to engage in research—animal research, specifically animals from Faerie—to see what other methods could help."

"But where? Oh..." My stomach dropped, twisted, and did a nauseating break dance. "Please don't tell me..."

She nodded. "They're updating your old lab since it was set up for veterinary research. I've sabotaged them as much as I can, but I can only do so much. Lawrence, you have to expose him."

"I don't know how, though. The Truth Seekers are aware. At least I think they are." I'd mentioned it to Barton, hadn't I? I couldn't remember. I made a mental note to do so as soon as I returned to The Aerie.

"Thanks. I don't dare. I'd risk exposing that I'm helping you with this..." She inclined her head toward her bag.

Competing desires—justice for Reine and protecting innocent animals from torture I couldn't even imagine—battled in the center of my chest. Perhaps I could connect them, make one lead to the other. If Maeve weren't in charge, that would stop the animal research, wouldn't it?

Or would unscrupulous Fae—talk about a redundant phrase with a few exceptions—continue?

Stones, I needed to get Reine back on her throne. This added more fuel to that already raging inferno of determination in my chest.

"All right, what have you got?"

She scooted the now-empty plate and her latte to the side and pulled a thick, yellowed, and folded piece of paper from her bag. She unfolded and unfolded and unfolded until a topographical map lay spread over the table. I recognized certain names from my time in Scotland and Reine's memories.

"It's an old map, but I've cross-referenced it with various reports, both physical and magical, and I'm fairly certain I've pinpointed the location of the order's headquarters."

Hope flared like a crystalline rainbow in my chest, but I tamped it down with logic. I couldn't be disappointed again. "Fairly certain isn't very certain."

"No, someone needs to go and scout out the location for us to be mostly or very certain."

I sighed, although after dealing with the Fae for as long as I had, I should be used to less-than-satisfying degrees of certainty. "So go to Scotland? And how can they be sure that's the right place?"

"You'd need someone who's energetically sensitive and able to hide. The security will be insane."

I rubbed my eyes. "I don't know anyone outside the Fae who... No, wait. I may know someone."

"Oh?"

"Yes, although I can't promise he'll cooperate."

Latonya shrugged. "I've done what I can. I'll leave you the map and references. I'm afraid I have to bow out of our little arrangement so I can devote my energy to matters at the CPDC."

"I'm in your debt, so please tell me how I can help you there. If I can."

"I may be in touch to ask you about creatures of Faerie if they start importing them."

"All right." I thought about Sir Raleigh, who waited at my house, and the conversation I'd had with Astrid. "Be careful. They may look similar to Earth realm animals, but they're much more dangerous."

She stood, as did I. "Thanks for the reminder. I'm afraid Cimex doesn't know what he's getting into. What he's getting us into."

As promised, she left the books and other materials from her bag, and then she slipped out of the back door. I gathered everything up and pondered our conversation, which had again left me with more questions. Like, what did the goings-on at the CPDC have to do with Reine's imprisonment, if anything? What kind of danger were they in?

And could I get Grand-Pied to go to Scotland and check out the Order of the Silver Arrow's headquarters for me?

All that would have to wait. My phone buzzed with a text from Elise—*"Got another one! Meet me at my office."*

I DROVE over to Elise's office, which took me a while due to traffic. Sir Raleigh popped on to my passenger seat after I parked. His green eyes glittered in a way I hadn't seen before. He resembled a Fae creature more than a cat.

"Do you sense something?" I asked.

Raleigh blinked but didn't answer.

"All right, you're here just in case something happens. Got it."

He didn't argue, so I assumed I was right in my guess.

We walked into the clinic. Elise's receptionist was packing up to leave but paused to show me and Sir Raleigh, whose eyes had returned to normal, back to Elise's private office.

"I'm glad you're here, Doctor Gordon," the receptionist whispered. "She saw something today that spooked her, but she's not saying what. I hope you can help her figure it out."

As far as Elise's staff knew, I was an expert on unusual injuries, since that's what she'd been reporting to me.

Elise had rearranged her office since I'd been there last. The small space still held bookshelves bursting with books on everything from veterinary texts to historical treatises on animal worship. Instead of the previous painting of a pair of Siamese cats, an antique mirror hung across from her desk and reflected the waning light from the windows.

I'd left Faerie just after the Summer Solstice, and my recovery had taken a good two months. Now we had passed the Equinox, and the days grew shorter. The sun would set in an hour, and it was already sinking toward the horizon with a deep golden glow. Normally it would have made me feel peaceful, but my heart ached without the bond. Another night without Reine. What fraction of the day she'd passed had mine accounted for? She'd once explained that the time differential didn't move at the same pace all the time, but the longer one spent in Faerie, the more human time passed.

"It's kind of a relativity thing no one understands," she'd tried to explain. *"A couple of days here is roughly equivalent to the same there, but a week here may be two there, and so on. It's not steady or exponential, though."*

Elise found me at the window.

"I'm glad you made it. Hello, Sir Raleigh." She bent down, and he sniffed her proffered hand, then turned his back, tail up. "I guess he's not happy with me today."

"I had a meeting I had to leave him at home for, so he's not happy with anyone."

Indeed, he huffed and curled up under her desk.

"He's really bonded to you, hasn't he?"

I glanced down to where a tip of gray tail stuck out from the shadows. It twitched, so I knew he was listening and chose my words carefully. "I'll never replace Reine, but I hope I'm an adequate temporary substitute."

She smiled, and her voice softened. "I know the feeling.' A woman of Indian descent, Elise had a high-cheeked combination of tan skin, black hair, and dark brown eyes that turned liquid with emotion. Most men would find her attractive. I had the first time we'd met at a conference, but I'd reached a low place in my failure to find my father's killer and hadn't felt worthy of a relationship. Then the next time I'd seen her had been when she'd helped out Sir Raleigh with a broken leg. He hadn't been chased by a revenant, but instead had been kicked out of Reine's energy field by an attack and had then sought me out to help find her. Elise and I had the mutual respect of veterinary colleagues, and she'd hinted that she was willing to comfort me in other ways, but I hadn't taken her up on her offer. The tension between us had settled into a warm acquaintanceship held together by our mutual mission to figure out what caused the increase in injuries from panicked animals falling from high places or running into things.

"Who's our patient today?"

"Come see. The owner is still here and is happy to talk to us."

A movement in my peripheral vision made me turn to look, but all I could see in the mirror's surface was our reflections, slightly distorted by the antique glass.

We left the office, and I asked, "How long have you had the mirror?"

"Oh, it's a family heirloom. My great grandmother had it in her parlor opposite the fireplace. She said it was to help reflect the glow, but I always suspected she used it to keep track of our expressions without looking at us. It fit perfectly on the wall in the office after I moved things, so I had to bring it."

Should I tell her something had made me uneasy? No, I reasoned, I would sound paranoid. More than I already did.

The cat's owner, an older man with grizzled gray and black hair and beard, sat and held the gray striped ball of fluff on his lap in the otherwise empty waiting room. He wore scrubs, and the sleeping kitten had a cone on. One paw was bandaged.

Elise introduced us. "Doctor Rizzo, this is Doctor Gordon, the specialist I told you about."

He took in my appearance with bright blue eyes. "I'm sorry for not getting up."

"Please don't disturb your friend," I said.

"Thank you. He's had a rough day."

Elise and I took seats across from him with one chair between us. Sir Raleigh slunk out and took up a position under my chair.

"This is my supervisor, Sir Raleigh," I explained. "What happened?"

He looked down at the sleeping kitten and ran a light finger over its fur. A faint purr vibrated the air between us. "I don't know. I came home from my shift this afternoon to find this little guy yowling at something in the spare bedroom. I went in and saw him on top of the wardrobe, which is about ten feet tall. I have high ceilings. He was poofed up and spitting at the mirror over the bed."

I couldn't help myself. "Did you see anything in the mirror?"

Doctor Rizzo looked between the two of us, then at Elise. "Would you excuse us for a moment?"

Elise shot me a puzzled look and stood. "Of course."

Once she'd left, Rizzo leaned forward and lowered his voice. "You're a gargoyle, yes?"

All my hair tingled at the roots. "Yes. And you are...?"

"Something not human. Can't tell you what. But I can tell you that something came out of that mirror and chased after my Jerry, who leaped to the ground and hurt his paw."

Sir Raleigh emerged from under the chair and stood with front paws on the seat beside Rizzo.

"What did you see?" I asked. "And do you mind if he takes a sniff?"

"And a grimalkin? Well, today is full of surprises. Sure." He held Jerry to the side so Raleigh could reach him.

The kitten opened its green eyes when Sir Raleigh sniffed, then licked him. The grimalkin turned his bright green gaze on me and said, "*Revenant.*"

"So that's how they're getting through... Doctor Rizzo, is the mirror in the spare bedroom an antique?"

"What? Yes, I got it at an estate sale. Too pretty to pass up. But I checked—it didn't come with any ghosts or other issues."

I didn't ask how he checked, and I understood why he'd dismissed Elise.

"And did your friend just say, revenant?" His bushy brows drew down. "As in Fae souls not yet fully reincarnated?"

"Yes, he did. The Great Rising is upon us earlier than expected."

He stood. "Then I have work to do, people to warn. I'm glad we met, Doctor Gordon. Please keep me updated."

"I would if I could. I can't breathe the air in Faerie."

"Ah, yes, the age-old problem. Well, well... History is about to change, then, isn't it? I'll be sure to cover my mirror. You do the same if you have any."

"Wait, do you know why the revenants are coming through them?"

"Some mirrors can be used as a portal to other realms if they're old and distorted enough."

I stood and rushed toward the back of the clinic. "Thank you for the info. I'm afraid I have to go."

Before I had to explain why, Elise's scream made us both jump. Rizzo placed the kitten on the floor, and we ran toward her office.

9

REINE

The orderlies brought me to my room, and I collapsed on the bed. Whatever I had released into the ground and the pond had left me drained, the core of my soul left open and raw like the inside of a scooped-out gourd. What kind of seeds had I planted with my fit?

I soon found out. The click of the lock and opening of the door announced....

"Hello, Healer Wilfrin," I croaked as though I really had spewed out lava, or at least boiling water.

"Hello, Your Highness. Would you care to tell me what all that was about?"

"I wouldn't." I bet the little arse would revel in the chance to say, "I told you so," and he'd take it whether I invited him to or not.

"I have a guess." Yep. "All of the feelings you've been repressing came out, didn't they, when you found your painting of your pet destroyed?"

I didn't answer. I hugged the Sir Raleigh stuffed animal to my side. Perhaps I could recreate the feeling of the real Sir Raleigh snuggled up to me while I slept. When he wasn't sleeping on my chest or my head. I'd left whatever Basil had sneaked in there in him because I could pretend he had a skeleton, which made him feel more real.

Gods, I *was* going insane, wasn't I?

"I can give you something to block the emotional pain."

That made me roll up on one elbow to glare at him. "No ambrosia. I've seen what it does. Trust me, there are better ways to sedate people."

"People, but not Fae. Your metabolisms don't process human drugs like they do. Do you not think we've tried?"

I pushed up to sit and crossed my ankles. "I think you're stuck in old models. How would you know if you haven't tried? There's a new drug called luridatone that works on lycanthropes. It blocks their animal brains. It could be worth a trial."

"As if we have the money or resources for a trial. Have you forgotten where you are?"

"Unfortunately, no." I looked around. "I'm in this creepy facsimile of my old room that lacks anything useful like hair pins. Are you afraid I'm going to kill myself by styling a French twist?"

"Standard precautions, but I will make a bargain with you."

I wanted to flop back and cover my face, but I held myself straight. "What kind of bargain? Those have gotten me in trouble."

He laughed in a squeaky little wheeze that made me want to strangle him. "I understand. No, it's nothing potentially harmful. You're a physician, and I could use the help."

"What?" Surprise nearly made me topple over. "You want me to assist you? Here?"

"Yes. I accept your challenge. You show me there's a better way to help Fae with psychological irregularities, and we'll stop using ambrosia."

I thought through his offer. "I don't hear anything in there for me. It sounds like you know you need to change your methods, and you want me to show you for free or out of some sort of altruism. Fae don't do altruism, remember?"

He cocked his head and tapped his pointy chin with a gnarled finger. "That was an assessment to make sure you are in your right Fae mind. You passed."

Hades, he was cleverer than I'd given him credit for.

"Good. So what is the real bargain?"

"If you help me in your capacity as a physician, you will no longer be locked in your room."

"Oh, yay, I can have free run of the prison, but I can't leave. I need more than that."

His ears drooped, but I didn't give into his attempt to manipulate my emotions.

"Very well," he said at last. "What do you want?"

I chose my words carefully. "I want free reign of the asylum." And yes, I meant "reign," not "rein," but I counted on him not to notice the difference. "I want to wear what I want, including the clothing I brought and other garments in that style. I want to be able to communicate with those on the outside and to invite guests to see me."

He wrinkled his nose. "Essentially, you want to treat this as your palace."

"I want to create circumstances that will be truly beneficial to my mental health." I shrugged. "How would it look for a Fae queen to go mad under your care?"

"Ah, and a side of blackmail. Well-played, Your Highness. Well-played." He thought for a moment, then sighed. "I can grant you all except the communication and the ability to invite guests." He held up a hand before I could object. "Those things are beyond my power."

An electric tingle emerged against my backside from fake Sir Raleigh. "But you would grant them if you could?"

"Yes."

"Then I will hold them in reserve until the time you can acquiesce to that part of my bargain."

He glanced over his shoulder and around the room, then nodded. "Be careful, Your Highness. You are dabbling in danger beyond your knowledge or control."

"I'll take my chances. What have I got to lose?"

"Unfortunately, the asylum likes to answer that question. By the way, it will have to return your clothing to you. I will arrange for a shopkeeper to come and offer you more garments."

"Thank you."

He inclined his head. "I will leave you now. With the door open."

When he left and didn't lock the door behind him, I picked up fake Sir Raleigh. The hard thing inside had grown warm. The change meant I couldn't ignore it any longer.

"Sorry, buddy," I said and found a seam, which I sliced open with my right index fingernail. I dug around inside and pulled out a black onyx mirror in a frame of platinum. The frame twined around the mirror in the shape of two snakes, one with purple gemstone eyes and one with blue. It reminded me of the caduceus symbol.

It looked like I'd have my communication device, after all. But what would it cost to use it?

I didn't ask the question out loud, but a vibration rumbled through the asylum.

I stood and looked around the room. "I don't know who or what you are, but I am a queen of Faerie, and I demand for you to show yourself or at least communicate with me in a way I can understand."

Another rumble, this one quieter, vibrated through my feet.

I sighed. At least I had told it—whatever it was—that I wasn't interested in its games. Whether it would pay attention to me was another question.

I opened the closet door to find the outfit I'd worn when I arrived there. It had been washed and pressed, and I gratefully ditched the dress and donned my jeans, light green T-shirt, and faux leather jacket. I closed my eyes, finally feeling a bit like myself. I didn't see my shoes or socks yet, but I hoped they'd appear as well. At least the slippers provided were comfortable.

I opened the door and looked both ways down the hallway. A glow at the end drew me toward it, and I found another space with a stained-glass window, this one of blues, turquoise, and greens. Ocean colors. I swallowed against the salty wave of nostalgia that rose through my torso and threatened to burst through my eyes. When would I see the ocean again? How many times had I looked at it when I was doing my medical training in the Caribbean and taken the view for granted? And how was Max, my colleague and friend who'd trained with me? The last time I'd seen him, he'd teetered on the edge of sanity from not being able to use his wizard powers in the Fae prison. I hoped that, like Lawrence, he'd recovered. I'd ask Basil, but I didn't want him to think I expected him to do all my errands. Plus, being in the asylum made me feel more like he was doing favors for me rather than serving me as a queen.

What did he want? I'd thought we'd come to a friendly arrangement, but his behavior during our meeting had been more "guy who wanted out of the friend zone" than friend.

I had other, more pressing questions. How had I not noticed the glow from the window before? It wasn't like the weather in Cruaidh changed much. Had I been preoccupied with my own situation to the point I'd ignored or missed it?

That didn't feel right. Had the asylum revealed something to me when I'd confronted it? I found that answer more disturbing.

Who would know? I didn't want to ask Wilfrin because he'd shown his limit to what he was willing to reveal. Did the asylum have an archive? Medical facilities had to keep records, right?

They did in the Earth realm, but as Wilfrin had reminded me, the rules differed in Faerie. I bet they didn't even have HIPAA here, which presented its own set of disturbing possibilities.

I wandered through the quiet hallways. How many Fae had come here and passed into their ten-thousand-year sleep? How many wouldn't rise again because of Wilfrin's liberal use of ambrosia, that addictive substance that eroded a Fae's soul such that it would dissipate at death? Who had set up that system, and why? Who had decided to play god with others' fate?

While my grandmother Tatiana had possessed her ego and her faults, I didn't think she could have been that cruel. But if she'd inherited the system of sending threats to the asylum, she would have been more likely to accept it and use it because that's what Fae queens did. I'd come to recognize many of those assumptions after returning to Faerie from the Earth realm. It was easier to see systems from the outside once I'd been away from them for a few centuries.

No, Tatiana and Lilith had created the asylum' Together. Just because a queen was of the light Fae didn't mean all her intentions were good. That was an Earth prejudice.

How many of my own systems and beliefs needed a good airing out and examination? I shuddered. That would be a question for another time.

I stepped outside into the cloudy late afternoon and found Olred and Larry Leafmore outside in the garden. Larry, my old teacher, had been sent to the asylum after he objected to my exile, and I had a fondness for him for that and because of humorous memories associated with his pedantic style of teaching. Now, as an adult, I had a new sympathy for him. How difficult had it been to try to shove knowledge about history and culture into the heads of young Fae who wanted nothing more than to be outside exploring their burgeoning magical abilities?

Olred blinked, and some of the fog cleared from her expression. The twin snakes of sorrow and anger twirled around my heart. Who could she have been if she had been treated humanely? If my grandmother hadn't sent her to the asylum to punish her for what she knew?

Or had that been my mother, Maeve? Olred had kept the secret of my mother's consorting with the Gray Fae, aka my father Ellerin. Had she threatened Maeve to expose the knowledge when my mother exiled me and Rhys to the Earth realm? Now guilt joined and danced with the other emotions. Somehow, I had been responsible for Olred's fate, as I was also indirectly the cause of Larry Leafmore's imprisonment.

Therefore, I owed it to them to make things better.

"Hello," I said, and I inwardly cringed at the tentativeness of my greeting.

"Hello, Princess Reine," Larry replied. "Lovely day, isn't it?"

As usual, I didn't correct him. I certainly didn't feel like much of a queen at the moment. "Yes. May I join you?"

He patted a place on the bench beside him. Olred continued to sit cross-legged on the grass, and she picked a couple of daisies, which she twined into a chain. The ones she picked immediately replaced themselves, so she picked and added those. I watched. The rhythmic motion of her hands and the continued growth of the flowers mesmerized me.

"She does that to keep herself from lashing out," Larry stage whispered. "She hasn't had ambrosia in a few days and is trying to stop them giving it to her."

"There's not much of me left, Princess." Olred spoke without looking up. Her gray brows bent toward each other with her efforts to focus. "I have to preserve what there is."

"I agree." Now I hesitated because I didn't know what they would think. Would they believe I'd gone to Wilfrin's side?

Olred's lips curved into a gentle smirk. "You look more far gone than I, with your wearing men's clothing. What do you think you are?"

I laughed. "I've gotten comfortable in these. On my travels, I mean. Those dresses just weren't me."

"And who are you?" Larry asked. "You've grown from the little Reine in my classes causing mischief with that redheaded girl. What was her name, Aoine?"

Aoine's betrayal still stung, but I forced a smile. "Yes, Aoine. She's the Lady of the Forest now."

Larry chuckled. "For now. She'll have competition soon enough."

"Larry," Olred admonished. "Now don't go telling tales."

"No, I want to hear them." I said turned to give Larry my full attention. "What do you mean?"

He demurred, "I'm not the court historian anymore, Princess."

I'd forgotten he'd been in that position, but that had also been several hundred years before. That's why Fae needed historians. We lost a lot of details with our long lives and memories.

"Have you met the guy who was? He was pretty useless. Couldn't even figure out an organizational system." Not to mention he'd been plotting against my grandmother. Luckily for him, he'd vanished when I'd taken the throne. Or maybe he'd gone to wherever Maeve stashed her allies. Filling that position was yet another thing I'd left undone. Hades, I needed to figure out how to take care of administrative stuff.

Larry chuckled again, and it sounded like his throat was reaching for a laugh but couldn't quite make it. I suspected those muscles hadn't been used much, if at all, in recent times. "I hadn't heard who was appointed my successor."

"I only met him once. He was a traitor to my grandmother by the name of Duke Henry Alderbranch."

Larry shuddered. "One of Maeve's pets. I'm not surprised he proved ineffective."

"So what did you mean by Aoine not being the Lady of the Forest for much longer? Who's her competition?"

He and Olred exchanged looks.

"You unlocked that box, Larry." Olred said with a shrug. "Do you trust her?"

Those words from my former nurse punched me right in the solar plexus, and I sucked in a quick breath, then gasped, "Why wouldn't you trust me?"

"You're the queen now, aren't you?" Olred pointed a finger at me. "Yet you haven't told us. Us! Your nurse and your teacher. Why don't you trust us? Do you think we're crazy? That we deserve to have been in this hellhole all these centuries? Why didn't you release us once you took the throne?"

Unfortunately, she had a good point. "I'm sorry. I was overwhelmed with my other duties and meant to, but every time I thought about it, something else came up."

"That's how they bury us here." Olred snorted. "They make us unimportant. Aren't you afraid you'll be made unimportant here, Your Highness? That your title will become as useful as this stupid daisy chain, which will wilt and disappear under the moon, even if we never see it? No Luna for the lunatics."

She cackled at her own joke.

"Olred," Larry warned. "Please calm yourself. You don't want them to find you like this."

Olred shook her head. "Like this or that or the other. Don't go complain to your mother. You share her blood, though her name is mud, and your fate is unlike any other."

She regarded me with complete sanity with that last line, and a sensation of icy lightning struck through me. "I..."

"It's important to remember where you came from, Your

Highness. Sometimes it's more important to look that way instead of where you're going. Not that we're going anywhere except inside. I'm tired." She stood, as did Larry, who held out his arm for her to take. I watched them walk toward the asylum and disappear inside.

Then I rubbed my arms and walked toward the lake, although I couldn't say why. The water bubbled, and I sensed it ran deeper than a typical pond would. What did that mean? Or did it reflect the instability of the consciousness and subconsciousness of the Fae in the asylum?

Olred's accusation and mockery made for an unsettled feeling that persisted no matter how much I tried to walk it off. I wished for someone, anyone, to talk to about it. No, most of all, I wished for Lawrence. He would understand and say something comforting.

I sensed the moon rising to my left, and although I couldn't see it, I turned my head in that direction. Was he standing under the same moon in the Earth realm? How much time had passed where he was? It's not like the relationship was linear.

A splash made me whirl to face the pond, and a series of large, concentric ripples spread from the center of it. Whatever was in there, I didn't want to know, at least not now. Not ever. The shivers had returned, and I recalled Ellerin fighting and then negotiating with the Kraken in the lake with the haunted boat.

Fae bodies of water, especially the ones in this part of the realm, had their nasty secrets. Like everyone. The question was, when would I be forced to face this one?

10

LAWRENCE

We reached Elise's office to find her cornered behind her desk by two wispy humanoid figures. They turned their glowing eyes and gaping mouths toward me and Rizzo, and I heard them chorus in secret conversation, "*Lunch.*"

I cursed my lack of magical abilities. These weren't animals whose behavior I could predict and manipulate. Sir Raleigh changed into his grimalkin form, a black panther with bat wings, and growled. He leaped on to the desk between the revenants and Elise, and she ducked out of the way of his lashing tail.

"Can you do something?" I asked Rizzo.

"Yes, but close your eyes."

"What?"

"You too, Doctor Elise."

Her eyes widened, and she screeched, "Are you nuts?"

"No." His voice took on a resonance that wouldn't brook questions, and tingles raced along my skin. "Close your eyes!"

I did as he commanded, then squinted against the bright golden glow. The revenants screeched, and the sudden cessation of the sound pressed on my eardrums worse than their high-pitched noise had.

"All right, you can open." He once again sounded like a tired provider who'd had a long day.

I blinked my eyes open and found he appeared normal. Sir Raleigh had resumed his cat-like appearance and also blinked dazedly.

"What...was that?" Elise sank into her chair.

"Those were revenants," Rizzo explained. "They're Fae souls that are in the process of waking from their long sleep, which is how they reincarnate. They take a while to flesh out, and until they do and gain their brains, they're ravenous spirits."

I recognized I had tensed and held my breath waiting for Elise's response.

"I... I see. And is that what's been scaring the animals?"

I glanced at the mirror. "Yes, they're coming through antique mirrors. There must be something keeping them from consuming the souls of the animals."

Rizzo chuckled. "Perhaps there's something of the Fae in them. They have high regard for animals, who they ally with. As for humans... They may not be strong enough after journeying through the mirror, but they will be soon."

"And what are you, then?" Elise pointed at him, then me. "Both of you?"

Rizzo bowed. "I'm not at liberty to say, Madame. Only that you're lucky I was here. I'd cover that mirror if I were you."

I thought through the mirrors at my house. I had a few that would require coverings as well. I'd also talk to Kestrel. I didn't think she had any antiques in her apartment, but then, I didn't know what she'd brought from John and Beverly's house.

"And what about you, Lawrence? How do you fit in with all of this? Please. Tell me."

Rizzo shot me a sideways glance. "That's my cue to leave.

But don't wait too long to claim your destiny, Doctor Gordon. As you can see, Faerie isn't the only realm in peril."

He left, and I faced Elise. What should I tell her? We had a strict code at the CPDC to not let the humans know what we were because, as with many minorities, they'd fear, then figure out how to exploit us. But she did have the books on her shelves about mysticism, so I suspected she already had a connection. And after today, she wouldn't be able to deny it.

I opted for an evasive answer. "I'm a veterinarian. I'm also not entirely human."

"I get that. Neither is Arthur Rizzo. And this guy..." She looked down at Sir Raleigh, who had flopped over and proffered his fuzzy belly. "Don't try to play cute with me, cat. I saw what you turned into. What the hell is your dad feeding you?"

I laughed, as did she. Sir Raleigh huffed, then rolled to his feet and jumped off the desk.

"You can tell me when you're ready. Thank you for your help today. I'm glad we know what's causing the injuries, although I'm not sure what to tell my patients."

"Make sure they cover their antique mirrors, for one thing. Make up something, like the way the light is hitting them is scaring the animals."

"And covering them will do it? Those things seemed powerful."

"They are, but they need the image of the room to come through. Covering them or turning them to the wall should do the trick."

"All right." She shuddered. "I'd ask you if you want to join me for dinner, but I need to get home. I have a few mirrors to take care of."

I didn't tell her I wouldn't have taken her up on her offer. I had to get the map Latonya had given me back to The Aerie so Barton, Desmond, and I could take our next steps.

After she assured me she could get home safely, I took my

leave. Sir Raleigh curled up on the front passenger seat and yawned.

"I should make you ride in a carrier. It wouldn't do for a vet to have an animal loose in the car."

He glared at me, then disappeared. I guessed he'd meet me at my house, where I'd be turning my mirrors.

Stones, I needed to get in touch with Reine, let her know the situation was escalating. The two revenants in Elise's office would have devoured her soul, I was sure of it, or at least tried to the point of causing major trauma.

Reine might be stuck in the asylum in Faerie for thirty years, but we in the Earth realm didn't have that long to wait.

We may not even have thirty days.

11

REINE

I found myself eating alone in the dining hall that night. Neither Larry nor Olred came in, and I worried that they were avoiding me.

Or that Olred had lost control of herself after she'd confronted me and had been dosed with ambrosia again in spite of my express wishes that Wilfrin let me try other things first. I would inventory the stores the next day and see what he had on hand, then see about making an order.

Ugh, what kind of red tape would that require? Would Queen Lilith have to sign off on it?

I also needed to see if Basil had made any progress toward setting up my allowance through the light Fae treasury. Surely I should be able to access my money and resources, at the very least the ones that belonged to me personally.

Eating turned out to be a fast chore since I was alone and lost in my thoughts. I returned to my room and pulled the obsidian mirror from my pocket. I hadn't let it off my person since finding it. I discovered that fake Sir Raleigh had been stitched back up—the magic of the asylum?—and I gave his plush ears a rub to apologize for my clumsy surgery.

After getting ready for bed, I pulled the bed curtains closed and cupped the mirror in my palms. I could have been fooling myself, but I could've sworn that it warmed. I breathed on its surface, then drew a symbol I knew would appeal to Basil—the Fae glyph for music. Did he still strum his guitar in the evenings when he spent time by himself? Or did he woo the female Fae of Lorien? The thought didn't irritate me. On the contrary, it amused me because I knew he wouldn't get anywhere with them. Or would he? Ellerin had managed to not only woo, but impregnate my mother, and he was already the Gray Fae, at least as far as I knew. I didn't know much of my own history, it seemed. Again, the curse of a long life with only so much memory capacity.

The glyph faded, and the surface of the mirror fogged within. I leaned back on the pillows and willed it to show me Basil. Which it did. He sat on his bed and strummed his lute, as I'd imagined him. There was no sound at first, but then a few notes trickled through. He played something in a minor key, and I recognized one of our old country songs about a lost love. When he finished, he looked up, and his mouth formed an "O" of surprise. He walked toward me, and I guessed he had an obsidian mirror hanging on the wall.

"Took you long enough to find my present, Your Highness."

"Please, you can still call me Reine when we're alone." Heat raced along my cheeks when I remembered I spoke to him from my bed and while wearing my nightclothes. It made for an intimate setting. He had removed his vest, and his flowing white shirt laid open and unlaced across his upper chest. The shirt framed a triangle of tanned, muscled skin with a smattering of golden hairs.

Intimate, indeed.

"I fear you've caught me at a disadvantage. I don't play for others anymore."

For some reason, I blushed harder. "I appreciate the private performance, then." Hades, could I sound any more flirtatious? I needed to reel it in. "The song was lovely. I haven't heard it in ages. Literally."

"Sometimes you need to express the yearnings of your heart."

I didn't know what to say to that, so I switched the topic to, "Do you know how long we'll be able to talk through the mirror? Does it have a time limit?"

"Not as far as I know. So you like it? I had the frame made especially for you as your healer self."

"It's lovely. And thoughtful. And somewhat illegal for where I am, but that's fine. I need to be able to talk to you securely."

His brows drew into a worried line. "Are they treating you well? My au—er, Queen Lilith said you would be well taken care of."

"Yes, the accommodations are fine. In fact, I've managed to earn some freedoms that will make my stay here more tolerable." Like I was talking about a bad hotel or something.

"Good. You're clever. What did you do to convince that little gnome to loosen the bars?"

"I had a screaming fit and threw an easel with my artwork into the pond."

A startled laugh escaped him. "How in the worlds did that do it?"

"Apparently Wilfrin had been expecting me to crack and express my emotions for a while. Nothing charms a male like being proven right."

His mirth passed from his face like the sun on a stormy day. "You're probably correct. But are you all right? Do you need someone to talk to?"

I did, but he wasn't the someone I wanted to discuss things with. "No. Look, I don't mean to rush you, but I still can't lock my door from the inside. Have you made any progress in getting access to my allowance from the treasury or my personal assets? I may need to contribute to an order, and I don't want to be further in debt to Lilith." *Or you*, I mentally added.

"No progress yet, but I'm working on it. I can lend you some of my own money if you need it."

I pulled my lower lip under my teeth for a second, then exhaled. "No, but thank you. I—"

Fog covered the mirror again, and for a second I worried that he'd hung up on me. Rude. Then the last face I expected filled the circle.

"Rhys!"

He glanced over his shoulder, and the view shifted so that I looked up at him from below. He must have had a small hand-held mirror like I did.

"Look, Sis, I don't have a lot of time. I wanted to tell you that no matter what they're saying about me, it's not true. None of it. I didn't hurt Lawrence."

"So you didn't shoot the dart that tranquilized him so they could throw him in the palace prison?"

"Okay, I may have done that, but I didn't throw him in the cell."

"Rhys..." I wanted to strangle him, but he was my brother. "Are you all right? Where are you?"

"I can't say. Only that I'm deep undercover like Ellerin was supposed to be."

"'Was supposed to be?' You're not making sense." Not that he usually did, but streams of anxiety for him raced through my limbs. And the old concern that he'd betrayed me sat like a leaden lump in my belly. "Rhys, did you betray me again?"

"No. And you know I can't lie. But it's complicated. Look, I'm just here to tell you to look to the Order of the Silver Arrow for what you seek. They have the evidence that will get you out of there before—" He grimaced and grunted. "I can't say. I'm under a gag spell. Just find it. And soon."

Fog obfuscated, then obliterated his image.

"Rhys! No, not yet. Before what? Why soon?"

Basil's image reappeared. "What just happened? Did you hang up on me?"

"No, Rhys broke into the call. I didn't know that was possible."

He frowned again. "It shouldn't be. That's a single channel mirror—it should only work for you and I to talk."

"So I can't use it to talk to Lawrence?" I didn't bother to keep the disappointment from my tone.

Neither did he. "No, I'm afraid I can't grant your deepest wish. What did Rhys have to say?"

"Nothing we didn't already know. He said to look to the Order of the Silver Arrow for the evidence we need. But I can't do that from here."

"And I can't leave here for long amounts of time. The revenant situation is getting worse, Reine. Really worse. Like we're going to have to do something drastic, but I don't know what. I've been looking through all the sources I can, but the information on them is spotty at best."

"I don't know what to tell you." Talk of the revenants tipped me over the edge of exhaustion. "I need to go to bed. It's been an intense day."

"I understand. Well, I don't, but I wish you a good night. Sleep well."

"Thanks. You, too."

His image faded, leaving me feeling even lonelier.

I TUCKED the mirror under my pillow inside the case, then curled up with fake Sir Raleigh against my chest. I wished Basil had managed to charm the stuffed animal so it would purr when squeezed. I would have tried, but I knew my powers wouldn't work in the asylum, or if they did, they wouldn't do what I needed them to. I didn't want to damage the plush grimalkin more than I had, for which I felt irrationally guilty.

Turning over didn't solve the weight of the guilt in my chest and stomach. I thought through everything I'd learned about the wake of destruction I'd left for a particular family in my attempts to find healing for Rhys' scar. That it had only required my grandmother's touch irked me even more. It would have been so much easier if Maeve had allowed me to talk to Tatiana, but she'd been playing the manipulator and deceiver, pitting us against each other even though we'd wanted nothing more than to be in each other's presence again. And now my grandmother had passed into her long sleep, and I found myself alone once more. And helpless. I was stuck in the asylum while my realm was in danger.

Tears trickled down my cheeks, this time for the loss of my grandmother, my main guiding adult since my mother was too busy being the Crown Princess of Faerie and having fun with her consorts and lovers. Then I allowed myself to think about Lawrence, whose name I refused to say or even think most of the time. I had to stop kidding myself. His presence lingered in my mind, and I would have given anything for him to wrap his arms around me and pull me to his chest. I didn't even need to have sex with him. Being with him physically, our energies mingling, breathing in the scent of gargoyle—water on stone— and putting my head on his strong shoulder would be enough.

I'd managed to reach out to others through my dreams while I was stuck in the time loop. Perhaps the asylum, being a place of supposed healing for the conscious and subconscious, would help. "Asylum, please, give me a solution for the revenants in my dreams."

Sleep claimed me, and I went into a dream that I wandered the halls of the asylum. Something beckoned me lower and lower, and I found myself in the basement. Rather than the dungeon I'd imagined it to be, it resembled a hospital I'd worked in during my internal medicine residency. The walls had been painted white, and each room had a bright fluorescent light that illuminated the depressing emptiness inside. Thankfully there was no morgue. I didn't want to be in a dream of revenants or reanimated corpses.

I walked down the hallway and dragged an IV with me. When I looked, I saw it went into the vein at my left wrist.

"What are they giving me?" I wondered aloud. "I don't feel anything." In fact, that was the problem. I felt divorced from my emotions. With a shriek, I ripped the needle out. Whatever they were giving me, I didn't want it. I needed to feel, to access all parts of my brain and the rest of my nervous system.

I sensed that someone didn't like that I'd ripped my IV out, and I found myself running down halls that twisted and turned and doubled back on themselves. No matter where I turned, I found myself in front of the door to one room. Finally, panting, I pushed the door open and entered the small, cramped office of some lower-level hospital administrator. Papers and charts littered the desk, and files lay in haphazard rows on the metal shelves behind the rolling office chair.

I turned to my left and found a large slab of obsidian. I gasped when I saw not my reflection, but Lawrence, who beat his fists against it from the other side. I ran to the mirror and stretched my fingers against its smooth, cool surface, which disappeared. Lawrence clasped my hands and pulled me through.

He tangled his hands in my hair, and our lips crashed together. I tasted the salt of someone's tears—they might have come from both of us. I squeezed him as hard as I could so I wouldn't have to let him go. Ever.

But like in many dreams, the illusion passed, leaving me crying and panting. I stepped forward in the utter darkness, and stars poked through the gloom. Grass tickled my feet, and now I lay on the lawn outside the asylum, close to where I'd found my picture lying face-down in the grass.

Find it, something whispered to me.

"I can't," I answered aloud. "I threw it in the lake."

Find it, the voice insisted.

"All right." I walked to the pond, which lay still as a mirror and reflected the clear sky. I peered into it and saw my easel and the picture lying below the surface on the shallow sand.

Find it. Find it. Find it.

"I found it! It's right down there. What do you want me to do?"

Grasp it.

I flexed my fingers. I had never liked manmade ponds. They tended to be scummy and slimy. But I reached under the surface of the water, which, as I suspected, turned out to be deceptively deep. Yes, it had that slippery feel of stagnant pond water and didn't smell much better, but I thought I could feel the edge of the pad of paper. I pinched the triangle and pulled it toward me. It turned out to be caught on something, and I gave it a good tug.

It loosened, and I toppled backward and let go. Instead of the wooden frame with canvas, a water wolf emerged from the water, snapping its jaws at me.

I reacted with my instincts and shot a bolt of fire at it. It yelped, and the sound woke me up...

...to the smell of burning fabric. I created a Fae light and found that the canopy of my bed, the part just over my head, smoldered from having been hit with a concentrated beam of fire like the one in my dream.

I looked down at my hands, then back up at the canopy.

"Heal," I commanded, not expecting it to work, but the hole disappeared.

Could I have figured out how to reach my powers? If so,

what did that mean about everything else I'd been told about the asylum?

With a smile, I turned over and went back to sleep, this time without dreams.

Good. I had a big day ahead.

12

REINE

The next morning, I found Healer Wilfrin in the apothecary, which was located on the first floor off the receiving lobby. The place reeked of ambrosia, which should smell pleasant to a Fae nose. As with anything, too much highlighted the unpleasant sickly-sweet odor to the point it evoked the start of rot.

"How much of that stuff do you have down here?" I asked and waved a hand in front of my nose.

"Enough. Queen Lilith sends us a shipment every month."

"Why?"

"So she can keep it out of the hands and veins of her courtiers, I suspect."

I clenched my fists like that would help me hold on to the sanity and souls of my light Fae subjects. "No more. Whatever else she sends gets disposed of."

"How?" He motioned to the barrels along the wall. "No one knows what to do with the stuff. It doesn't decompose. It doesn't evaporate."

"Store it somewhere. Perhaps the asylum will tell you where," I added to see what his reaction would be.

He glanced over. "I can assure you, Your Highness, that the asylum doesn't like it any more than you do. But I will see if something comes to me."

I pondered his combination admission and vagueness.

"Is the asylum sentient?"

He looked toward the ceiling. "I don't know. It has its preferences and rules, but I can't say how I know."

"Are you sure they're not *your* preferences and rules? Perhaps your subconscious is projecting your wishes on the stones around you."

"I invited you to help with the patients, not me," came his sharp reply. Interesting. "What part of that brings you down to the apothecary?"

"I want to make an order. What sort of budget do we have? If Lilith is sending the ambrosia and providing the food, we must have some sort of budget for other things." Unless it was going into his pockets, but if so, he didn't seem to be using it for clothing. He wore the same robe as I'd seen him in on my first visit several months prior. But his type of minor Fae creature did like to build treasure stashes...

"We do, but it's limited. And if you're asking to get things from the Earth realm, that's more expensive. What do you want?"

"I'd like to try some basic psychotropic medications to see if we can prevent outbursts. That way they won't have to be quelled with ambrosia."

"And by those, I assume you mean the antidepressants and anti-anxiety medications from the Earth realm."

"Yes. Or whatever those analogues would be here." I thought back to my biochemistry and pharmacology classes. "There's an experimental drug called Luridatone, as I told you."

"And where do you suppose we get it? From whom?"

"Hmm... I suppose we could offer to be a clinical trial site.

But that would take a lot of time, and they might not appreciate the slowness of our results once we got it."

Speaking with him made me realize how I'd become accustomed to being queen and having others take care of things for me. I'd been like that as a princess, too. Then I'd become self-sufficient in the Earth realm but still found ways to delegate.

"Veronica!" I snapped my fingers. "I bet she knows someone. She's connected to witches all over the Northeast."

"It sounds like you have more research to do, Your Highness. And then once you find the supplier, you still have to get it here."

"Right." I sighed. "It's not like I can pop out to the Earth realm and pick it up. But Basil may be able to."

"Troubadour?" Wilfrin wrinkled his nose. "Since when does he do anything that doesn't benefit him directly?"

I smiled. "He's changed. Grown. He's enjoyed being on my Council of Three, and he has quite the head for research and a good memory, as one would expect of a bard."

"And he has a longer history here. Don't forget, just because you high Fae can't lie, it doesn't mean you're always telling the whole truth."

"I'll be the judge of my people, thank you very much." As the words left my mouth, I had to admit I'd snapped at him because his words brought up doubts I'd had myself. What if Basil wasn't being completely honest with me? Did I really know his motives?

But at this point I was too dependent on him to risk offending him by challenging him.

Wilfrin chuckled. "It sounds like you have a lot to think about. Why don't you go on and explore the asylum, figure out if it has any messages for you?"

"Maybe I will." I turned to leave, then turned back. "I do want a message sent to Veronica. I'll write it out. She may also be able to send me some funds for our project."

"Commerce with a human? My, my, you are full of surprises."

"Yes. As this place is. By the way, what's on the lower floors? It's not a dungeon, is it?"

Wilfrin shrugged. "I wouldn't know. I've never been down there. It has a repellent energy I'd rather not challenge."

AFTER I LEFT THE APOTHECARY, Wilfrin's words echoed in my brain. He hadn't gone into the basement of the asylum? How did he know, then, that there wasn't anything down there that could be harmful to his patients or staff? My Earth-realm training listed through possibilities such as black mold, a gas leak, rats... I reminded myself I was in Faerie, which meant worse possibilities.

That meant I needed to go down and investigate. If he wanted me to help him heal, I had to know what other potential obstacles I faced.

The next question was how to get down to the basement level. All the stairwells I'd been in or found stopped at the first floor.

Where had the one in my dream been? And did I have access to my powers again? I didn't feel connected to them like I had before coming to the asylum, but what I thought and reality could be two different things.

I smirked. Fae don't do therapy, but I'd just generated one of the tenets. I would do well to remember it.

"All right," I whispered. "Show me the path to the basement."

Nothing happened, but I stood in the receiving hall. I moved to the main hallway on the first floor and whispered my command again. I was glad none of the staff were around to see me mumbling to myself. That wouldn't help my desired image of totally sane and healthy, whatever was left of it, but didn't most geniuses talk to themselves?

Again, nothing happened...at first. Then all the lights went out, leaving the illumination coming from the window at the end of the hallway. This one didn't have colored panes, only clear, and I blinked when I reached the little parlor at the end. The lamp over the painting—this one a Flemish landscape with mountains, a valley, and roiling clouds over both—flared on. The frame stood about two feet off the ground, and the painting itself was taller than I, giving the illusion of looking out over something pleasant.

"That's not the door to the basement, that's art," I grumbled. Then I paused and reminded myself, "I'm in Faerie. Illusion is the game here. And what better illusion than to hide a secret stairwell behind art that's meant to stop the viewer by calming them?"

I glanced behind me. No one was walking through the corridor, so I stepped to the edge of the painting and pulled. It stuck to the wall, so I tried the other side. It moved a centimeter, then stuck.

"Huh, well, if no one's used these doors, that makes sense. I'll test my magic."

I placed a finger on the crack and imagined a thousand little fingers growing up the inner edge of the frame and separating it from the wall.

With a groan that echoed down the hallway and straight into my soul, the door swung open. A dust cloud blew out in the shape of a mini-tornado and knocked me backward. I grasped the back of a chair for balance and countered with a cleaning spell to contain the mess like the one I'd used in The Aerie to clean the cabin I'd rented. Unlike in the Aerie, the dust devil fought back. I gritted my teeth and fed the spell my strength until the dust contained itself in a nice little brick.

I trembled when I straightened from picking up the dust

brick and took inventory of my strength. My conclusion—I had access to my powers here, but it took more effort to use them. I suspected I had to overcome both the magic-dampening spell of the asylum itself and the repulsion to being in the lands of the dark Fae, which required energy to deliberately ignore.

"Right, then, monitor the soul-budget and spend wisely." I smiled again. Who knew this adventure would lead to me doing therapy on myself? The psych intern who had joined us on psychiatry rounds when I was a medical resident would have been so proud. So would Selene.

Selene... I closed my eyes and deliberately brought the face and form of my frenemy to mind. The image made me feel wistful and worried. Had she recovered from the trauma we'd been through with the automobile chase and crash, and then her being mortally threatened in the cottage in the woods? Probably not, but at least she'd have the support of her fiancé Gabriel, and she was a psychologist, so she would hopefully know what help she needed to seek.

Having saved her with the help of the dimension-walker and Gabriel with the bargain that landed me in the asylum made me feel... I had to be honest and face my doubts. Had it been worth it? But then, Gabriel hadn't been my main concern. Lawrence had, and I couldn't question the wisdom of saving him, even beyond our mate bond and his death possibly being fatal to me.

I placed the dust brick at the edge of the corridor behind the painting so it would keep the door from closing completely and trapping me. Would I find the bones of other Fae who had stumbled upon the doorways, or had the defensive dust spell kept them out? Or had the dust been what remained of their bones? I rubbed my hands on my pants even though the dust brick hadn't shed any particles on them. I produced good dust bricks when needed. They made good surprise weapons.

I stepped into the alcove behind the painting and allowed

the picture to close. The dust brick held and let in a line of light.

"Illumina," I whispered, and a ball of Fae light appeared over my hand. I willed it to hover over my head, and it illuminated the dark stone-lined space. Writing covered a three-foot-square panel made of smooth, dark marble on the wall to my right, but I couldn't make out what it said. It looked like Old Fae, which I'd never been proficient at translating. I would need to bring a piece of paper and crayon and get a rubbing so I could research it later. Or perhaps Larry could interpret it for me.

The space reached back a couple of meters and ended in a black rectangle that turned out to be a spiral staircase wide enough for one person to ascend or descend. Tight quarters for battle if I encountered anything sinister, but that tug toward the basement resumed. I wished I had Sir Raleigh with me for his guidance, but the best I could do was trust my instincts and my dream.

I took a deep breath, which revealed the odors of old stone and stale air. I opened my Fae sense as well—no surprises in the near vicinity. Since I didn't smell or sense anything unexpected, I exhaled and descended.

13

LAWRENCE

I raced back to my house, then threw some clothes in a suitcase and gathered up what I thought I'd need. I'd just reached the outskirts of the city when my phone rang with an incoming video call from Kestrel. I pulled into a gas station parking lot, then answered and set the phone in the holder on the dashboard.

"Hey, are you okay?" she asked. "I was getting the scalp tingles."

"Is that a new manifestation of your Trickster powers?" With her, I never knew what would pop up.

"Sometimes. I may have, uh, done a spell to alert me when you were heading toward danger."

Well, that was comforting. Sir Raleigh nudged his head under my hand.

Kestrel grinned. "Is that Sir Raleigh? Give him a scratch for me."

"Will do. And yes, it's him. How long has your scalp been tingling?"

She glanced to the side. "A few days. I decided I'd call when it didn't stop."

Part of me wanted to scold her for attaching a spell to me without my consent, but I couldn't do it. Sure, we'd had an argument before I'd been captured and dragged into Faerie, but she'd apologized once I was able to get in touch with her from the hospital in The Aerie. In the meantime, she'd gotten herself moved out of my house and into her apartment in Athens, where she'd be starting at UGA in the spring.

"Are you in danger? What happened?"

I told her about the black lightning bug attack, then the revenants, and she shuddered. "I still have nightmares about both of those."

"And Ellerin appeared with Sir Raleigh after we got rid of the black lightning bugs."

"Oh, him." She didn't look thrilled to hear the mention of her biological father's name. She'd grown up thinking my friend John Graves was her father.

"Yes, and he says the situation in Faerie is getting worse. It needs its light queen."

"I'm sure it does." She didn't care much for Reine, either, since Reine had kept Kestrel from using necromancy powers to save John from a fatal stab wound. "Has anyone else interesting appeared?"

"Only the former water nymph Astrid, who said that Rhys is missing."

"I can't keep all these magical creatures straight. Life was easier when it was just us witches and shifters."

"You have a good point." That was also when her parents had been alive, so I wasn't going to argue with her that life had also been somewhat boring. Then Reine had come into our lives and mixed things up more than any of us could have imagined.

But it was also indirectly due to her that I'd been reunited with my mother and had connected with my half-siblings. I just wished I could skip landing in the hospital in The Aerie as a prerequisite to seeing them.

"So what are you planning on doing? You said that the black lightning bugs and revenants are gone."

I should've figured I wouldn't be able to misdirect her. "Kestrel, I'm going to have to go back into Faerie. Ellerin said I need to do so as a crown prince of the gargoyles."

She went so still I thought her picture had frozen. Then she blinked and wiped her left eye with the back of her wrist. "But if you do, you could die."

"And if I don't, I couldn't live with myself. It's not just Reine I'm worried about. There are hundreds of thousands of magical creatures in Faerie that will be destroyed if the revenants run amok."

"So let them. They've been torturing humanity for millennia."

"That's not fair. Some of them have been good influences." Granted, those were the minority.

"And even if it wasn't for that, crown prince? Then what would you have to do? Would you have to live in The Aerie? Would I ever see you?"

"Yes, you'd see me. I'll come visit."

"When would you have time? We're Americans. We have no idea about royalty and its duties. Your mother could have you traveling all over the world. All over the realms!"

"You're thinking too far ahead. I haven't committed to anything."

Her mouth took on a stubborn pout I'd seen all too often on her mother's face. "No, but you're seriously considering it. And weren't you the one who told me I needed to plan ahead, that the future held too much uncertainty to be unprepared?"

I hated it when my words got thrown back at me, especially when she was right. "Fine, I'll think about it more before I agree to anything. But I don't have much time."

She put the phone down, and the sounds of thumping and rustling came through.

"Kestrel, what are you doing?"

"Packing. I'm coming to The Aerie to talk some sense into you. At the very least, you need to tell me to my face, my in-person face, that you're going to risk everything. Again!"

"Kestrel, you can't. You don't know how to get there. It's hidden, remember?"

She picked up the phone, and her face had gone blotchy with her almost crying. "Random powers, remember? I bet I can find it."

"Please don't. It could be dangerous."

"You're one to talk. I'll see you soon."

Then she hung up on me. When I tried to call back, the call went straight to voicemail. I groaned and rubbed my eyes.

At least wait until tomorrow, I texted. *Don't try this in the dark.*

She didn't respond except to thumbs-up my text. All right, that gave me some reprieve.

Sir Raleigh rubbed against me.

I ran my hand over his soft back. "I can't blame her for being upset. That's the worst part. I feel like I'm being torn apart between all these people who need me."

He paused and looked into my eyes. I sensed he knew the feeling.

"You feel torn between Reine and Ellerin, huh?"

He nodded, then hopped over the gear shift and curled up on the passenger seat. I blinked. It always startled me when he communicated with me in non-feline ways even though I knew full well he was a grimalkin, a Fae creature, and only a cat in appearance.

"We need to go to the grocery store. She'll need to eat. And then I'm going to have to tell her I'm heading back to The Aerie. I...have responsibilities."

He looked back over his shoulder at me, and this time I felt he communicated something like, *If it looks like a crown prince and acts like a crown prince... When are you going to stop denying it, dumbass?*

Or perhaps I was projecting. Either way, I had a lot to think about. It didn't help that I didn't have a job in Atlanta, and my house felt too big and empty without a certain Fae to make it a home.

I STAYED the night in a hotel and told myself I was just heeding my own advice to not try the winding mountain roads in the dark, but I knew the real reason. I couldn't face my mother, Micah, and all the others who had pinned their hopes on me becoming Crown Prince in spite of my protests. Most of all, I couldn't face myself. Had I crossed the line of he who doth protest too much?

I could figure that out the following day. Unfortunately, my subconscious tortured me with dreams of Reine being lost in a white-tunneled maze and Kestrel going into the woods and not coming out. John and Beverly appeared in that dream and scolded me for not protecting their daughter.

When I arrived in The Aerie, I parked at my mother's house, placed the map in my leather satchel, and walked to the hospital. I took the long way around through the woods and tried to escape the memories that threatened to ambush me at every turn. There was where the path split off to go to the cottage Reine had rented and where we'd had steamy shower sex. There was the little chapel. There was the path to the mountain, where Reine and a few others of us had defeated Grylja during the Solstice festival. The gargoyles would cele-brate the Equinox in a few days in downtown Aerie, and I dreaded the celebration without Reine.

Sir Raleigh also seemed subdued. He trotted along beside

me and appeared lost in his own thoughts. Not for the first time, I wondered what he pondered. Did he, too, recall being here with Reine, chasing the white snow creatures that served as spies for the ice witch, and then the brief reprieve we'd had before Reine went back to Scotland to rescue Max and Gabriel? And me, as it turned out.

We turned onto the trail that would take us up by the hospital. Caves still pocked the hillside. Had ordinary creatures moved in now that the witch and her creatures had been vanquished? Or would they remain empty? What had lived in them before? Nature didn't allow potential housing to go to waste.

I'd texted Barton when I left my mother's, and he waited for me by the wishing well that someone had dug by the hospital parking lot. His dark brows were drawn together, and I had to ask, "And what are you wishing well?"

He smirked. "Nothing interesting."

"No? I thought you may be wishing to stay here. How long is your assignment?" I didn't say the name of the organization he worked for—Truth Seekers—out loud. We walked toward the hospital and the employee entrance Desmond and I had used.

"Until the politics here are settled." He shot me a look that told me my decision about becoming Crown Prince was a big part of that.

"So if I put off my decision, you'll be here indefinitely?"

He chuckled. "It's not that simple. And it's cute that you think acknowledging you're the CP would settle the political situation here."

"Oh?"

"Oh?" He mimicked and held the door open. "Your mother didn't want to tell you, but there have been some...challenges."

I stifled a growl that wanted to grow into a roar. "And she didn't tell me why?"

"Because she didn't want to interfere with your recovery."

"I'm afraid we're running out of time on many fronts, then."

We entered the morgue, and Desmond waved us toward his office. "Sorry, have a patient."

Barton preceded me, and a flash of light made me turn, but Barton pulled me inside. "Sorry, trade secret."

A giggle floated through the air, and spider-foot prickles crawled from my scalp to my shoulders. "What the hell, Barton?"

He shrugged. "All I can tell you is not to worry, it's legal."

Desmond walked in. He wiped his hands on a towel, and some of that prickly energy wafted off him until he took a deep breath. "I hear you found something interesting for us."

"Yes. How's your day going?"

He didn't take the bait. "Well enough. Let's see what you've got."

I opened the satchel and spread the map on his clean desk, which only had a light on one corner, a nameplate, and a cup of pens on it. "My contact said that the CPDC pinpointed the location of the order's headquarters here. But that was back in the seventies. Do you think they would have moved?"

Barton hovered his finger over the map. "It's possible. They're a secret society, after all. Moving around would maintain their security."

"But they're also an old one," Desmond argued. "Those tend to get complacent. Plus, there are only so many drafty old castles around." He grinned at me. "It's legally required for them to maintain appearances, especially in the dungeons."

I wanted to ask how he could be in such a good mood after having completed his morbid task, but I recalled that gallows humor would be part of the job. What had that energy been?

"I don't want to just jump in there unless we know for certain where they are," I argued. "We'll need to sneak up on them, and they're bound to have guards."

"What about popping over and doing recon?" Barton indicated an area by a river. "There's probably enough magical energy here to manage a jump."

"But they'd feel us coming a mile off." Desmond seemed to enjoy playing devil's advocate. "Are you still allied with that dimension walker, Lawrence?"

"I don't know. We haven't spoken in a while."

Desmond studied the map. "We'd need a Fae or one of them to check it out. Assuming they haven't upped their magic game after Wolfsheim was defeated."

"Reine was there," I blurted out. She'd told me about the werewolf Gabriel battling the leader of the Order of the Silver Arrow.

"So I'd heard." Barton shook his head. "Trust me, I almost asked for her autograph when I figured out who she was."

"And you don't have any Truth Seeker information that would help us?"

"No."

The brevity of his answer startled me. "Just...no?"

"No. I don't. And don't ask me to request it."

"Is everything okay?"

"We don't have time to get into that." Desmond folded the map and handed it to me. "See if you can get in touch with that dimension walker. Or that Fae he hangs out with."

"I'll do my best. Time is running short, though, so we may have to go in without complete knowledge." I told them about the encounter in Elise's office.

Desmond and Barton exchanged an interesting look when I mentioned Arthur Rizzo and how he'd chased the revenants back into the mirror...or something.

"You're lucky he was there," Barton said. "And that he decided to help you."

"Would he help us again, do you think? And what is he?"

Desmond barked a laugh. "No, he can't help us. He's stuck close to his assignment in the city. As for what he is, I can't tell you. That's proprietary information that goes way above you in the supernatural hierarchy."

"That's pretty much what he told me." I swallowed my annoyance at Desmond withholding information. It felt like all our avenues were closing, so I opted for another track. "How's the breathing device coming along?"

"We're almost ready with another prototype." Desmond put a hand on my shoulder. "I promise, I'm working as quickly as I can."

I later came to regret my rudeness, but the sleep deprivation, secrets, "proprietary information," and inside communication broke the seal of my normal emotional control. I shrugged his hand off, turned toward the door, and shot over my shoulder, "Just don't let your other jobs, whatever they are, get in the way."

Then I walked out and let the door close firmly behind me.

14

———

LAWRENCE

Sir Raleigh hesitated when we stepped into the sunlight, and he rubbed against my leg as if to ask, "Are you okay?"

My thoughts whirled. "No, but we need to keep going. I'm going to stick to the woods and river trails as long as possible, though. I don't want to face awkward questions." I didn't know how I'd handle them, if my irritation with Barton and Desmond had been any indication.

As if I didn't have enough to worry about, I recalled I had to be concerned about Kestrel losing her way in the thick forests of the Smoky Mountains. But maybe it was good she wanted to test her powers. I still shuddered at her threat to join the Normals, which was little better than a cult trying to convince paranormal creatures to live as humans. It couldn't be healthy to deny the mystical part of oneself. I should know. I'd tried.

When Sir Raleigh and I reached the shadowy part of the woods, which had grown more so since the spell the witch had placed over the town had lifted, one of the shadows detached from the trees to walk with us. I jumped back, but Sir Raleigh trilled in greeting in time to keep me from going into gargoyle mode. Thankfully. I liked the jeans I wore too much, and I would've been unhappy if they'd gotten ruined. Reine said my ass looked awesome in them.

I opted for the formal, "Well met, Ellerin."

He chuckled. "Are you sure? I almost scared the gargoyle out of you."

"So you did the shadowy thing on purpose, then?"

He fell into step beside me. "It never hurts to stay in practice. How often do you change and fly now that you've been here for a couple of months?"

"Once a week."

He nodded. "And how often did you do that when you were living in Atlanta?"

"Once a month. On new moon nights, mostly, if there weren't clouds to reflect the city light pollution and make me visible."

"And how does that feel?"

"What are you, a freaking therapist?"

Sir Raleigh looked up at me with a disapproving glare.

I returned it. "Don't start with me. How often do you change into your big, scary grimalkin self?"

He whipped his tail up, giving me a good look at his butt-hole, and trotted ahead.

"He probably could stand to do it more," Ellerin mumbled. "He's getting more cat-like with each day."

"Maybe that's how he's comfortable."

"Is it?" His sideways glance said he was asking about more than Sir Raleigh.

Stones, the longer I'd lived, the more I'd thought I had come to know my preferences. Had I gotten comfortable instead of continuing to grow and explore? Was there such thing as comfortably off-balance?

Those were questions I never had to ponder as a veterinarian working for the CPDC.

"Does this conversation have a point, Wanderer?" I had to admit the question came out grumpy.

"Yes. I was wondering if you'd pondered our discussion from earlier, about how Faerie needs you to return as the crown prince of the gargoyles." His mouth quirked into an amused curve. "It sounds like the townspeople decided you are."

I sighed from the depths of my soul. "I know. That's why I'm taking this path instead of the easier one by the road."

"And so you're avoiding them because you don't want to commit to the role. Do you even know what it means?"

"No. Kestrel brought up a good point. I've been an American for so long I've lost touch with what silly monarchy titles entail. I don't know if I want to commit to staying here, though."

"Because you have so much to go back to."

An image flashed into my brain of sitting on my screened-in back porch with Scotch in hand looking down over my back lawn and listening to the stream behind the trees. Those had been peaceful moments, but since my best friends John and Beverly were gone, had those times on my own been happy? Only when Reine had been there. And sometimes with Kestrel, although she rarely sat still long enough.

"You have a point," I conceded. "I have my house, but that's it. I don't have my job or my lab. My closest friends are dead." I sighed against the weight of the double grief settling like a dank fog in my chest. Had I allowed myself the chance to properly mourn them? No, because that would mean having to acknowledge how angry I was at Beverly for her roles in her own and eventually John's death. I wanted to miss her, not be pissed.

"Grief is a complicated thing," Ellerin agreed.

"Were you reading my thoughts?"

"No, but you were thinking so loudly flashes came through."

"Great. I'll have to remember to shield around you."

"It will come more naturally when you assume the crown

prince role. Again, there are benefits to go along with the responsibilities."

We reached the statue of Uncle Augie. Legend had it that he would return to flesh instead of stone when the gargoyles needed him. I patted him on the head.

"Like what?"

Ellerin inclined his head toward Augie. "That would never happen to you. Gargoyle royalty can stay in their magical forms indefinitely in defense of their realm."

"So there's a catch."

"Isn't there always?"

"True."

We crossed the small bridge and descended the stairs to the river path.

"There he is!" A group of journalists ran toward me, and Sir Raleigh hissed, then darted behind Ellerin.

"Remember, there are benefits. We can continue this later." He whipped his cloak around himself and disappeared, leaving a confused-looking Sir Raleigh, who then hid behind my legs.

"Some brave grimalkin you are," I teased him, then steeled myself for the onslaught.

"I HAVEN'T MADE any firm decisions yet," I told the reporters. "I am considering many things right now."

Sir Raleigh peeked out from behind my legs. I couldn't see what had caught his attention, but I figured it was a bug or something.

"But you took charge and acted like a crown prince yesterday," Hazel Archwork, the evening news field reporter for The Aerie's one local television show argued. "Surely that must have felt good. Your cleverness and leadership saved us all!"

I held out my hands. "Let's not exaggerate. We don't know

what black lightning bugs can do beyond cause uncomfortable bites." But I recalled Barton's colleague who had taken ill after one. I should've asked if they were a gargoyle or something else.

"When do you think we can expect a decision?" Hazel persisted.

Before I could answer, Sir Raleigh opened his mouth and yowled. I looked down, expecting to see he'd been bitten by something, but he continued to stare straight ahead, his eyes wide and focused on something I still couldn't see.

"What's wrong with your cat?" a male reporter, Harold something-or-other, asked.

"I don't know." I didn't correct them that he wasn't a real cat.

Sir Raleigh yowled again, and they covered their ears. I almost did, for he brought forth every ounce of pain and longing I had for Reine, every regret for time I'd voluntarily spent apart from her. I bent down to comfort him, and his eyes showed me the reflection of what had distressed him.

"Reine!"

Then he leaped forward. The reporters scattered. A couple of them fell into the river.

But the grimalkin didn't connect with anyone. He just vanished.

"What the stones was that?" Hazel asked. She stepped forward from the confused group. Someone helped Harold out of the water. The other reporter had made it over the lip of the river barrier and was checking his equipment. I wanted to laugh at the way a bunch of supposedly strong, tough gargoyles had scattered from a small cat-like creature.

"I don't know." I also didn't know where he'd disappeared to. The way he'd howled beforehand, I suspected he'd found a portal to go to Reine and had managed to unlock it. Although Ellerin had summoned him, Sir Raleigh was her creature now.

The distraction had changed the energy of the group, and I used the confusion as an excuse to bow out. "Thank you for your questions. I'll call a press conference if I decide to pursue the Crown Prince role further. I need to do more research."

"Speaking of more research," Harold said and wrung out his ridiculous flat cap. "I'd like to know what your connections are to Faerie. That was a grimalkin, wasn't it? Aren't those Fae creatures?"

"Yes, they are." I could understand Harold being unhappy about his unintentional swim, but his tone had gone from grumpy to hostile. I avoided identifying whether Raleigh was a grimalkin or not.

"That's the cat that was with that Fae when she was here in the spring," Hazel pointed out. "I recognize the one white paw. He always seemed to know more than he let on."

"And he wasn't with you at the battle at the bridge," Harold pressed. "Did he come through from Faerie? Did your girlfriend send him to see how the black lightning bugs fared with their attack?"

Now when I held my hands up, they were in my defense. "Raleigh—the cat grimalkin—doesn't belong to the same Fae who sent the black lightning bugs. Reine wouldn't do anything to harm this town or its inhabitants. Have you forgotten already that she was instrumental in getting rid of the ice witch and restoring the fertility to the gargoyles here? How many pregnancies have we confirmed since then?"

Hazel cleared her throat. "Ah, we don't know for sure. People are too afraid to announce anything in case it goes wrong."

"So you don't have any evidence," Harold crowed. "I bet the witch had nothing to do with the infertility problem here. It's probably because of the leadership of The Regent."

Since my mother's bargain with the ice witch had caused the infertility issue, I couldn't argue with him. But I could rebut, "There's no infertility problem anymore. Just wait a few months. You'll see."

"Oh, will we?" Harold sneered. "Or are you and your mother stalling until you can find a new scapegoat for the fact that things haven't been right here for decades?"

I opened my mouth to argue, but Harold continued, "You can't say anything, Crown Prince. You haven't been here to see the mismanagement, the daily affronts to gargoyle decency and the way keeping other creatures and humans out has stifled our economy, caused what young people we had to seek their future elsewhere until we're left with this..." He spread his arms, and water dribbled from the edges of his sleeves. "This shell of a town with its sham leadership. If your mother is the true leader of The Aerie, the best thing for our community, prove it."

"She did the best she could. There's no way to show you what *could* have happened if she'd taken a different course."

Logic wouldn't prevail, and Hazel shot me a worried glance over her shoulder. More gargoyles had rounded the bend and crowded in behind the reporters.

"Prove it!" Other cries joined Harold's. "Prove we're no longer cursed!" "Prove the Regent isn't holding our babies hostage." "Prove you didn't have anything to do with the black lightning bugs!"

Hazel looked me in the eye and said, "If I were you, I'd get out of here, and quickly."

"I agree. They're turning into a mob." I turned and dashed up the stairs that led into town, then darted on to the path that went behind the hotel. It wasn't as well kept as the others or as scenic as the river path, but I could at least hopefully be sure no one would follow me. They might guess I'd gone through town.

But at least one person anticipated my route. When I reached a point on the path that crossed the road, a police cruiser waited for me.

∽

THE PASSENGER WINDOW ROLLED DOWN, and my sister beckoned to me. "Get in! There's a mob out to get you. And Mom."

I climbed into the car, and she rolled up the window, then made a quick three-point turn to head out of town.

"Thank you," I said. "How did you know?"

She slid me a glance. "I have connections in the press. They warned me."

"Hazel."

"I can neither confirm nor deny." But she winked.

"It makes sense. Your girlfriend is the town gossip, so the field reporter seems a logical connection. That's how Hazel gets a lot of her scoops, isn't it?"

She sighed. "You're not the one who needs to be asking questions right now, big brother. What in Uncle Augie's petrified stones did you cause down there?"

I plopped my head back against the headrest. "Things were going well until Sir Raleigh saw something."

"The cat thing that was following you around? What did it see?"

"*He* saw Reine, I think. And let out a couple of blood-curdling yowls, then jumped through a portal only he could see. Unfortunately, that meant he jumped straight at the gaggle of reporters that had cornered me."

"Did he injure anyone? I didn't hear any calls."

"No, but he startled them, and a couple of them fell in the water, including that odious Harold whats-his-name from the newspaper."

She wrinkled her nose. "Oh, him. Harold Ironkeys or something ridiculous like that. Claims to be of Old English gargoyle stock."

Ironkeys... The surname tickled my memory, but I couldn't bring anything into conscious awareness.

"Yeah, he got a good dunking, including his stupid hat."

She laughed. "I've never heard you so disgruntled. And I

would have paid to see that." Her mirth disappeared when she glanced over at me. "But it didn't go well. What, exactly, happened?"

I filled her in on how things had gone sour. "And now they're out to take down Mother, or something ridiculous like that."

Minerva sighed. "Yeah, that's not new. Someone tries it every decade or so. People get tired of the same old rule. Even if things are going well, they feel like they could be going better."

"Well, to be fair, they always could be."

"And there you go with the logic. But they could always be worse. I'll get Karen to keep an eye on Ironkeys. He's tried to call for an election to make himself Regent a few times, and it's never gone anywhere, but you never know."

Minerva turned off the road into a long driveway, which wound around a couple of wooded bluffs before crossing over a lawn. She pulled into the two-car garage of a stone cottage-style house.

"You make a good point. Is this your place?"

"Mine and Karen's. We haven't said anything to Mom about it yet. I can tell she's trying to accept me for who I am, but it's hard for her. I think she hoped I'd produce her first grandchild."

That my mother's grandmotherly hopes had rested on Minerva stung. "Had she given up on me?"

Minerva turned off the ignition. "Sort of. She didn't know if you would ever find your way here."

"And why didn't she send someone for me?"

She got out of the car, and I did as well. She led me through a door into a modern kitchen.

"Fancy," I commented.

"We're not truly primitive here. And she didn't send anyone for you because she knew you were looking for your father's killer. She didn't want to distract you. I don't think she could have anticipated what you'd find. Or why."

"You're very right about that. That brings us back to the question of who maimed Rhys and why."

"Yep, but that's a mystery beyond our little town." She switched on the coffee pot and pulled two mugs down from the cabinet. "Coffee?"

"Don't you have to get back to work? I'd love a tour, but I don't want to keep you."

She grinned. "I'm off. I just dressed and took the car so no one would mess with me."

"Ah. Smart."

"See? We are related."

The earthy cinnamon aroma of coffee wafted through the kitchen, and for the first time since leaving my mother's house that morning, I felt grounded, no pun intended.

She gestured toward the kitchen table, which sat in a little alcove to the right of the door to the garage. It had windows on two sides opening on the back and side lawns. I walked over and basked in the sunlight—or would have if I'd been in a basking mood. In truth, Sir Raleigh's abrupt departure saddened more than upset me even though he'd caused trouble.

Minerva brought over the two cups and a plate of cookies on a tray. She had the family dark hair and stone-gray eyes, but she had gotten Mother's high cheekbones and pointed chin, which gave her a mischievous, gamine appearance even in her Regent Security Forces uniform.

"You look sad," she said. "Here. Mom would always give us cookies when we came home from school crying."

"I'm not crying." And if a tear wanted to leak from either eye, I'd catch it before she saw it. We sat at the table, and I took and bit into a cookie. "Delicious. Is that Mother's butter cookie recipe?"

"Brought from the old country, or so she said."

"She would make these for me when I was a kid, too. When we had enough butter and sugar."

Minerva looked at me over the rim of her coffee cup. "You had a very different upbringing than we did. But don't change the subject. What's eating you, big brother?"

I looked into the murky depths of the coffee cup. "I don't know. No, that's not true, I do." I sighed and hoped that it would open my throat so I wouldn't weep. "I guess I hoped Sir Raleigh would stay with me. Having him with me was like having something of Reine, you know?"

"I don't, but I believe you. No..." She walked around the cupboard peninsula that separated the kitchen table alcove from the rest of the kitchen and pulled out a worn rolled leather case. "I do know." She placed the case on the table and unfolded the leather, which had that cedar smell of time and oily sheen of use.

"Are those chef's knives?"

"Yes." She smiled. "Those were my father's. He loved to cook. I got those genes, though, not Micah, so he gave these to me when he got sick." She rolled up the case. "I use them sometimes when I want to feel connected to him."

"So you do understand."

"At least a little." She patted my hand. "You're not as alone here as you think, Lawrence. Micah and I are your family as much as Mom is, but you don't seem to believe it."

I opened my mouth to object.

She stood and continued, "Not that Micah isn't a perfect turd sometimes. But that's what little brothers are, right?"

I grinned. "You were the twin born first, I take it?"

"Yes, and I never let him forget it. That also makes me the middle child, so I reserve the right to be a brat to you."

Her words and teasing warmed a place in my chest that I hadn't realized was there. I'd made my definition of family Fae-shaped, but it was entirely possible I hadn't made it big enough.

15

REINE

My Fae light illuminated the spiral stairwell but couldn't show me what waited around the next tight curve. I switched to directing it with my left hand and summoned a silver knife, which I clutched in my right. I suspected that the magic of the asylum would definitely not approve of my wielding a weapon, but so far it hadn't kept me from going behind the picture into the secret stairwell, defeating a dust devil spell, or otherwise flexing my powers.

Which felt damn good. I'd been reluctant to use my full power as Queen of the Light Fae, especially when caught in the time loop because of the risk of a spell having unintended consequences. Perhaps if I had used my powers, claimed my identity earlier, I wouldn't be in this mess.

Or maybe I'd be in a worse one. Legend had it that certain healers could block a Fae from his or her magic, which would eventually cause depression, insanity, and death. Some healers. And as the fragments of my past had showed me, I hadn't exactly used good judgment in my long life.

Not that I was showing great judgment now.

I reached the bottom of the stairs and hesitated. My Fae

light only illuminated about three feet around me, but that was enough for me to make some startling conclusions.

First, why wasn't the floor dirtier?

Second—what was it made of?

Third, ditto for the walls. The floor and walls shone a smooth white, which didn't make sense for a dungeon or basement.

Some instinct made me reach to my right, and I found a metal switch. When I flipped it, torches illuminated along the walls, but instead of flames, they all had Fae lights hovering above their stalks.

Fourth... This looked surprisingly like the hallway in my dream.

What could it show me? Could I get to Lawrence? Even if I couldn't touch him, to see him and know he was okay would be enough. Touching him would be too much temptation to run away from the bargain I'd made, and I couldn't risk sabotaging the retrial I hoped Basil would arrange once we found Sir Gerald Brigadine's original letters. If I were to be released, I wanted it to be with no doubt or asterisks next to the decision. Fae Queens didn't do asterisks.

"Well, I supposed I should follow the path my dream showed me, see where it ends up," I murmured like I was talking to Sir Raleigh. I missed his guidance.

I wandered down the hall, which had a surprising lack of doors. I couldn't tell, but I thought I should be farther along in the asylum, that I'd gone beyond the footprint of the upper floors. Did this labyrinth stretch under the entire property? And how much of a labyrinth was it if it only went in one line without any branches?

I paused and closed my eyes. I focused on my third eye and cast about with my Fae senses. Ah, the minty green residue of the cleaning spell hovered in the corners and swirled with the lavender-edged dark of the obfuscation spell that kept the corridors of the asylum a maze for the residents. Interestingly, that hadn't caught me on this visit, although I'd noticed it on the previous one. Could I be my own guide in this place? How?

When I opened my eyes, I found I stood in front of a wooden door that hadn't been there previously. Tingles raced in little ant feet over my skin and made a cap of prickles on my scalp. I sensed that if I were to go through the door, I wouldn't be able to unsee or un-know what was behind it.

I glanced around, willing for Sir Raleigh to appear and give me some answers. Of course he didn't. No, this had to be my decision. I could turn around and resume my previous life, or I could open the door and see what other paths could be possible.

The decision begged to be stated aloud. "All right, then. Let's go through."

I opened the door and found another light switch. This one illuminated the empty room from a Fae light chandelier on the ceiling. The white box stood about five meters on each side, and I turned, seeking some clue for what the room had to show me. When I revolved to face the back of the room, I found an obsidian mirror like I'd seen in my dream the night before.

I smiled. Dreams had their meaning, and some turned out to be more than mere brain drippings and processing of the day. I supposed my wanderings from the night before had held a deeper purpose, after all.

The mirror didn't show me anything. Well, that wasn't quite true. It didn't show me myself, but it reflected the room. I could have been invisible, and I checked my hands to make sure I wasn't.

"Show me Lawrence," I commanded. Light flashed across the surface, and Lawrence's image appeared. He stood on a path by a river, and I couldn't see who he spoke to, but he appeared to be having an animated conversation that didn't necessarily make him happy, according to the tightness in his jaw. I ached to run my hand over his cheek and soothe the tension.

Sir Raleigh poked his head out from behind Lawrence's legs, and he opened his mouth. I didn't hear anything, but I could imagine his wail of "mrrrrowl!"

"I'm sorry, sweetness," I told him. "I didn't mean to make you sad. Look, I'm fine."

Another silent yowl, and Lawrence looked down at him, then in my direction like he was trying to see what had set the grimalkin off. It felt like he was looking at me, and I waved even though I knew he couldn't see me.

Sir Raleigh launched himself at the mirror, and I scrambled for a command to make their images disappear.

"Show me—" I said but couldn't finish the command because Sir Raleigh barreled into me and knocked me over.

I LAY on the floor and looked up at my grimalkin for several seconds, maybe minutes. It took a while to focus my vision, even beyond the tears of relief. I didn't know what protocol Fae had, but I suspected I might have a concussion from the hit and the fall. I placed a hand on the back of my head and healed whatever it was.

With a trembling hand, I scratched behind Sir Raleigh's ears, and he purred. The sound broke me. I clutched him to me and rolled to my side, crying in fear—what would happen to him here?—and joy. I'd figure something out, even if I needed to hide him. He lay next to me and purred with his entire body until I calmed. Then he wriggled out of my arms. He went to the base of the mirror and stood on his hind legs, then placed his white paw against its surface. It reflected him, and when I rolled to my knees and then stood, I saw myself in it.

But it wasn't the me I expected in my Earth realm clothing.

No, I stood in a long white gown with an over-bust corset of dark blue threaded with gold. The overskirt had the same dark blue material with silver embroidery.

The longer I looked, the more details came into focus. What had originally looked like a fancy ball gown turned into a coronation gown, but not that of the light Fae. I'd worn a gown like that, but of white with turquoise and gold accents. I had seen a painting of Queen Lilith at her coronation, and her dress was of midnight blue with silver and black. This dress appeared to be a mashup between the two with something else.

Then the crown built itself on my doppelgänger's head. It started out platinum with diamond and emerald, but then incorporated elements of the dark Fae crown as well including sapphires and onyx. And there were moonstones, which neither light nor dark Fae used in our jewelry because they were sacred to the goddesses we pretended to worship.

Sir Raleigh made a "prrt?"

"I don't know. It looks like a coronation outfit for all of Faerie." But Faerie had always had light and dark queens, hadn't it? The image before me turned and smiled. She held out her hand, and a man dressed in the regalia of a king stepped into frame.

"How?" I whispered. I almost put my hand to the mirror, but I didn't want to take the chance that Lawrence—healthy and whole and in Faerie—would disappear.

The images still disappeared in a whirl of smoke, and I blinked the fog away. Had it been a spell of some sort? The prickling sensation returned.

"Do you dare accept your destiny?" a voice asked. It sounded like my grandmother, but older and wiser yet.

"Who's there?"

"Do you dare accept your destiny? It will not be easy. You will sacrifice much. Lose much. Gain much. Suffer much."

"And if I don't?"

"Ah, you are a daughter of the Earth realm. If you don't..." Another image filled the mirror, this one of Lorien, but the streets were empty except for the glowing white shadows of the revenants and their white owl harbingers. One of the revenants stumbled and fell, and it solidified into flesh—the Fae coming out of the larval reincarnation stage and into its revived form. The other revenants fell on it and devoured it. Then I knew what had happened to the previous residents—all devoured.

As horrific as the scene was, it gave me a clue as to one of the problems I needed to figure out. How to not just defeat the revenants but also preserve them so they would make it to their changes and bring the wisdom of ancient times into the modern.

"If I don't, all of Faerie will be destroyed."

"And Earth and Nightmare and Collective Unconscious realms."

"What happened? What caused the Fae to turn into that form when they awoke? How can I change it?"

"And now you're asking the right questions..."

The mirror disappeared, and Sir Raleigh squeaked and darted behind me. In its place another wooden door appeared. "Enter...

I opened the door and stepped through into a delightfully familiar smell.

16

─────────

KESTREL

What the hell was my Uncle Lawrence thinking? He couldn't go back to Faerie after Reine. She'd made her decision. If he couldn't tell she'd pretty much broken up with him, he wasn't nearly as smart as I thought he was.

All right, she'd agreed to be imprisoned in the asylum in Cruaidh—not a pleasant place, as I recalled, although they had good desserts—because he'd gotten himself captured by her bitch of a mother. Must be a Fae thing. Not that I could talk. My mother had been so unsatisfied by what she'd thought was my lack of power that she'd made a dangerous deal and gotten herself killed.

As Scar said in *The Lion King*, "I'm surrounded by idiots."

My phone buzzed with a text from Lily. She was technically my future graduate supervisor, but she'd taken me under her wing when I'd gotten to Athens, showed me around, and sometimes we hung out. She wasn't into the bar scene, and I was just old enough to legally drink, but I didn't like the smoky, noisy bars, so we would go to bookstores or coffee shops that stayed open late.

"What are you doing tonight?"

"Sorry, gotta go see my Uncle Lawrence."

"How's he doing? Still recovering well from Fae lung burn?"

She knew what he was, so it wasn't weird for her to ask. She used slightly different terms than Reine had. Uncle Lawrence and I had deduced she was some sort of high dark Fae, but I hadn't pried.

I video called her, and she picked up.

"What's wrong?" she asked when she saw my face. "You look like you're ready to smite somebody."

I laughed, although my cheeks stayed tight. "It's my Uncle Lawrence. He's thinking of accepting the gig as Crown Prince of the gargoyles. And I can tell he's already plotting to go back into Faerie after Reine."

I'd filled her in on that sitch, too, since at our first conversation we'd talked about Reine being missing. No, she'd gotten herself stuck in a time loop and Lily's professor, Doctor Grand-Pied, who was a dimension-walker, what most people thought of as a Bigfoot, had to go rescue the people trapped with her. She'd figured her own way out. Not that it had done her much good.

That bitch be trouble. Why couldn't my uncle see that?

The one little secret that Lily didn't know about all our drama was that Reine and I were actually half-sisters. I'd kept that one to myself.

Lily had been quiet for a bit while my mind ran all over the place, so I asked, "Do you know anything about the whole Crown Prince thing?"

"Actually, I do."

"And..."

"I need to talk to your Uncle Lawrence. But it can't be on the phone. I need to be in person to see what sort of energy is there."

"I..." Surprise knocked me to my ass on my secondhand loveseat. "You what? Is this Fae stuff?'

"Shhh! You don't know who's listening. I don't want another visit from Grimm and Gilmore."

"I don't blame you. That vampire dude creeps me out. Agent Grimm is kinda cute for a dimension walker, though." They didn't like to be called Bigfoots even though Grand-Pied had played with the term for his name.

"When are you going?"

"I'm leaving as soon as I get packed. I want to get up there before dark."

"Up where? Isn't your uncle back in Atlanta?"

"No, um, he's gone back to The Aerie. So I don't know if you can come with me. They had a dark Fae attack."

"What kind?"

"Black lightning bugs." I shuddered again thinking of them. They'd "welcomed" us when we arrived in Faerie that spring, and it hadn't been a pleasant greeting. Nasty little creatures.

"In that case, I really need to go with you. Your uncle may be stepping into Fae politics he has no idea of. His mother, too. She's the Regent, right?"

"Yes. I think her name is Agnes."

"I've heard of her." Lily drummed her fingers on the arm of her couch. "This is troubling in so many ways."

Now I shivered for Uncle Lawrence and his family. "What do you mean?'

"There's a prophecy that the Great Rising will bring about the unification of Faerie under one queen who has the blood or mark of all three aspects of it. She will have for her consort the gargoyle prince, and the gargoyles will be welcomed back into the realm."

"Wait... Aerie is only one letter off from Faerie. But that doesn't sound like a bad prophecy, except all the gargoyles would die."

"No, that's the other part, that there will be a great battle for the hearts and souls of the realm that will reach down to the smallest creature, which may mean microbes."

"Okay. They're having revenant issues. Is that what it could mean?"

Lily scrunched her eyebrows. "I'm trying to remember all the bits of it. I think there's something about a great sacrifice being made."

"There usually is with that kind of prophecy." But I'd gone cold. "Who or what is being sacrificed?"

"I don't know. I'd have to look again, and that scroll is back in Faerie."

"Great. All right, you can come with me. I'll swing by after I pack."

"Okay." She sighed.

"What?"

"I really hope this doesn't get me in trouble with the Normals. It's totally against their rules."

"They seem to have a lot of them."

"You have no idea..."

17

REINE

I walked through the door and into a library. Not just any library, but the largest one I'd ever seen, and I'd visited and researched in more than a few . Graceful wooden archways stretched overhead, and shelves of books and scrolls lined the walls at least three stories high. Bridges and ladders afforded access to all of them. Natural light poured through the skylights, but there were no windows, and the sky above me didn't look like the dull gray of Cruaidh. Wherever this place was, it was in a separate reality from the asylum, but somehow still contained within it.

"What do you think, Sir Raleigh?" I asked in a hushed tone. It didn't feel appropriate to speak loudly even though I was the only one in there. That I could see. Did dozens of individual patrons sit at the tables behind the books that lay open on them? It looked like I had just walked in on a busy day after the library had been evacuated.

Being a nosy Fae—I admit it—I wandered to the first table and peered at the book that lay open. It appeared to have just been started.

A History of the Schoole for All Faerie, in the Capital City of Statera, established in the Year of the Goddess 1257.

I didn't know either the city name or the year. Fae didn't anchor ourselves to time like humans did, so I'd have to see what calendar it referred to. I sensed it was old, and since when had there been a "Schoole for All Faerie?"

"Queen Healer Reine!" Healer Wilfrin's voice echoed through the library, but I couldn't see his blue ears peeking up over the tables or poking out around bookshelves.

I jumped back, and guilt over being caught where I shouldn't be jolted through me. But *something* had led me there...

"Yes?" I called, not sure if he would hear.

"You have a visitor coming! She'll meet you in the receiving parlor in an hour."

"Who is it?" Yes, it felt ridiculous shouting my business all over the secret part of the asylum, or wherever I was, but I needed to know if it was someone important enough to actually attend.

"It's the Lady of the Forest and another guest who didn't want to name themselves."

Aoine, the supposed Lady of the Forest. I rubbed my hands together. I couldn't wait to confront her for testifying against my character at my trial, claiming I'd spurned her hospitality. She'd been trying to put me in a different prison, of blackmail. Besides, I wanted to see what Larry had meant that she might not be the only one. Or had he said the real one? Dammit, I needed to start taking notes when I talked to my old teacher. He'd probably love that.

"I'll be there."

Now for the next problem—how to get out? The door I'd entered through had disappeared, leaving a smooth wall covered with tapestries. I peered behind a tapestry but didn't see an exit.

Sir Raleigh sat and licked his white paw.

"Can you tell me how to get out, O Wise Grimalkin?"

He shot me a look that told me he understood I was mocking him but huffed and trotted over to a large portrait of a Fae queen that I would have sworn hadn't been there a minute before. "What is this place?"

The grimalkin sat in front of the portrait and looked up. I caught my breath—she wore the same coronation outfit and crown that I'd seen on myself in the mirror, but she sat on a throne and held a sword in her right hand and a wand in her left. She reminded me of the Empress card in old Tarot decks. Empress, not queen.

I pried the frame away from the wall and found a stairwell leading up.

"Well, I guess it's go up the way I came down, huh? Are you coming with me?"

He leaped into the hole, and I followed him. I created the Fae light just before the painting-door slammed shut behind me. We ascended the spiral staircase, but I didn't see any landings for exits.

"Is this a passageway that responds to will?"

Sir Raleigh continued climbing, so I guessed I needed to figure this one out for myself. "Fine. I would like to exit in the doorway behind the painting on my hall in the asylum."

The next curve brought us to a dusty landing, and both Sir Raleigh and I sneezed. Great. I guessed since we were coming from the staircase, we didn't activate the dust devil spell, and I dared not try to clean the dust with my own magic in case I brought unintended attention to us.

"We'll just have go through and get dirty."

The painting opened with some resistance but no sound, and Sir Raleigh and I emerged into the aquamarine stained-glass light of my hall.

I took a quick shower and wrapped myself in a towel. When I went to the closet to grab clothing, I found that in addition to my Earth realm-style clothes, my wardrobe had been upgraded into satins and silks—material befitting a queen.

"That's more like it." I'd dress the part when needed, so I pulled out a turquoise satin dress with white underskirt and three-quarter sleeves. Even better—it fastened on the side, so I didn't need help.

I also found hairpins on my vanity and styled my hair in an updo that allowed curls to frame my face.

"Mrow?" Sir Raleigh asked from the indentation he'd created on the bed by curling up on the thick comforter.

"You'd better stay here. I don't want to push the bounds of our benefits. At least not yet."

He yawned and gave me a full view of his teeth, which appeared larger and more menacing than the average cat's. Then he rolled to his side facing away from me and covered his face with his white paw.

Message received: I was dismissed.

I still gave him a scratch behind his ears and told him, "I'm glad you're here." I kissed his head.

I had to purse my lips to wipe the goofy smile from my face. I'd missed the little guy. Grimalkin. Cat. Now if only I could figure out a way to sneak Lawrence in...without it killing him, of course.

Aoine hadn't arrived in the receiving parlor yet, so I pulled the blue silk cord in the corner. One of the orderlies came in.

"Yes, Your Highness?"

"I'm about to have a visitor. Would you have some tea sent to us, please?"

She nodded, although I could tell she wasn't thrilled with

the order. Well, what did they expect? I wasn't going to act like an average patient.

She'd only been gone a few minutes when Aoine swept in. Her forest green eyes took in all the details, and I was glad I'd taken some extra time with my appearance.

"Your Highness," she said and curtsied. "It's been too long."

I nodded to acknowledge her following the protocols. "Yes, please have a seat. Tea will be arriving in a moment. Do you have another guest with you?"

"I did, but she got detained on the way in. She may or may not be joining us."

"Who is it?"

"High Princess Desdemona. She's been wanting to meet you since you arrived but has been detained with other matters."

By "other matters," I wondered if she meant herding her small troop of revenants and scaring travelers. Rhys, Basil, and Lawrence had had an encounter with Desdemona and her creepy pets. Had the poor spirits changed into their final Fae forms yet, or did her enchanting them and giving them the appearance of nightmare creatures interfere with the process?

"I wasn't aware you knew her."

"I don't know her well. She approved my petition to visit, and that's when she asked to tag along."

The tea arrived, and I dismissed the orderly. "I'll pour."

"Oh, no, you musn't!" Aoine fluttered her hands. "You're the highest-ranking Fae here. I should serve you."

"It's all right. I got self-sufficient in the Earth realm." I smiled and hoped she got the hint—I wasn't about to let her slip something into my beverage or food. They'd given us a stacked tray of small sandwiches, buttery cookies, and scones.

"Well, if you insist..."

"I do." I poured the tea into two of the three cups and handed one on its saucer to Aoine. She dropped a sugar cube into hers and stirred in some milk. I drank mine black. It had pleasant earthy notes.

Aoine helped herself to some of the delicacies, which she placed on one of the small plates provided. The tea service had a *fleur de lis* pattern around the edges of the plates and cups, all of which had been rimmed with gold. "I do apologize for not coming sooner. We've found that the revenants are less active near the road in the Gray Zone at certain times, so I felt it prudent to wait."

"I understand. One attacked my carriage during my transport here. Do you know what the status is? How many have been seen, and how many attacks?"

She took a bite of scone after I asked the question, which made me think she needed time to come up with an indirect answer.

After she swallowed, she said, "I don't know all the details. It seems to me that the threat has been exaggerated. We've had to make some adjustments, but..." She shrugged.

Hmmm... I wanted to ask her about her testifying against me, but I needed to warm her up a little more.

"How are things at the Castle in the Forest? Any interesting new creatures?" I recalled what I'd learned about Sir Brigadine's fate. "Or ghosts?"

"They're the same old, same old, I'm afraid." She patted my hand. "I'm not here to talk about me. How are *you* doing? You looked terrible at your trial."

I blinked. Point to Aoine for the unexpectedly direct attack. "I'm doing as well as could be expected, considering all the nasty surprises I've had lately."

"Yes, your plea bargain. Tell me—were you really guilty of all those things?"

"No. And you tell me—was I really guilty of rejecting your hospitality? You certainly spun it that way."

She cast her gaze down and to the side. "I am truly sorry. All

I can tell you is that I was under duress to make those statements, and you *had* left my castle in the middle of the night after the banquet."

"Yes, after your guards tried to capture me."

"As I told you when you arrived, they've been overly protective of me. They didn't trust you leaving the banquet early. Everyone knows you can't resist dessert."

I couldn't help the blush that bloomed in my cheeks when I recalled what else had happened when I'd finally gotten dessert that evening. Lawrence had brought it to me, and then we'd become dessert.

"Ohhh..." Aoine clapped her hands. "Do tell."

"I can't. But I didn't miss dessert."

She covered her mouth in pretend shock and laughed. "Oh, you naughty thing. Was it that hunky gargoyle you were with?"

Hearing her call Lawrence "hunky" made me slide into our old schoolgirl banter rhythm. "I'm not one to fuck and tell."

Her eyes widened in real shock. "Language! What happened to you in the Earth realm?"

"Many, many things. Including a human following me and trying to gather evidence of my misdeeds."

"Fae don't do misdeeds, we're only misunderstood."

I did smirk at her repeating the lesson we'd heard many times. "I know. But the human disappeared somewhere around your lands. Do you happen to know where?"

"I don't. I wasn't aware that an unusual death happened in my forest."

I doubted that. She had an exquisite attunement to her lands as the Lady of the Forest. Plus, she'd not said she wasn't aware of any deaths, just an unusual one. What did that even mean? For Fae as old as us—several centuries—"unusual" had a narrow definition.

"Well, please do let me know if you do find out where."

"You need to question his shade?"

"Something like that." I didn't want to admit more...or the depths of my desperation.

Aoine, always the schemer, sipped her tea, then asked, "And what will you give me if I do?"

Ah, there it was. The Fae bargain. How many would I have to make to get out of the asylum?

"What do you want? You're already a high-ranking Fae."

She sighed. "Yes, but there's a shadow over my reputation. Someone interpreted the ball I threw you as an effort to recruit you to a movement that was resisting your grandmother. Word got out, and I've been shunned since. I would like my reputation restored, and that will happen if I am known to be the friend and confidant of the Queen of the light Fae."

I raised my eyebrows. "'Interpreted?' It's clever of you to say it that way, but that's exactly what you were doing."

"I was throwing a party for a friend who had returned to Faerie for the first time in centuries. It just happened that some other troublemakers were there."

"And yet I know some of those 'troublemakers' managed to keep their positions, like the useless archivist. What are you really playing at?"

Now she blinked, and tears sparkled in her eyes. "I've missed you. Can't we be friends again? I feel so icky and vulnerable saying this, but it's lonely being the Lady of the Forest."

I'm not sure I believed this explanation any more than the last one, but it must have had some truth to it if she had been able to state it so directly.

"I'm still stung about the trial and the trap, Aoine. It's going to take me some time to trust you."

"Then it's a good thing we're Fae, isn't it? We have plenty of it. I'll prove my goodwill and search for the shade of the man you seek, and if I find him, then I'll let you know and leave it up to you as to whether you welcome me back as a friend."

If anything, her offer made me trust her less, but I nodded.

"Very well. Bring me the information I seek, and we'll go from there."

"Good." She stood. "This has been lovely, but I need to go. I want to get back across the Gray Zone before dark. Even if the revenants are ebbing, there are other nasty things out there."

"I agree." I stood as well. "Thank you for coming to see me. It's been lovely to speak with someone from home."

"I'll write you! And you can ask me for anything you want. I'll get it in. No bargain necessary."

"Thank you. I'll consider that. Do you know if High Princess Desdemona will visit soon?"

"I don't. As I mentioned, I didn't see her, only corresponded with her."

"Thanks."

She curtsied again, then took her leave. I sat and poured more tea, then took a bite of the raspberry lemon scone I hadn't touched yet. I nearly choked when a voice from the corner asked, "Did you actually believe any of that bat shit?"

18

LAWRENCE

Minerva called Micah and told him to retrieve my car and stuff from Mother's house. I could hear him grumbling, but he complied and got most of it. I'd have to go back for a couple of things I'd had hanging in the closet, but otherwise it was fine. He arrived about an hour later, during which I'd taken a nap in one of Minerva and Karen's guest rooms. I hadn't realized just how tired all the morning's activities and excitement had made me, and it frustrated me. If I were to go into Faerie, especially hauling a heavy apparatus, how long could I realistically last?

Micah didn't come alone. Mother emerged from the passenger side of the car, and I could tell from the stern lines of her jaw and lips that she wasn't happy.

Minerva took my stuff up to the room I'd be staying in, and once she returned and we all sat in her living room with fresh coffee, Mother looked at Minerva, then me.

"Tell me everything that happened." Her tone sounded more like the Regent than a mom, and I found myself involuntarily sitting up straighter, ready to report.

"A bunch of reporters cornered Lawrence," Minerva started, but with a curt hand gesture, Mother cut her off.

"I need to hear it firsthand."

So I told her about the encounter and how Sir Raleigh had disappeared in a dramatic fashion, causing a couple of them to get dunked. Did I see a twinkle of amusement in her eyes? Maybe. But she maintained her serious demeanor until I finished, then gave me a curt nod.

"And Minerva, when did you decide to get involved?"

"Karen got a call from one of them that they were looking for Lawrence for more questioning, and it could turn dangerous. She texted me, and I deduced where Lawrence had likely gone and the route he'd taken and intercepted him."

"Am I that predictable?" That didn't sit well.

"No, but it's what I would've done."

Mother rubbed her eyes. "Gargoyles don't run away, but it's also necessary to make decisions according to logical odds." She sighed. "I suppose this was going to come to a head at some point. Harold's been getting more and more vocal over the past few months, ever since the witch's spell was released. There have been rumors of a movement, a petition, for me to step down and for them to elect a new Regent."

"No!" Both Micah and Minerva objected.

"You're a good Regent, Mom," Micah said. "Sure, you made mistakes, but you did what you thought was best for us, and it mostly worked out."

"Except for the lack of births, yes." Mother shook her head. "Maybe it is time for me to step down, but I'd prefer to take the hereditary option and pass along the position to one of my children."

Micah and Minerva looked at each other and at me, and the words, *Not it!* Hovered in the air between us, although none of us said it.

"In spite of the cat's antics, Lawrence has the best optics, especially after he got rid of the black lightning bugs," Minerva pointed out. "The scandal will blow over, and I bet more than a few people will be amused to hear about Harold and that other reporter ending up in the river." She drummed her fingers on the arm of the sofa. "Karen's already working on spinning it in the gossip stream as them being scared of a little cat."

Micah snorted. "I hate to admit it, Sis, but that's going to be the best PR."

"Why does Harold have it out for you?" I asked Mother. "Since I'm still a relative outsider, I feel like I'm missing part of the story."

"I don't know. Like I said, it's been more over the past few months since your Fae girlfriend and her brother were here." Mother didn't frown, exactly, but her brows drew together into her thinking face.

Minerva did the same, and the resemblance between the two of them showed more strongly. Minerva tapped her coffee cup with a nail. "Now that I think about it, his behavior strikes me as defensive, like he's trying to deflect suspicion from himself."

"For what, though?" Micah asked. "It's not like we've had any major crimes since the murder, and that was solved."

"And the perpetrator punished, although not in a traditional way," Minerva finished. "Partially due to the actions of our heroic older brother."

I held up my hands. "Whoa, I don't need a whole PR campaign. I'm not running for Regent."

"No, but if you're going to be the Crown Prince, you need good optics." Minerva pulled her phone out and tapped in a note. "Reminder for me to talk to Karen about it and see what other resources we can marshal for you."

"Aren't you the head of the security force here?" I teased, but even I could hear the edge of desperation in my voice. "Not the

Regent PR pool." I pictured myself as a cat being cornered by a pack of water wolves.

"Security means many things, Big Bro. I know you haven't made your decision yet, but it won't hurt to get some good press regardless. It will help Mom out, too."

She knew I couldn't argue with that. Darn it, why did I have such a perceptive sibling? And smart, too. Had that created tension between the twins? As far as I could tell, Micah was happy for her to take the lead. It meant less for him to do.

Mother leaned forward. "Lawrence, I know this is a lot, but the encounter this morning shows that you need to make a decision. Do you know when that will be?"

"I need to do some more research. Like, what does being Crown Prince entail? What are the benefits and costs? Could I maintain a home and life outside The Aerie?"

"We can talk about that, but I'm afraid some of the knowl-edge has been lost to history. There are rumors that a Crown Prince can compel others to obey him if it's for the good of the realm."

"Oh, really?" My voice went higher on the last syllable, and the three of them looked at me.

My phone dinged with a text—Kestrel.

"I'll be right back."

I escaped into the yard.

19

———————

REINE

The voice startled me, but I snapped into Fae mode—*don't show weakness.*

I carefully placed my teacup on its saucer, set the saucer on the tea cart, turned the plate so the handle of my cup would match the angle of the others, and stood. I could almost feel the creature behind me quivering with impatience and uncertainty.

Finally, I turned and smoothed my skirt. A middle-aged Fae with a gray streak in her chin-length ebony bob emerged from the shadows. She wore a black catsuit, and that along with her dark brown eyes and ruby red lips matched the descriptions that Rhys and Lawrence had given me of the dark Fae Crown Princess Desdemona. The question was, would she turn out to be as big of a bitch as my mother?

"You missed tea."

She smiled, but her gaze twitched to the tea cart, upon which plenty remained. "Good thing I'm not hungry, then." Her voice matched her appearance—husky and dangerous, almost a purr.

"You're late, Crown Princess."

She stiffened at my use of her title. "Fae royalty have their own timelines, or did you forget during your long exile in the Earth realm?"

"I didn't. But it's courteous to be on time for one who outranks you. I'm still waiting for my curtsy."

Considering she matched my mother in years, if not surpassed her, I guessed she'd try to avoid that formality. I wouldn't let her.

"You'll be waiting for a while, then."

I shrugged and turned. "This interview is over."

"All right, fine."

I glanced back to see her give me a half-assed curtsy, which looked all the more ridiculous in her black catsuit.

"What do you want?" I crossed my arms. "I don't have all day to wait for you to get to the point."

"Because you're *so* busy here in the asylum, I can tell. Have you found anything...interesting?" She raised her eyebrows like she knew there were things to find.

I didn't let on. "I haven't explored much." It wasn't a lie. I hadn't, but I'd explored enough, and I definitely planned to further. "Look, I don't have time to banter with you."

"No, I imagine not." She walked around me and looked me up and down. "You've settled in quite nicely. Docilely, dare I say. I'm curious as to what your game is..." She sneered my title, "Your Highness."

"No game. I made a bargain. I'm keeping my side of it."

"Yes, for your precious gargoyle lover and your pathetic Earth realm friends. Tell me, are the gargoyles as...big as they say when they're in their creature form?"

Before I could put conscious thought to the reaction, I had her by the throat and lifted off the ground. She clawed at my hand, and I dropped her.

"You will speak to me with respect."

She staggered to her knees, then flopped back on the couch.

"Nicely done," she croaked. She rubbed her throat, and I could sense her healing the bruises. "I didn't think you had it in you."

I crossed my arms again. "And what is your game, Desdemona? Did you stop by to check on me for your mother? You can tell her I'm still being a good little patient."

Desdemona crossed her legs and wiggled her foot, giving me a good look at the point of her stiletto heel. "I'm not here for her. I'm here for me. She doesn't share her plans with her daughter. You know what that's like."

I didn't respond.

"Anyway..." She stood. "I came to find out whether you're actually up to something in cahoots with my useless cousin or if you're a coward hiding out here while the revenants take over Faerie. I'm leaning toward the latter."

I still didn't say anything. The fact that I had gotten stuck in the asylum showed the extent of my abilities to judge whether a course of action would be a good one.

She waved her fingers toward her nose and inhaled. "Ah, there it is. The smell of self-doubt."

"So what if it is? It wouldn't hurt you to have some humility. You may find it easier to get the information you want."

She laughed so hard she doubled over. Then with a flash, she straightened and threw a wooden-handled iron dagger at me.

I dodged, but it caught my shoulder, and I hissed at the searing sensation and sizzling sound. As for the smell...

"You light Fae smell like cooking mushrooms when you get iron-burned."

I whipped out my ice energy lasso and aimed it for her neck, but she batted it away with the sword of fire that material-ized in her hand.

"You know how they say there aren't any weapons allowed in the asylum?" she asked. "That's only for the inmates. What-ever you summon won't hurt me."

"Who sent you to assassinate me?" My mind riffled through my mental rolodex of enemies. Unfortunately, it was a long list. "And is Lady Aoine in on this?"

"Her? No, she's not that subtle." Desdemona and I circled each other, but she blocked the door, and I couldn't get around her.

"Was it my mother?"

Desdemona laughed. "Ah, mothers. Why do the Fae ones always suck so hard?'

Suck... A plan formed in the back of my mind. I needed to keep her talking so I could figure out all angles since I'd only get one shot.

"I don't know. Because they're threatened by powerful daughters?"

She cocked her head, considering. "Yes, I suppose so." She feinted at me, and I leaped back. "You only have so far you can go, you know. I'll have you up against the wall soon. Then I'll pin you to it."

"You're enjoying playing too much, Des. That's what Basil calls you, isn't it? Tell me, how long have you been in love with him?" I reached behind me and found the silk pull-cord, which I severed with a thought so I held a length in my hand.

She blinked, and her smile returned, but less feral than before. "There's nothing between me and my cousin."

"No, there isn't. He's been trying to get in my petticoats, in my bed, since the first time he met me. I can assure you, he's not a great kisser." Well, I didn't know exactly, but compared to Lawrence's kisses, the one Basil had given me had been boring.

She snarled and lunged at me. This time I was ready. I dodged to the side, and she buried the sword in the wall. I wrapped the cord around her neck and pulled it taut.

"I don't want him, but he doesn't deserve you." I whispered. "He's too good and noble for you." A bead of sweat escaped her hairline and rolled down her cheek.

"Are we talking about the same Fae? And you shouldn't be this strong," she objected in secret conversation. *"You're a light Fae."*

"You're wrong."

The pinprick scars where Ashlee Wyatt the vampire had fed from me heated, and I allowed my eye teeth to grow into fangs.

Desdemona fell to her knees, and I dropped the rope but grabbed her by the hair. Her hands hung limp by her sides. I bent over, yanked her head to one side, and pricked her skin with my fangs. Two droplets of blood trickled on to my tongue. "Dark Fae taste like chocolate raspberry. Let this be a warning to you. I am more powerful than you, and I will destroy you if you come after me again. Understand?"

She nodded, and I let her go. I stepped back and caught myself on the back of the couch.

What in Hades had just happened? I blinked, and the crimson blood lust cleared from my vision.

Desdemona stood, and I waited for her to grab the sword and try one more time to run me through. She might have succeeded if she'd tried. She appeared as weakened and as drained as I felt.

This time when she turned her dark gaze on me, she showed respect. "So, it is true."

"What is?" The certainty that I'd revealed too much nearly made me groan.

"That you're not all light Fae. You're the daughter of the Wanderer. And you have some dark in you from somewhere." She smiled. "You're the one powerful enough to take down my mother."

"I have no desire to do that. We need Faerie to be in alliance, not conflict, in order to defeat the revenants."

"No, we need Faerie to be united. Do you have any idea how many Fae, both light and dark, are on your side? The romantic angle made your story even more palatable." She placed one hand on her chest, and sighed, "The Fae queen who gave up her freedom for her gargoyle lover's life." She made a circular hand motion. "Good for you. You have power, Queen Reine. You need to use it."

"Or what?" I didn't want to hear what she said. It wasn't like public adulation would get me out of here or allow me to go back in time to pick a different bargain. But then, I would never have found the ancient library, which I hoped had the keys to all my problems. Or was I putting too much faith in books?

This time her expression held no mockery. "Or we're all doomed. Your mother is doing something to weaken the boundaries between the Gray Zone and our lands. Soon the revenants will overrun the lands of the dark Fae, including Cruaidh." She snorted. "I thought if I killed you, I could make her stop. By the way, my mother wasn't on board with this plan."

"But she knew?"

"She did."

"And she didn't do anything to stop you." I didn't ask it as a question, but she shook her head.

"You're a thorn in her side as well. Some feel she's keeping you prisoner here and that she made up the story of you choosing the bargain, although you remain, as ever, the hero for saving your lover. If you die in here, well, that solves both her and Maeve's problems, doesn't it?"

"Except the revenants remain a threat." I sighed. "And that's the problem I need to focus on."

She held out her hand. I hesitated but took it. An electric shock passed between us, and I tried to draw my hand back—I didn't know if I wanted what she offered.

Desdemona held tight, and the power of her words echoed through the room. "I swear you my oath of loyalty, Queen of the Fae."

"Light Fae," I corrected.

"No, Queen of All Fae. You may not accept it, but I can see it.

You shouldn't have been able to defeat me like you did. You shouldn't be able to call upon dark, destructive forces or channel a vampire's bite. But you did." She grinned.

"I'm not so delighted. Don't breathe a word of any of this to your mother."

"Oh, don't worry. She'll find out soon enough, but not from me." She released my hand. "I'll come visit again soon. Perhaps we can really have tea."

I surprised myself by saying, "I'd like that" and meaning it. Then I recalled the cloaked rider, who had repelled the revenants on my journey through the Gray Zone. "Were you the one who helped me with the revenants?"

Desdemona grinned. "You would ask me that." Then her expression turned serious again. "I'm losing my control over them. But again, I'll do what I can."

We both felt the words she didn't say—*Even if it's no longer enough.*

20

LAWRENCE

Kestrel's text told me she'd figured out the way to The Aerie—"I have an eel for that too!" she typed, referring to the system Reine had taught her for accessing her magic. I'd be interested to know what that particular talent had showed her and if it made us vulnerable in unexpected ways.

And there I went thinking like a Crown Prince again.

After I walked back in my sister's house, my mother stood and hugged me.

"I apologize. It's not fair of me to pressure you to follow my dreams for you, for us. You're your own gargoyle. You always have been, and that's one of your strengths. I'll be happy and proud for you no matter what you decide."

"Thank you." How many times had I longed for that kind of reassurance during those long, lonely years when I'd been searching for my father's killer? Then after survival became more of a necessity than revenge, when I'd been trying to figure out what I wanted to be or do with my long life? I'd arrived at helping animals when I'd rescued a horse stuck in a mud bog and hadn't looked back.

Until now.

"I have a, uh, guest coming," I said.

Mother, Micah, and Minerva all looked at me with surprise.

"Kestrel?" Minerva guessed.

"Yes. She's insisting on coming up here and talking me out of being the Crown Prince and whatever other foolhardy things I'm thinking of doing."

I expected Mother to be angry, but she smiled. "Good. I'm glad I'll finally get to meet her. She sounds like an amazing young woman."

"Her magic is... Well, she's not Fae."

"Thank goodness," Micah muttered.

I shot him a look. "She's half Fae. Half Earth witch."

Now frowns met my words. Minerva fiddled with a tassel on a pillow. "What does that make her?"

"A trickster."

They all gasped.

"We've never had one of those here." Mother tapped her chin with her right index finger. "How in control of her powers is she?"

"Not very, but they don't leak out or anything weird. In fact, she spent most of her life up until a few months ago thinking she didn't have any magic."

"What happened?"

Minerva smirked. "Reine happened, I'm guessing."

"Yes, but things would have come to a head, anyway. It's too long a story to tell now. Where can she stay?"

"We have plenty of room here." Minerva motioned to the upper floor. "There are at least three furnished rooms we're not using."

"We should only need two, but thanks."

"Don't you want to stay with me? Wouldn't she?" Mother asked. "I'm sure this thing with the journalists and the cat will blow over soon. There's no need for you to stay so far away from everything."

I patted her on the shoulder. "I'd still feel better here, especially with Kestrel being as she is. I don't know that the townspeople need to be exposed to yet another creature so soon."

"I thought you said her powers didn't show?"

"They don't, but I don't want to take any chances. Something may happen if she feels threatened."

"I understand."

But I could tell she didn't like it.

I TEXTED Kestrel the address Minerva gave me and helped my sister prepare one of the other guest rooms.

The headlights of Kestrel's car wound up the drive about an hour before full dark. I'd become accustomed to the long sunsets in The Aerie, which had something to do with the magic that had kept it hidden for so long. Although the spell had been broken, parts of it lingered, like over the river through town and along the horizon. Reine had told me that it would gradually decay, and the parts that remained wouldn't be harmful to anyone, gargoyle or not.

I walked out to the front porch to welcome Kestrel, but the first voice I heard was familiar and unexpected.

"Is this it?" Lily the dark Fae princess asked.

"It's his sister's place. He told me to come here." Kestrel emerged from the car and stretched. "Hey, Uncle Lawrence! You remember Lily. She insisted she come with me."

"Did she bring any friends?" I peered into the thickening shadows for signs of Agents Grimm and Gilmore, the two representatives of The Normals who had threatened me and Kestrel after we'd encountered Lily in Atlanta.

"No, they don't know I'm here." Lily emerged and looked around. Her dark hair brushed her shoulders. I noticed she wore it long, likely to cover her pointed ears. Now that I saw her in more open surroundings, I could see the resemblance between her and Desdemona, the dark Fae princess who had led an attack on me, Rhys, and Basil in the Cavern of Whispers under the dark Fae capital of Cruaidh. She must be a daughter or granddaughter...or the missing princess.

That realization slotted into my brain and almost made me groan. How much more trouble would that mean for us? Nothing to be done for it now.

"Kestrel, I'm happy to see y'all, but a heads-up would've been nice."

Kestrel ran up the stairs and gave me a tight hug. "Are you okay? You're thinner. And your aura isn't as bright as it was. You're still not all the way better."

"No, but I'm healing more every day. Lily, welcome." I held out a hand, and she shook it. "I don't know why you're here, but I'm sure we'll make sense of it all. Are you two hungry?"

"Yes, starving," Kestrel said. "What smells so good?"

Mother emerged wearing an apron over her usual attire of white shirt and pencil skirt. "Summer vegetable chicken stew. Oh, who's this?"

I introduced Lily, whose mouth had dropped open when she saw Mother.

Lily bowed deeply, and when she rose, she said, "Regent, I am honored to meet you. I wasn't expecting to have this privilege so soon."

"Please, we don't have to be formal here. And this must be Kestrel. Welcome, dear." She hugged a surprised-looking Kestrel. "Come in and let me take care of you girls. You must be famished. We've got the stew, and Minerva made her famous yeast rolls, and her girlfriend Karen made her award-winning apple pie..."

"I'll get the luggage." I walked down the two steps, and Kestrel followed me.

"I'm sorry, I should've told you. But she was afraid she wouldn't be welcome, especially after..."

"Yeah, this could get interesting." But I smiled at her. "Let me know what I can carry."

"We don't have anything heavy. We don't plan to stay too long."

"I'll be fine." Stones, between my mother, Minerva, and Karen, I had enough females fussing over me. Would I have to endure it from Kestrel as well? At least Lily didn't seem to be the fussing-over type.

I led Kestrel to the upstairs room Minerva and I had prepared. It had a queen bed.

"Will this be okay, or do you want me to ask Minerva to make up the other room, too?"

"No, this is fine. I told her sleeping arrangements may be tight."

"Nonsense." Minerva swept into the room. She examined Kestrel with a look that wasn't friendly, but not exactly welcoming, either. "So this is Kestrel?"

"Yes, ma'am." Kestrel held out a hand. "It's nice to meet you."

Minerva hesitated but accepted the handshake. "It's nice to meet you as well. Did Lawrence tell you I'm the head of the security forces here?"

Kestrel went white and squeaked, "No."

"Min," I warned. "She's no threat."

"Yet she brought a dark Fae, a high dark Fae, into our enclave. Into my home. I think I have the right to ask some questions."

"It's fine," Kestrel told me with a shaky smile. "I'm pleased to meet you, Agent, and I'm happy to give you whatever information you require."

Kestrel had told me she wanted to leave it behind, but her

PBI training and etiquette lessons shone through. I stepped back physically and mentally to allow her to handle the situation.

Minerva gave me a curt nod of acknowledgment but didn't shift her gaze from Kestrel. "You have some training?"

Kestrel winced. "I was a junior agent with the Paranormal Bureau of Investigations."

"And you're no longer with them?"

"No."

Minerva paused, and I could tell she was pondering whether to pry further. Kestrel's reasons for leaving the PBI were none of her business, and I almost stepped in to tell her, but I held my tongue.

"What was your intention coming here?"

"Originally to talk to my Uncle Lawrence. I needed to see for myself that he's okay and of sound mind."

Minerva's lips twitched. Trying not to smile? "I can assure you he is. We've had some interesting occurrences here in The Aerie recently."

"I've heard."

"And why did you bring your friend without telling him?"

Kestrel glanced at me. "There's a history there, Agent. She says she has important information for him that she could only deliver in person, but we weren't sure of her welcome."

"And you believed her."

"Yes."

"Do you trust her?"

Kestrel shifted her weight, and her hands twitched—interesting tells. "I do to a certain extent. I believe she has information to convey, but I would be cautious what you say around her."

"Is that all?" Minerva arched an eyebrow.

"I trust Uncle Lawrence to make a good decision, but he always told me to gather as much information as I could before stepping on to a new path. I want to make sure he does, too, and I trust *him* to know what the Fae says that is pure truth and what is consistent with their tendency toward deception."

Now Minerva did smile. "She's a smart one, Big Brother. I can see your influence."

"Thanks. But her intelligence is all credit to her own curiosity and her parents' efforts and genes."

"Thanks," Kestrel's reply emerged with wry tone. "But you've had a good influence, too. That's why I don't want to lose you to whatever this is up here."

Micah poked his head around the door frame. "Uh, y'all, do you mind? Things are getting tense downstairs between Mom and the dark Fae, and I don't know how much longer Karen can stall a full-on fight."

WE DASHED down the stairs to find Mother standing at the stove clutching a ladle like a weapon or wand—or both—and Lily leaning against a counter with arms crossed and a sulky droop to her features.

Karen rushed between dining room and kitchen setting the table. Her blonde curls stuck out like she'd been running her hands through them, and her anxiety showed in the sweat that rolled down her forehead and darkened her pink T-shirt across her chest and under her arms. "Oh, good, glad y'all came down. Good timing. Dinner's ready."

"Lily?" Kestrel walked over to the dark Fae.

"It's fine. You'd think the gargoyle Regent would know I can't answer some things about Faerie."

Mother blew out an exasperated sigh. "Try *any* things about Faerie. How are we supposed to trust you if you won't even say where you're from or who your family is?"

"That's not the information I came to convey."

"Can't this wait 'til after dinner?" Karen asked. "You may feel better after eating."

Lily narrowed her eyelids.

Kestrel elbowed her and smiled at Karen. "Yes, dinner would be great. Thank you."

Karen shot Kestrel a relieved grin and handed her the basket of rolls. "Minerva usually makes these for special occasions. It's delightful to finally meet our Lawrence's niece by choice."

Kestrel's smile turned pained, but she said, "Thank you. I appreciate the effort." She didn't say whose effort, so I hoped both felt appreciated.

We sat around the table, and Mother and Karen brought out bowls of stew. I offered to help, but Karen waved for me to stay seated.

"You probably have a lot to catch up on."

"True. How's the apartment?" I asked Kestrel.

"Good. The previous inhabitant left some food rotting in the fridge, but I got rid of it without any problem."

"She blasted it to another dimension," Lily said with a delighted tilt to her mouth that made her look like she could be a graduate student, not a young adult Fae, which made her at least a hundred years old.

"Lily's been helping me with my powers," Kestrel added.

"At what price?" The words escaped me before I could weigh their politeness.

"No price." Lily rolled her eyes. "I'm not allowed to do that anymore. I'm technically not allowed to help Kestrel, but if she's going to live among humans, she needs to be able to control her magic."

My relief at Kestrel not being indebted to Lily was quickly swamped by a wave of worry that Lily was recruiting Kestrel to join the Normals.

"Don't worry, Uncle Lawrence, I'm not thinking of joining them," Kestrel told me via secret conversation, then winked at what must have been the totally shocked expression on my face.

"That was one of the first ones I taught her to access," Lily added.

"Out loud, please," Mother admonished. "It's rude to engage in secret conversation at the table."

"Yes, Mother," I said at the same time Kestrel and Lily responded, "Yes, Ma'am." We all laughed at that, and for a second it felt like a "normal" family gathering, at least as normal as four gargoyles, a Trickster, and a dark Fae could make it.

"I apologize for seeming stubborn," Lily told Mother. "I promise, I'm not trying to be rude, but I'm limited in what I'm allowed to say."

"We'll give you some time to talk to Lawrence after we eat," Mother told her. "But I wish you could at least tell me what you think about the black lightning bug attack."

"I... I suppose." Lily took a spoonful of the chicken stew. "This is delicious. It reminds me..." She cast her gaze downward. "Never mind."

"It's okay," Kestrel told her. "We won't tell anyone."

"All right." Lily took another bite and closed her eyes. 'It reminds me of something we used to eat when I was a child, and we were traveling."

"It's an old recipe for Traveler's Stew," Mother said. "I've been making it for Lawrence since he was a boy, and then these other two as well. It can be made with canned chicken while camping."

Lily opened her eyes and nodded. "That makes sense. Thank you for good memories of my childhood." She didn't follow her statement with something about not having many, but her words strongly implied it. I'd thought she'd joined the Normals to run away from her responsibilities, but what if it had been more? I'd met Desdemona, and that Fae was bat-shit out of her mind.

"What happened today?" Kestrel asked. "I thought you were staying closer to town."

"Perceptive, as always, kiddo." I ruffled her hair, and she batted my hand. I told her about the encounter with the reporters, and she groaned.

"That's hilarious, but I'm sad that Sir Raleigh is gone. I was looking forward to seeing him."

"He must have found a weak spot that allowed him to go through when Reine looked through a portal on her side," Lily explained. "And grimalkins make for very loyal and stubborn protectors. Don't take it personally that he left you, Doctor Gordon."

"Thanks, I tried not to." But it still stung. Maybe I needed a pet.

The food seemed to loosen Lily's inhibitions. "And as for the black lightning bugs, those were always Maeve's favorite ways to poke her enemies and test their strengths. How did you defeat them?"

"I treated them like animals and went from there."

"Smart. You'll be a good Crown Prince. Assuming you decide to follow through with that plan," she added in response to Kestrel's glare.

We'd all finished eating, and Mother shooed us into the living room. "Why don't y'all go ahead and have your chat while the rest of us clean up and fix dessert? Minerva..."

My sister made an about-face from following us. "Yes, Mother."

Lily shook her head when we reached the living room. I sat on the couch where I'd been before, and Lily took the recliner. "I like your family, Doctor Gordon. They seem so nice and like regular folks. I was a little scared of the Regent at first."

"Everyone is," I assured her. "But she's happy to have young people to take care of."

"Lily, tell him what you told me," Kestrel urged. Before I could ask why she didn't relay the message, she said, "I don't have all the answers to the questions you may ask."

21

LILY'S TALE

obody does generational trauma like the Fae royalty. We're not encouraged to be our true selves. No, we have to conform to the perfect image. Powerful. Beautiful. Haughty. And educated, but not by traditional, pedestrian means like reading for ourselves.

My mother Desdemona got impregnated by a scholar to spite my grandmother. I was the first dark Fae child of my generation, so they wondered what or who would come out. My grandmother hoped for a mini-her, a far cry from my mother with her rebellious ways, and so she planned to name me after herself. My mother convinced her that would be too confusing for the history books, so they called me Liliana instead.

Unfortunately I followed in my mother's footsteps and disappointed my Grandmother's grand ambitions. Instead of playing with spells and manipulating other Fae, I always had a book in my hand. History, biology, Fae literature—trust me, it's more than fairy tales—even geography interested me. If we had universities, I would have wanted to be a professor, not a princess. But I was Fae enough to drive my grandmother up the palace walls by challenging her own lack of knowledge. Finally, after my grandmother's efforts to curb my curiosity failed, she sent me to work in the archives.

I remember the haughty expression on her face when she declared, "If you're going to have your nose in old, dusty piles of paper, you may as well be useful." She thought she was punishing me, but instead sent me into what I thought of as heaven.

The archivist, an old Fae named Plachul, took me under his wing stubs. Yes, he'd been a servant who had worked his way up to archivist. My grandmother appreciated him because of his deference. He never tired of answering my questions, and he helped me to figure out my true love—Fae history. So much of it had faded into legend or the mists of forgetfulness, and I was determined to find out the truth. As much truth as can be found in history.

But our history had always bothered me. Like, if we were so similar, why were there dark and light Fae? The rubric was that the dark Fae engaged in destruction and the light in creation, but those boundaries always felt blurry to me. Fire both creates and destroys, right? So does water.

I won't bore you with philosophy. One day Plachul decided to replace some shelving that had started to crack. We emptied the bookcase, and when I helped him move it away from the wall, we found the door to a hidden chamber.

I got excited—could we have found a secret stash that held the answers to all my burning questions?—but he shook his head and warned, "This isn't for us, Princess. We can't let anyone know it's here."

Of course, I argued that it could contain documents from before the battle between light and dark Fae. We could finally answer questions about our history we never thought to ask.

Plachul, ever the teacher, told me to move beyond my curiosity and use my Fae powers to sense beyond the door.

I placed my hand on the wall and snatched it back. Whatever was behind there repulsed me with a slimy feeling down to my toes. We agreed it was dangerous magic and that we should hide it again.

We've all read the fairy tales. When something is forbidden, it becomes an object of obsession. I convinced Plachul not to cover the door again, and I would sit and stare at it for hours. What could it be hiding? What was so important, so mysterious, that it required a repulsion spell?

One day when Plachul had run into town to get more ink and parchment, I opened the door. I told myself it would just be a peek, but my first glimpse showed me rolled-up scrolls on shelves inside. I threw the door open to let the light in. No air rushed out or in, which clued me in to the time bubble spell that had kept all the documents in pristine condition. I could also detect the second layer of protection, the one that I'd already sensed. It was a sacrifice spell. Whoever went into the room would die, but just the first.

When Plachul returned, he found the door open and me furiously looking through references for the key to undo the sacrifice spell.

I should have thought through my actions because I'll never forget the last conversations I had with him and my grandmother...or Plachul's disappointment.

"I warned you, Princess. Did you truly think that kind of magic wouldn't set off an alarm?"

Panic shot through me. "What do you mean?" But I knew. The sinking of my heart into my gut told me my grandmother had more than one intention when she banished me to the archives. I hadn't thought enough like a Fae, though, to figure it out.

He cocked his head and cupped one ear. "Ah, yes, here they are."

The door burst open—my grandmother entered with her top four guards. "What did you find in here, Liliana? Oh!" She walked over to the door and peered in but didn't break the plane. "Hidden archives. And a sacrifice spell to protect them. Those must be some juicy secrets."

I rushed to block her, but her magic held me back. I pleaded, "We're currently researching how to break the spell. I'll let you know when we figure it out."

"No need." She gestured to her guards, two of whom took Plachul by each arm. "We'll take care of it now."

"No!" I reached out to stop them, but I hesitated to use my magic for fear of damaging the books. Plus, time bubble spells are notorious for distorting magic and intention around them. By the time I'd decided to take the risk, it was too late.

They flung poor Plachul through the door, and he screamed, writhed on the floor, and batted at his skin like a thousand wasps stung him. The silence when he lay still poured into my ears and hardened my heart against my grandmother.

She walked in next. "Ugh, all these scrolls. Liliana, be a dear and let me know if there's anything important in them." Then she turned and left me with the room and Plachul's body, which had already started turning into dirt.

I whispered the prayer to send a Fae soul to its long sleep and hoped I'd said it in time and that the spell hadn't blocked him from accessing his reincarnation. I cried as I gathered up his remains and brought them to his family. His mate accepted them and didn't ask questions, but I saw the suspicion in her eyes. She knew I'd had something to do with his death. Or perhaps I felt that rarest of Fae emotions—guilt.

I studied the scrolls, but I didn't inform my grandmother of what was in them. They were from the time before the Rift, and they included mostly prophecies, both that the battle would happen and what would need to occur for Faerie to be one realm again. First, they stated that a Fae queen would mate with a gargoyle Crown Prince. Then, somehow the realm would unite, and gargoyles would return to Faerie.

I attended Plachul's service and left from there for the Earth realm, where I hid with the help of the Normals until you two found me. Now I'm here, and I feel I was meant to bring you this message and this warning—should you rescue Reine, should you fully accept your role as Crown Prince, you do not know what ramifications there will be either here in The Aerie or in Faerie. But whatever you do, remember, most Fae are not to be trusted, and one of the rare good ones died so I could bring you this information.

22

LAWRENCE

Holy stones, Lily was the missing princess Liliana. Reine had told me about her. I hadn't thought she'd exiled herself to the Earth realm. Or escaped.

After Lily related her tale, we sat in silence. In my case, I processed what she told me and said a prayer to whatever deity was listening for Plachul's soul.

"So what you're telling me is that if I accept the Crown Prince position, I'll possibly start an apocalypse in Faerie?"

Lily nodded. "Something like that. Those of us who know of the prophecies and the history always figured that there's no way a Fae queen would ally with a gargoyle, and there was even less of a chance that she'd mate bond with one. So even if someone had the ambition to be Queen of All Fae, that barrier would prevent it."

Kestrel regarded me with a mixture of curiosity and disgust. "How did that happen, Uncle Lawrence? It's while we were there, wasn't it?"

"Yes, in Aoine's castle. No, I'm not giving you details."

Lily didn't have any such scruples. "It's an interesting

process. A Fae has to have sex with a gargoyle while he's in gargoyle form."

Kestrel covered her ears. "La, la, la, I don't hear you, I'm not picturing anything, la la la."

"Lily, really," I scolded as I tried not to laugh. "You don't need to show your dark Fae to that degree."

She shrugged, and her smirk came across as utterly unrepentant.

"The question is, let's say I'm already showing signs of being the Crown Prince... How much danger does this put us in?"

"That depends on how many Fae know about you and about the prophecy. I'm guessing not many. I wouldn't have found out about you had I not been approached by this one." She inclined her head toward Kestrel. "Then again, I'd heard gossip. But there's still the prophecy bit."

"And those are the Preservationists, the ones who want Faerie to reunite and for the revenants to be protected so they can share their knowledge once they're fully resurrected?"

"Yes. That's them. I can't confirm or deny that I'm still in touch with some."

"What do they know about me?"

"So far they've dismissed you as a rumor to discredit Reine. Honestly, though, her going into the asylum to save you has complicated things. You're now a romantic hero, which is bringing up questions."

"Great..." I sat back and sighed. "I can't undo what's been done. And I can't help what I've already done."

"Which is...?"

I studied her. Should I trust her? But she had the knowledge I needed. "I've already used the compulsion power. Twice. Once to save Reine. Once to save her and myself."

She nodded. "Not gonna lie, you already have the CP vibe. With whom?"

"Once was with a dimension-walker, and once with—what?"

She pursed her lips and whistled before saying, "You compelled a *what?* They're supposedly impervious to Fae or gargoyle influence. To any but their own, really."

"Was that Professor Grand-Pied?" Kestrel asked. "That wasn't very nice."

"He still made his choice, but I nudged him in the direction." I placed my hands over my face. "I'm not proud of it. This isn't a nice power, Kestrel. I hope you don't have it."

She shrugged. "If I do, it's not like I'm going to use it. I have ethics, Uncle Lawrence."

I thought I did, too. "I didn't mean to. It came over me."

"Meaning you're meant to the be the Crown Prince whether you like it or not." My mother walked in. "Yes, I was listening. I'm not going to say sorry, either. When were you going to tell me, Lawrence?"

She regarded me with a sternness that recalled how she'd cowed me when I was a boy. But I didn't react with the same emotions. I had a few centuries behind me now, and I'd learned to stand up to a Fae princess who'd become a queen. "When I was ready, which wasn't going to be until I figured it out."

Mother sat beside me and ignored Lily's very red face and Kestrel's wide-eyed stare. "Lawrence, when will you learn that you don't have to do everything by yourself anymore? Yes, being Crown Prince has responsibilities, but you'll also have the support of your family and your people."

"And it's important to get as much as you can." Minerva came in with Karen in tow and handed me a glass of white wine. "Sorry, not sorry, we were eavesdropping, too. You may need this."

My stomach gave a can-can kick to my solar plexus. "Why?"

"Because..." She turned on the television, and the news came on. "Because this."

Hazel sat at the news desk and reported, "And an unusual

incident happened today on the River Path with Regent's son Lawrence Gordon and his pet."

The screen switched to the view of one of the cameras and showed Sir Raleigh launching himself toward it, then disappearing. Then jostling and a couple of splashes.

"What was that?" the male anchor, whose name I couldn't remember, asked.

"That was Harold Ironkeys and Tommy Stonecrest jumping out of the way of the cat...and ending up in the river." The corners of Hazel's eyes crinkled, and she tucked her bottom lip under her top one like she was trying not to laugh.

Her co-anchor didn't bother trying. He chuckled and asked, "You mean two full-fledged male gargoyles went for a swim because they were scared of a cat?"

"Well, to be fair, his eyes went wild, and he leaped at us. I wouldn't want to be on the business end of those claws."

"What did Doctor Gordon have to say about all that?"

I put my head in my hands. As if Harold didn't have it out for us enough, this public humiliation would make him hate us even more.

The cameras panned to show the sidewalk and parking lot outside the studio. There seemed to be some sort of rally going on. Or riot.

"And now we have the scene outside our studio. Our sources say there's another scene, a similar one, in the parking lot behind City Hall. What's going on, Tommy?"

Tommy, who had apparently dried off, held the mic to his mouth, but the chanting in the background kept breaking in.

"We want our Crown Prince! We want our Crown Prince!"

"Yes, the gargoyles of The Aerie are chanting for Doctor Gordon to take the position his mother has offered him and become the Crown Prince of the gargoyles. Sentiment seems to be in favor except for a small but vocal minority."

Indeed, occasionally booing came through.

"What do his supporters say?"

"That we need someone in leadership who has experience with the Fae. And the opposition is afraid he's gotten too cozy with them, although no one's seen the blonde Fae he was with earlier this year."

"Good asylum timing, Reine," Kestrel muttered.

"And what about the events of the last few weeks?"

"Supporters are quick to point out that no one was seriously hurt in either due to Doctor Gordon's fast thinking and decisive actions. They attribute the disappearance of the Fae cat today to his influence and applaud him for getting rid of it before it really hurt anyone."

"And are you unhurt from your swim?" The male co-anchor asked.

"Yes, although I may still have some water in my ear." He tapped the side of his head. "But Hazel, as you know, the main question is, 'Where is Lawrence Gordon?' He hasn't been seen since the incident at the river."

Hazel looked straight into the camera, and I felt her gaze found me. "I'm sure wherever he is, he's planning his next move to impress us all." She swiveled to face a different camera, which still picked her up, but without the directness of the first one. "And coming up, we have an update on why fuel prices are rising in The Aerie. Stay with us."

Minerva switched off the television. "What a mess," she sighed. "Lawrence, I'm going to need to assign an officer to you. I don't trust the 'small but vocal minority.'"

"I don't need a babysitter," I grumbled, but Kestrel's stricken expression made me backpedal. "I mean, that's fine, as long as they don't act like a codependent guard dog."

Lily inclined her head toward Minerva. "This is part of the price of being the Crown Prince. You're going to be in the public eye. It does work out nicely for Reine to be in the asylum, though."

"She's right. You need to distance yourself from the Fae, at least for now." Karen's phone rang, and she smirked when she answered. "Hello, Hazel. Yes, we saw. Now why would you think I know where Lawrence is? Hang on." She switched herself to mute. "She wants to do an interview with you tomorrow. What should I tell her?"

Everyone looked at me, and my tongue stuck to the roof of my mouth. "I, ah, I..." I swallowed and looked at my mother.

"Remember, if you do it, you can't undo it."

"I know. But if I don't, what will they say about me? It could make the announcement of my decision seem more reactive than active."

For once, my strategic mind didn't have an answer for me. I was a scientist, not a politician, for stones' sake!

But if I was going to be the Crown Prince, I needed to act decisively. I nodded to Karen. "Tell her I'll do it."

As soon as I said the words, the energy in the room shifted. The urge to change came over me so powerfully I had to run outside and strip under the full moon. I leaped into the heavens with a roar.

23

———

REINE

Desdemona's visit left me shaken and trembling. I made my way back to my room, where I laid on the bed. Sir Raleigh sniffed my face.

"Do I smell different? I feel different. I don't know what happened down there."

What had come over me? What had I *allowed* to come over me? The second question disturbed me with its ramifications. Had I channeled something, or had that dark energy been lurking below the surface since Ashlee Wyatt had drunk from me with my permission?

Sir Raleigh snuggled against my side and purred.

I ran my hand over his soft fur. "I'm glad you're not judging me."

What had Desdemona been playing at with her little ambush? She'd seemed pleased with the outcome. I recalled what Aria, a medium and witch in the Earth realm had told me, that a web tightened around me. I thought I'd managed to escape the one she spoke about, but there was always another spider. This one felt bigger and more important. I sensed I'd be getting more visitors and surprises, and they'd come at a faster rate.

That decided me. I could lie on the bed and feel frightened for myself and try to see into the future, or I could go and learn all I could about the asylum, its builders, and its purpose in my own future.

I changed back into my Earth realm clothes, which had been magically cleaned. It was almost dinner time, so I walked outside to catch the sunset, what little I could see of it behind the clouds, and also to get a look at the asylum from the outside. The obfuscation spells inside the structure had kept me from getting a good sense of its true shape and scope, so I hoped that stepping back and looking at the whole thing from the grounds would give me a better perspective.

There was probably a life lesson in that somewhere.

Sir Raleigh tried to come with me, and I felt bad about shutting him in the room.

"Can you disguise yourself? You are a creature of the gray Fae."

He cocked his head. Then his shape went blurry and dissolved into a plume of gray smoke, which mostly disappeared when he kept to my shadow.

"Neat trick. I guess you have some extra powers here in Faerie, too, huh? The asylum must not dampen gray Fae magic. Or maybe it's using it..." I'd associated the confusion spell with the dark Fae, but obscuring things fell under gray Fae specialties.

Huh. That meant when the asylum was built, or at least when it was turned into an asylum, the gray Fae had been involved. Somehow that didn't comfort me, although I was half gray, as I'd learned.

My mind went through the lessons drilled into my young Fae brain by Larry Leafmore and other teachers, whom I could barely remember. Dark Fae magic destroyed. Light Fae built and grew. Gray Fae didn't exist. Heh, that would come as a surprise to them all later once Ellerin taught us all that the gray confused and obscured.

So had my encounter with Ashlee the vampire changed my percentages? I'd always thought I was a little more light Fae than gray, considering Ellerin had started off as light Fae. Unfortunately, no Fae Ancestry.com existed to confirm what I'd thought, that I had sixty-forty light to gray Fae genes.

I walked into the waning light and caught sight of the pond, which reflected the sky like a pool of mercury—pretty but deadly. I'd battled water wolves and called upon fire, a force that could build or destroy, and used it in conjunction with Rhys' magic to defeat them, or at least escape in the moment. Could I call on all Fae powers?

And did I want to know? The vision in the mirror felt like a dream, and I could easily convince myself it had been. I'd have to do some experiments, obviously in secret.

I caught my wandering thoughts. A chill breeze ruffled the curls that had escaped my updo during my battle, and I pulled one out of my mouth. I walked as far as I could from the asylum while avoiding the pond and turned to look at the structure.

It had been built in the T-layout of some of the Earth asylums, which was interesting because the back wing, which bisected the other two, wasn't visible from the windows in the right- and left-wing rooms. All the rooms on the backside of the asylum had an unobstructed view of the back lawn and pond. No back wing visible at all, which made me wonder—why and how? Did they need to keep the patients calm, and the dark gray stone of the rear wing would disturb them and remind them they were essentially prisoners?

I walked toward the asylum and kept my attention fixed on the rear wing. I zigzagged and noticed it didn't move against the rest of the building like I expected. In fact, one sun ray escaped the clouds and illuminated it for a second, and in the full light, it disappeared.

I stopped and blinked to confirm what I was seeing. "What in the Hades is going on?"

"Good evening, Princess." One of the inmates, a docile male Fae whose name I couldn't remember, greeted me. "It's nice to get a little bit of Mother Sun, isn't it?"

"Yes. I'm sorry, would you remind me of your name?"

"Oh, it's not important here." He waved his hand. "But if you'd like to call me something, Sigil will do."

"Thank you, Sigil. You can call me Reine."

"Oh, I couldn't! Princess will do."

I couldn't help it. I smiled with delight at his demeanor, which mixed determination with deference in a way only an experienced courtier could. Who had he been to my grandmother, and why had he been sent here? That would be a conversation for another time.

"Sigil, tell me. What do you see when you look at the asylum?" I could still see the back wing.

"Well, it's a long building. Two wings off the central corridor. But I'll tell you a secret."

"What?"

He lowered his voice. "If you walk around inside, it doesn't make sense. There's something missing."

"What do you mean, 'something missing?'"

"Things don't line up. I'm sorry, I was a footman, not an architect, but if you walk around for a bit you'll see."

"Thank you. I appreciate your perspective."

"Of course, Princess, of course. By the way, I'm glad you've got a little puff of smoke to keep you company. Hello, kitty. Don't worry, I won't tell anyone."

He wandered on, and I looked down at Sir Raleigh, who should have been invisible, but whose face had appeared.

"Some people can see more than we give them credit for. At least my impressions were kind of confirmed."

I HAD JUST PACED out the width of the illusory hallway when the spot in my chest that anchored my connection to Lawrence twanged. That's the only way I could think of to describe it. Like a guitar string, it vibrated and filled me with a joyous note of... something. What had happened? The connection hadn't severed. If anything, it reappeared stronger than ever. I found myself grinning down at Sir Raleigh.

"Do you know what that was?"

His green eyes glowed slightly in the gloom. *Mirror!*

He took off down the hallway, and I followed him to the picture at the end. This one was of a shimmering stream below waving branches. The shadows of the branches cast leafy patterns on the surface of the water, and the perspective was of looking down from a height. It made me dizzy.

The painting opened without protest, and no dust devil came out to attack me, so I surmised I'd disarmed the spell in the entire place. I found the spiral staircase where I expected it to be, and Sir Raleigh and I dashed down it until we reached the bottom. I didn't have to go far to find the room with the mirror. I thought I'd started figuring out the layout, but it continued to elude me. And frustrate me—I usually had a great sense of direction.

The desire to see Lawrence ached so deeply in my heart and my gut that I only had to say, "Show me," to the mirror, and it complied. It showed me Lawrence in gargoyle form flying through the sky against a waxing moon. Glowing wispy clouds framed his strong form, and I imagined running my hands over his muscles. He wore boxers, and I smiled at the memory of making love to him as a gargoyle. Silly us. We'd done it to satisfy our curiosity and get each other out of our systems. We hadn't known that it would create this bond between us...a bond that bordered on addiction.

"I can't forget him, Sir Raleigh." I hadn't thought through that when I made the bargain of his life for my freedom. Would he take Barton up on his previous offer to sever the bond? I wouldn't blame him, although I would mourn because my attachment to him went beyond this mystical thing to true love.

"Bonded," the voice whispered to me. "He is your Crown Prince."

I blinked in surprise. "Crown Prince? You mean he's accepted the role his mother's always wanted for him?"

"Yes. And you must consummate."

I snorted. "It's going to be hard to do that from here, mirror lady. I wish we could."

"Your wish is granted."

Lawrence landed in a clearing by a pond. The water reflected the clouds, moonlight, and branches, not unlike the painting through which I'd entered. Then I found myself looking up at him as though through the surface of the water.

"Reine?" He knelt and dipped his hand in the water. "Are you in there?"

"Can I go through? What about my bargain?"

"Silly Fae," the voice said. "You have yet to think through your words, said and unsaid. You can go, but you must return once you've consummated your new bonding."

I hesitated. Would a taste of Lawrence satisfy my current hunger, or make it worse? But I also sensed something larger at play, a process that we'd started without realizing.

I reached through the mirror and grasped his hand. He pulled me through, and I emerged from the pond into the cool night air.

Our eyes locked, and the lightness of elation made everything more vivid. I inhaled a few deep breaths, and the scents of greenery and the soft summer air filled my nose and lungs with their welcome. How had I forgotten how precious those things were?

But more precious was the gargoyle standing in front of me, holding my hand. He had his own perfumes of sun-warmed rock, moonlit night, and the slight tang of exertion from his flying.

He gazed at me, and wonder softened his harsh gargoyle features. "How is this possible?"

"It's a gift for you accepting your role as Crown Prince. Or something. I haven't worked it out yet."

"Nor have I, but you look beautiful."

I gazed down at my dripping form. Somehow my clothing had changed from my Earth realm clothes to a sheer light blue dress with dark accents, and the water made it cling to me in sheer, translucent form.

"Whoops."

"What?" He chuckled, and his mirth rumbled through him. "I think you look fine." Then his expression sobered. "How long do we have?"

I appreciated that he knew we had rules to follow, as much as I didn't want to. "I don't know. I have to return after we consummate, whatever that means."

"Oh, I think you know what it means." He cupped my breasts in his large hands and thumbed my nipples, which made me arch with the shocks of pleasure it sent through me.

"Oh, gods." I whispered a quick drying spell so I wouldn't be a soggy shag. Well, not in a bad way, anyway. Being near him, feeling his strength, running my hands over his taut muscles... Yeah, I was getting plenty wet. No part of me—head, heart, and other parts that had ached for him—could resist the force that drew us together.

He pulled me to him, and we kissed. I wanted to talk, to catch up, but the new level of lust that came with whatever had happened fogged my brain and made me stupid. Maybe we could talk through the mirror?

His tongue plumbed my mouth, and I wound my fingers through his hair, holding tight so we wouldn't be separated again.

Later. We'd talk later.

We came up for air, and I gazed into his eyes, which had gone from his usual gray to dark with his own lust.

"What happened?"

He shrugged. "Long story. Your cat started it. Well, escalated it, anyway. Is he with you?"

"Yes, he found me."

"Good." He bent his head to kiss me and met my lips briefly, then kissed his way across my jawline to my ear, which he gave a quick nibble, down my neck... With each one, my knees went more and more weak until I had to cling to him to remain standing.

To remain in the present without worrying when I'd be snatched back to the asylum. To draw on his strength, which complemented my own so well.

"You're so supple," he murmured. "So mine." He held me up without apparent effort, then picked me up and laid me on the grass beside him. He furled his wings.

"Now we can get down to business," I told him and made his shorts disappear and reappear hanging on a nearby branch.

He laughed again. "And what about your clothing? It's very pretty, but in the way."

With a thought, I removed it and hung it next to his.

"Your magic is even stronger than it used to be. I can feel it."

"I know. Long story there, too." A story I didn't want to get into at the moment. Unlike our shared dream of the picnic area, this encounter held the weight of something important. And although I didn't know what, it had the potential to change both our paths. Gods, I hoped it would merge them again.

"You're a gorgeous creature of moonlight and mist." I couldn't be mad that he'd called me a creature, not when he devoured me with his eyes. Every part his gaze crossed shivered like he'd physically caressed me.

"And you're an amazing creature of stone and water."

He ran one hand over me, and every cell thrilled at his touch. He bent to kiss me again, and this time it was tender and wondering. He cupped one of my breasts and teased the nipple, then broke the kiss and took the other one in his mouth.

The twin pleasures almost made me come right there. But that wasn't how it was supposed to be.

"Get inside me. Now."

"At your command, my queen." He propped himself up on his elbows and covered me. "Let me know if it's too much."

Formerly I would have laughed. Now, I assured him, "You'll never be too much."

His cock nudged at my opening, and I commanded my muscles to relax and let him in. He was even bigger than I remembered, but I fit him. Oh, gods, did I fit him.

He paused. "Is this okay?"

"Oh, yes."

He thrust slowly, and I bit his shoulder. His chuckle rumbled through me. "More?"

He withdrew, and I clenched. "Yes, more. I know you won't hurt me."

"Never. And I trust you'll tell me what you need."

"You. I only need you."

And when he moved in and out, I had to wait to come until his rhythm told me he was almost there.

The orgasm exploded through me in shocks of more intense pleasure than I'd ever had before, sending waves of heat through my whole body. This night. This gargoyle. This *rightness*.

This transcendent love. Our hearts beating in the same passionate rhythm.

He shuddered, giving me another set of waves, then let out a long groan. He released into me, and I welcomed him, all of him.

He removed himself, then rolled onto his side and gathered me to him. He folded one wing over us.

I snuggled against him. "I don't think I can move for a while."

"Keep wriggling your ass against me, and I'll make sure you can't."

I laughed. "I'm not used to you talking dirty. I like it."

He kissed my shoulder. "I wish I could do this every night. And day. And afternoon."

Now sorrow crashed through me. What would happen now? "Me too. I'm sorry."

He turned me toward him. "For what?"

"For not thinking through the bargain with my mother. The one that trapped me."

"Don't worry, we're working on it."

"But I do worry, and it's my problem, not yours."

"After all that, you don't think it's my problem?"

"Fair point. It can't be your problem. You'll die if you come to Faerie." I opened my eyes so I could roll over and look at him, but before I could move, I found the glowing green eyes of Sir Raleigh looking at me through the obsidian mirror. "Hades."

"What?"

"It's time for me to go back."

"No!" He held me tighter.

I rolled over and kissed him deeply. "I'll figure out a way to come back. Conjugal visits may be allowed. I'm still figuring out the rules."

"You Fae and your rules."

I stood and summoned my clothing to cover me. It was my

Earth realm outfit again. I reached in the pocket and found the obsidian mirror, the little one Basil had given me. Would it work if I gave it to Lawrence?

Before I could decide, the forest faded, and I found myself looking through the big obsidian mirror at Lawrence. He rolled to his knees and covered his face for a moment. He took a deep, shuddering breath, and my heart broke for both of us. What was the point of a monumental joining, one that would have repercussions in both realms, if we couldn't stay together?

The picture faded, leaving me with the reflection of my stricken expression. Only my eyes, the same green as Sir Raleigh's, looked like they'd been recharged.

"I shouldn't have gone through," I told Sir Raleigh. "We're doomed to be apart. Doing things like that will only make it worse."

He looked up at me with his inscrutable cat expression, then rubbed against my legs. I picked him up and held his purring form to my chest. If he minded when my tears fell on his gray fur, he didn't object.

The obsidian mirror buzzed in my pocket.

"What the hell, Basil?" I muttered. "Now isn't a good time."

I pulled out the mirror, which showed me Basil in his bedroom again. I hadn't minded previously, but now I wished he'd chosen somewhere less...personal...to communicate with me from.

"Reine, what in Hades just happened?"

"Uh." I couldn't exactly tell him epic sex with a gargoyle with the permission of the asylum. And it had been pretty epic.

"Did you feel the energy shift?"

"Um, I have no idea what you're talking about." In truth, I didn't. I hadn't been in Faerie to experience an energetic change.

"Where are you, anyway? You look like you're somewhere modern. Besides the impressive slab of obsidian."

My inner adolescent wanted to comment that it wasn't the only impressive slab I'd seen that night. I tamped it down, but a little giggle bubbled to the surface. I did feel a little different, maybe?

Sir Raleigh wriggled out of my grasp and landed with a light thump on the floor.

"I'm in the asylum still. I found a weird space underneath it."

"Seriously, it looks like you're in a spaceship. What have you been doing down there? Did you find something? Bespell something?"

I walked away from the mirror toward the spiral staircase. I was the queen, I reminded myself. I should be interrogating him, not the other way around. "Tell me what you felt."

"It woke me." Indeed, his hair stood up in tousled bedhead waves that many Earth realm men would have probably killed for, and his nightshirt stood open and showed his muscular chest, which most would have considered sexy but seemed puny compared to the one I'd just been snuggled against.

"What did it feel like?"

"It's hard to explain. Like a pressure change, like a bomb went off or something, but instead of destruction, it was...tingly."

"Tingly? What the hell does that mean? Hold on, I'm going into an enclosed space. I don't know if I'll lose the signal."

"This is a mirror, not a cell phone."

"Then why does it buzz when you call me?" The gloom swallowed me and rendered Sir Raleigh almost invisible except for his one white paw. We raced up the stairs.

"Would you prefer I shout from your pants?"

A giddy snicker bubbled through my throat. "No, good point."

"Where are you now? You've done some exploring."

"In a staircase." The Fae lights in their sconces flickered like yellow and orange flame and gave it a medieval glow.

"It's like you're traveling through time."

"Well, it is wibbly wobbly here in Faerie. But let's get back to the tingly."

Now he smirked, and I had to add, "Not like that."

Damn, the staircase went higher than I remembered.

"It's almost a lightness, a feeling of hope. Since the Great Rising started, there's been a heavy, almost oily feeling to our atmosphere. You may not have noticed as much because your first visit back occurred just after its start."

"You're right, I hadn't, but I didn't have the same perspective." I had just been happy to be home. "That changed?"

"Yes. Not completely, but there's a shift."

"And according to one of the laws of human physics, whenever there's an action, there's an equal and opposite reaction."

The stairwell finally gave me a landing, and Sir Raleigh and I dashed out. Instead of the backside of a painting, we exited through a wooden door.

And stepped out on to the roof of the asylum, which was taller than it should have been. And I wasn't alone.

24

LAWRENCE

After Reine disappeared, I knelt and took a long, deep breath so I wouldn't break into sobbing. Our separation had been painful before, a dull ache that I'd habituated to. And then when she'd sacrificed her freedom and gone into the asylum, it had faded.

Now the anchor to our bond throbbed with the pain of a shard of crystal lodged in my chest, and I knew it wouldn't ease until we were together again.

We had to figure out a way for her to get out of the asylum. We had to find those letters.

And determine what could be done to change the atmosphere of Faerie. From what Lily had said, the pre-division era had been a time of harmony. What if Grand-Pied had been wrong, and changing the atmosphere back wouldn't hurt any species that had evolved there since? Ten thousand years was hardly any time in the Earth realm. Hell, a hundred thousand years wasn't. Perhaps in Faerie it was the same.

I put my shorts back on and once again thanked whatever gargoyle had come up with the stretchy undergarments to keep us from dangling when we changed. Yes, in our history, we'd flown naked, but as a modern gargoyle, I liked to have my bits covered, saved for a certain Fae.

Gods, that had been amazing. It always was between us, but damn... Something had definitely been different. If I'd known accepting the title of Crown Prince would make the sex that epic, I would've done it sooner.

No, I wouldn't have. I commanded my brain to come back to reality, to the practical problems at hand.

With a leap, I took to the air. The pain in my chest didn't seem to impact my ability to fly. If anything, I flew stronger and faster, fueled by some inner strength I didn't know I had.

When I landed, I found Lily waiting for me.

"She came to you." It wasn't a question, so I didn't answer. I found my clothes, which someone had folded for me, and motioned for Lily to turn around. She complied.

I shifted and dressed. In my human form, the pain dulled. But I also felt uncomfortable and restricted, like my gargoyle form had been my natural one.

"What happened, Lily? You can turn around."

"You accepted the Crown Prince role. You took your victory flight and called your mate. She came. You consummated the new role, and now everything is going to change."

"What do you mean?"

"Don't you feel it?"

"I feel the changes in myself, which you didn't warn me of."

"I didn't know. The documents I found only talked about the Fae perspective."

"Figures." We walked back into the house, where I found a piece of apple pie waiting for me. Minerva had also left a package of hot chocolate powder and a mug out. I filled and switched on the electric kettle.

"Did you already have dessert?" I asked.

"Yes, it was delicious. You're lucky to have the family you do."

"I know." But I hadn't appreciated them until they rallied around me. And now everything had changed. Since she'd pointed it out, I could feel it. I'd always had a sense of The Aerie's boundaries, but now I could mentally trace them and feel in my spirit whether they were threatened. I sensed the weak spot over the river where Maeve had sent her little friends.

Maeve... How would she react to these developments? How would Lilith?

"What is it?" Lily brought me out of my thoughts with a light touch on my arm.

"How much more danger is Reine in now that whatever just happened happened?"

She bit her lip.

"Don't try to Fae-coat it, Lily. I need the truth."

"A lot. She's in a lot more danger."

"Stones." I plopped on to the chair.

As if to underscore the peril, my phone rang. I checked the screen. "It looks like your professor is calling."

She nodded. "If a dimension-walker reaches out to you, it's not good news."

"I know." I tapped the answer button. "This is Lawrence Gordon."

25

REINE

Wilfrin turned from where he'd been gazing over the city. From this height, I could see over the buildings and to the city walls, which were made of smooth black stone that would defy any attack or attempt to scale them.

"Where are we?" I asked. It looked like the roof of a Victorian building, complete with low wall around the top. But the asylum's roof was sloped.

"The roof of the invisible annex. I see you've found it. And your pet came to you."

Sir Raleigh unleashed a low growl, which startled me into acknowledging the feeling of not-rightness.

"Yes, you can't stop a guardian grimalkin with your silly rules."

Wilfrin snorted. "Silly rules, indeed, Your Highness. Can't you see you're in the middle of a grand game? You've been making your moves according to rules you can't even sense."

The truth of his words struck me through my core and chilled me. "What game, Wilfrin?"

"The game your grandmother started when she and Lilith transformed this place. It used to be a school."

The manuscript I'd looked at popped into my memory. "In the city of Statera."

"Yes, and you've come to this point because the city didn't die when Faerie divided."

"You know the history." The desperate need for him to tell me engulfed me, and I commanded, "Tell me everything you know."

He shook his head, and something underneath his cowl glowed for a second. "I'm immune to your compulsion, Your Highness. I outrank you here. And I've seen the future."

"You may outrank me, but you have help." I snapped my fingers (although I didn't need to), and the charm on its chain around his neck floated out from under his clothing and in front of his face.

He grabbed at it, but its chain lifted over his head and made his ears come together in a comical angle before they fell into a droop.

The charm levitated to me, and when it touched my palm, I recognized the magic. "Maeve. You've been working for her."

His ears drooped lower, as did his head. "Yes, Your Highness."

A whole new set of questions popped into my brain and flowed into the compulsion spell, which had slowly taken hold. "Why? For how long? Does she know the permissions you've given me?"

When he lifted his face, his wrinkles had assumed an arrangement that resembled a defiant, deranged blue prune.

"Why? Because she agreed to send me help if I aided her, and then to give me the position of Grand Healer when she assumes the throne. You think I'm a quack taking the easy way out with the ambrosia, but I can assure you, I'm doing the best I can."

A spark of compassion bloomed in my chest. "I know you are."

"And for how long? Since after your last visit. She approached me and asked me what Olred had told you, what she'd revealed. I told her Olred had said nothing of substance, and she rewarded me."

"Yet you still allowed me freedoms."

He rubbed his face. "I didn't think you deserved to be here. And I suspected the asylum wouldn't dampen your power for long. It wasn't designed to hold a queen."

"So you allowed me privileges so I wouldn't grow unhappy? Defiant? Insane? That doesn't make sense. You're withholding something, Wilfrin."

Now he sounded like he was trying to hold something in, and he covered his mouth with both hands, but his words came out rushed and muffled.

"Maeve wants you to find the hidden library. She wants the knowledge to defeat the revenants and become the Queen of All Fae."

The charm in my hand turned fiery orange and burned, and I dropped it. The crystal shattered, and its high tinkling sound turned into that of a swarm of angry bees. The shards rose in a whirlwind and engulfed Wilfrin, cutting and burning his clothing and flesh. He screamed.

I flung a cooling, healing spell at him with one hand and a defense spell with the other. The burning crystals disappeared, and he fell to the roof in a pile of tattered cloth and oozing blue ribbons of skin and muscle. Although I'd done some emergency medicine and had treated battle wounds in my own time as a healer and then Earth realm doctor, I'd never seen anyone —human, Fae, or other—as mangled as him. One of his severed ears lay by his shoulder, and I avoided kneeling on it, but I had to do something.

"Gods, Wilfrin, I am so sorry." How had I not suspected that

Maeve would layer in a betrayal spell with the protection charm? And now she'd know that Wilfrin had spilled the truth.

"It was inevitable, Your Highness. I foresaw my death when I came up here."

"Then why did you?"

His arm moved toward the pocket of his robe, and he withdrew a wooden-handled iron knife. He lifted it, and then it clattered to the ground between us when his grip failed.

"Because she said I needed to kill you when the revenants massed at the city walls."

"And then she killed you." And she'd made me an accomplice. The quartz in the charm hadn't needed to glow, but it did. She'd lured me into killing her informant, or at least contributing to his death.

"It's the danger of dealing with the High Fae." He grasped my hand. "Avenge me, Your Highness."

His entire body quivered, he let out one gurgling cough, and then lay still.

I squeezed his little blue hand. "I will do so, Wilfrin. For you, me, and all of Faerie, I will." I whispered the prayer in Old Fae that would send his soul to its long sleep so he would reincarnate in ten thousand years.

I stood, and Sir Raleigh twined around my ankles. I looked toward the walls, now seeing the bright white glow on the other side and the swooping gwynwyfvar spirits above. The walls should be able to withstand any attacks, physical and magical, but that presumed the attackers were alive.

"We need to figure out the secret to defeating those things, Raleigh. Down to the library we go."

∿

THE ROOF FADED, and after a brief and not pleasant falling sensation, Sir Raleigh and I landed with a soft thump on the floor of what I'd started calling the White Room. The obsidian mirror reflected our truth at that moment—haunted eyes, bloodstained clothes, windblown hair. All right, that was me. Sir Raleigh looked like himself, and he pawed at me to get up and stop gazing at myself.

I'd just seen a Fae killed in the most brutal manner, and I was partially responsible. My mind kept going through the interaction. Could I have done something differently? But if I hadn't taken the charm from Wilfrin, he could have killed me with the blade he'd shown me.

The voice of the spirit of the asylum mocked me. "Uncertainty is part of royal life. Haven't you figured that out by now? It's a classic paradox—the more power you have, the more danger you're in." Or maybe she chided me. I couldn't tell. I'd started thinking of her as an AI—Artificial Intelligence—a darn good one. But Fae didn't have that technology. They also didn't have secret chambers with smooth white walls that could have come straight from an alien spaceship. Our decoration tended toward medieval chic or Victorian excess.

I scrambled to my feet. "Who are you? What do you want?"

"The answer to the first question is too long to give you in the time you have. And we desire the same thing."

"The preservation of Faerie?"

She laughed. "Good answer. You are meant to be queen if you put your realm above your own desires."

The mirror continued to show my reflection. "I don't look very regal."

"It's a poorly kept secret that queens have to get their hands dirty." Then a scoffing sound. "Something your mother never learned."

"You're right about that. But I need to know how to defeat the revenants. They're at the city walls. Mirror, show me."

It obliged, and the sight ran electric chills through my nervous system. Revenants—there must have been thousands of them—massed outside the walls of Cruaidh. Lilith's soldiers and sorcerers at the top of the walls shot both projectiles and spells, but to no effect. The gwenhwyfvar owl spirits swooped over the soldiers, and one fell. He couldn't get purchase on the slippery wall, and his scream took on an extra edge of agony and terror when he fell through the spirits and they piled on him, devouring his flesh and soul. The silence in the wake of his voice and life being cut off rang in my ears.

I swallowed my dinner for a second time so I wouldn't throw it up. "How much time do I have?"

"An hour, give or take. Use your time in the library wisely."

The mirror disappeared, and the door to the library replaced it. Sir Raleigh and I ran through, but instead of wonder, hopelessness now crushed me. How would I find what I needed in the mass of books and scrolls? A year might not be enough time, and I only had an hour.

Fifty-nine minutes, forty seconds, to be exact.

I thought back to my medical student days. What would I do if I needed to find information on an obscure topic? I'd been to medical school in the Earth realm in the eighties, before the internet and online library databases, so our best resources were our—

"Librarian?" I called out. "Is there a librarian here?"

A woman's form shimmered into view in front of me. "How can I help you?" She had the pointed ears of the Fae, and she wore horn-rimmed glasses. Her dark hair had been pulled into a messy bun, and she folded her hands in the sleeves of a scholar's robe.

"I need to know how to defeat the revenants."

"I'm sorry, you need to make your query more specific."

Son of a Fae... Who knew I'd need fucking keywords here? Or to rethink my approach to the question. If she couldn't tell me how to defeat the revenants, I needed to figure what characteristics they had that I could exploit. But they were pure spirit, weren't they?

Even pure spirits had some substance to them. The feather weight of a soul and all that.

"What are the revenants made of?"

She gestured to the table to our right, and a dozen scrolls appeared. "Those are the collected research of the ancient philosophers on the makeup of the Fae soul."

All right, not exactly what I was going for. I didn't have time to go through philosophy texts, as fascinating as that might be. A different query, then.

"When did the first revenant appear?"

She nodded—a sign I was getting closer? The dozen scrolls disappeared to be replaced by three thick books. "Those are the tomes of the earliest history of the Fae, including the first Great Rising."

"The first... There was one before this?"

"Yes, in the eleven thousandth year of the realm. A plague had decimated the population in year nine eighty-five."

"Oh. I didn't know. Did the revenants attack the population and cause another period of mass death?"

"Much has been lost to your time. And that rising didn't result in any issues."

"Why not?"

She waved her hand, and all but one of the books disappeared. It fell open to a page, which I read aloud, "'The spirits, being given form within an hour of their rising, only hungered for a handspan of minutes, resulting in only two Fae deaths.'"

"Huh. So they used to not be a threat. What changed?"

The book closed, then opened to a different page. "'It was determined by the Queen of All Fae that the gargoyles, having defeated the Fae by tying to them their lives, must be expelled. She spoke the Spell of All Breath, which changed the atmosphere of Faerie and made it poisonous to the gargoyles.

However, it preserved the risen souls in the state of hunger for days, not merely minutes. Thus the Gray Zone was created to contain them with the dark Fae on one side and the Light Fae on the other to guard and keep balance."

"This...wasn't the history I learned. I heard it was a battle between the Fae that divided the land into light and dark."

The book started to disappear, and I held on to it. "No, I want to keep this one."

"Then you have to check it out, which will require you to fill out an application for a library card."

"How soon would the application be approved?"

"Within a day. A few hours at least, a day at most."

Hades, I didn't have time to go through that. What other questions could I ask?

"I need to know the Spell of All Breath." Maybe I could somehow reverse it to make Faerie habitable to gargoyles again and turn the revenants into Fae before they could hurt anyone.

The librarian didn't say anything. She merely blinked at me through her thick lenses.

"What?"

"That spell is not in the catalog. It is proprietary information that only the Queens know."

"But I don't!"

She shrugged. "That spell is not in the catalog. It is proprietary information that only the Queens know."

"Where do queens learn it?"

"It is in their palace archives."

Hades. But if I could get into Lilith's archives, I could find it. "Thank you. I appreciate your help."

"My pleasure, Your Highness. Please be forewarned—if you find and reverse the spell, you will face a battle and the consequences will be more than you anticipated."

"How so?"

She shrugged again. "That's the price of high magic-work.

Be careful what you wish for. It may come true." With that, she disappeared, and I found myself back in my room.

"Lovely time for riddles," I muttered, then pulled the obsidian mirror from my pocket. "Mirror, connect me with Desdemona."

26

———

LAWRENCE

"Hey, GP, what's up?" I tried to sound casual, but my tap-dancing heart betrayed the fact I felt like I was being called into the principal's office.

"First, where's Lily?" He always spoke in a growl, but this time its lower timbre made his question a threat.

"She's here. I'll put you on speaker."

"Hey, professor," Lily called. "I'm fine. I had to come up and take care of some things, but I haven't done anything stupid."

"That's not what Grimm and that idiot Gilmore said. They spoke of danger of slipping back into old patterns. Which brings me to my next question—what the hell did you just do, Gordon?"

Epic sex with my girlfriend came to mind as my immediate response, but I replied, "I accepted the role of Crown Prince of the Gargoyles?"

"That was a question. Did you or didn't you?"

"I did."

"Congratulations. I'm sure your mother is thrilled." His deadpan tone almost made me laugh, but I held it in, especially when he asked, "But you consummated it. How?"

Again, my flippant side, which Reine brought out, almost said, *big dick energy*, but I gave him the answer he needed. "The asylum let her out for a conjugal outing. She disappeared after."

He didn't say anything, but a huffed sigh let me know he stayed on the other end of the call. "This complicates things."

"How so?"

"The two of you have put in motion a process that no one anticipated would happen, at least not for another millennium."

"I told you," Lily mouthed.

"And if you cannot go and claim her as your queen, and she cannot have you by her side as Prince Consort, the result will be a twisted, perverted version of Faerie that will pose grave danger to the Earth realm and those beyond it."

"You didn't tell me that," I whispered to Lily.

"I didn't know!"

"Why would she? Most of the information has been lost to history. Hold on."

The air shimmered in front of the kitchen table, and Grand-Pied stepped through. I'd never seen a dimension-walker actually do their thing, and I envied the ease with which he popped from one place to the other, especially without knowing the exact location of The Aerie.

Lily asked before I could, "How did you do that? Have you been here?"

"No, but that's proprietary Dimension Walker information. And now I'll be in trouble, too." His harsh features spread into a smile. "It was bound to happen, and I'll handle it. Gordon, how do we get your woman out of the asylum?"

"I've been working on that." I related to him the bargain she made for my life as well as those of Gabriel McCord and Max Fortuna and how she'd been accused of interfering with the lives and livelihoods of a human family. Well, mostly human. Vampires had gotten mixed up in there somewhere.

"So her bargain was tied to her plea bargain?"

"Yes, so if she's able to prove her innocence, her bargain will be voided." Or mostly so. I wasn't sure of the exact wording, but it stood to reason that if the plea bargain wasn't needed, then it would retroactively cancel her debt in the original bargain. Fae logic didn't always agree with the logic of the rest of the species.

"Where is the evidence?"

"In the letters of a man named Gerald Brigadine, whom Maeve killed so he couldn't talk. He was the one who actually interfered with the humans as he trailed Reine through history for the Order of the Silver Arrow. He'd been caught in the same time loop."

Grand-Pied tapped his chin. "So it stands to reason that the letters are somewhere in the Order's archives."

"If they didn't turn them all over to Maeve."

The dimension-walker scoffed. "I know of this organization. They're too smart to have given her the originals, or if they did, they made copies."

I almost held my breath, hoping he'd offer his help.

"You still have to get the papers from the Order," Lily pointed out. "They're not going to just hand them over, especially if Maeve still has them under her finger."

"No, we'll have to be sneaky about it." Grand-Pied gave a sharp nod. "Gordon, gather your allies. I'll be back tomorrow, and we'll plan our heist."

"Our...heist?"

"Yes, we're going to get those letters. It's more practical than sending you into Faerie with scuba gear, don't you think?"

"Yes, but how did you—?"

He disappeared before he could respond. I shook my head. "Why do I have the feeling he's been monitoring the situation even though the Normals forbade him to?"

Lily laughed, again sounding like a much younger Fae. "Because he has. That's part of the reason why I came up here.

He told me to. Luckily our girl Kestrel was happy to have me along."

"And why?"

Lily rolled her eyes. "You humans and gargoyles... You do things that you don't realize have consequences far beyond what you can imagine. Why do you think we have laws against interference? You're not playing games with only the gargoyles and Fae."

"No, I'm getting that message now. What did he mean by 'a perverted version?'"

Lily went paler than her natural goth hue. "You weren't there for the nightmare creature debacle but imagine if the revenants were to take over. Soon there wouldn't be any Fae left, and they would continue to feed on whichever of their own took on flesh. The ones remaining would end up being insane...and insanely powerful. And they wouldn't stay in Faerie."

I shuddered, remembering the ones in Elise's office. "I'm getting the idea."

"The good news is that Reine, being on the path to becoming Queen of All Fae, now has access to the hidden archives. Hopefully she can find the answer to the revenant problem."

"And if she does, but we still can't get her out? At least we wouldn't have to worry about them coming into the Earth realm."

"Then you can't be her balance, and we risk her turning into the Dark Queen of All Fae, which would be worse."

"Oh, Hades." At least Grand-Pied had agreed to help, but we still faced odds stacked against us.

I could almost hear the tick-boom of the clock we raced against.

∾

AFTER GRAND-PIED LEFT, I hung my head and covered my face. Collect my posse? A heist? What did Grand-Pied think this was, a paranormal version of *Ocean's 11*?

Again, I felt the gap between my scientist-veterinarian self who went to the gym and took an occasional kickboxing class and the action hero the situation called for. I had only had one lesson in fighting, and I hadn't done well at it. My gargoyle self had brute force but lacked finesse. My human form had strength but lacked the means to make it count when it mattered.

But with the triple threat of what would happen to Reine if she stayed in the asylum, the destruction of Faerie, where I did have allies and friends, and the impact on the gargoyles, which were affected by the goings-on in Faerie, I didn't have a choice.

"Uncle Lawrence?" Kestrel walked into the kitchen and narrowed her eyes against the light. "I must have fallen asleep while reading. When did you get back? Where did you go?"

"Lily..." I warned. "Tell her the truth."

"I'm sorry, Kestrel. It was Fae business. I needed you out of the way for a while."

Kestrel glared at Lily. "What kind of Fae business? Why did you exclude me? Don't you understand—he's the only family I have left!"

I hadn't questioned her absence, which made me feel worse and prompted me to confess, "Kestrel...I consummated my choice to be Crown Prince with Reine."

"How? I mean, ick, I don't want those details, but how? Isn't she trapped in an asylum or something?"

"It let her out, briefly." Lily shrugged. "Even Fae get conjugal privileges with their mates."

"Ew, ew, ew..." Kestrell covered her ears. She shook herself, then looked at me. "What happens now? I know this isn't the end."

"You're right. It's not. The stakes are higher now, and we need to prove her innocence, get her out of there."

"But she made a bargain."

"A Fae bargain," Lily pointed out. "There's always a loophole if you're clever enough to find it. And she attached it to her sentence for her crimes."

"Are you sure the stakes are worth it? And do you know for sure it will work, Uncle Lawrence? Like, for sure sure?"

My throat constricted with the memory of her asking me a similar question when she'd turned twelve. I'd told her that often magic emerged for young women when they hit puberty. She'd asked me then if I was "for sure sure" about it, with the same desperation in her voice, the plea for everything to be okay.

"Yes, the stakes are worth it. Reine's sanity is at risk. The future of Faerie could depend on it, as could the safety of The Aerie..." I paused. As Lily had pointed out, The Aerie was only one letter off from Faerie, but I hadn't considered possible reasons why. Gargoyles had once lived in Faerie. The Aerie was slightly out of the Earth realm, suspended in a different dimension.

"Lily, was The Aerie originally part of Faerie?"

Kestrel smirked. "I'd already made that connection."

Lily smacked her. "Showoff. And supposedly. That's one of the facts lost to history, but there's a theory that it was."

"And what will happen if we manage this and Reine claims the throne of all of Faerie with me as her consort?"

"I don't know. Well, I've read theories, but nobody knows with any certainty..."

"Lily..."

"It's possible that The Aerie could get pulled back into Faerie. But again, that's a theory based on vague hints and conjecture."

"But you can't breathe there!" Kestrel protested. "You could all die."

"If the magical barrier holds, the original one, not the one the witch made, you'll be fine." But Lily didn't sound sure.

"All right, another problem to deal with, and one we don't know if we have. What's the greater danger, leaving things to spool out as they are or proving Reine's innocence and preserving her sanity and that of Faerie?"

"Definitely the first," Lily replied without hesitation. "That's the one we're more sure will happen."

I hated dealing with conjecture. That's why I'd gone into science—cold, hard facts made more sense and could be proven through the scientific method. How had I managed to get drawn into this world of magic and Fae logic?

Love. Love had drawn me in. And even if Reine and I hadn't shared a bond, I would still want the best for her regardless of whether we could be together.

Kestrel sat at the table with me, and Lily placed a mug of hot chocolate in front of her.

"Did you drug this?"

"No, it's only the chemical powder that passes for hot chocolate and hot water."

"Okay, thanks." She blew across the top, then sipped it. "Well, Uncle Lawrence, it sounds like you have your work cut out for you. How can your trickster adopted niece help?"

27

REINE

Desdemona agreed to fetch me from the asylum. I couldn't petition the asylum director for a reprieve since he lay in pieces on the secret roof. I'd need to make arrangements for him to be interred, but I only had a limited amount of time before the revenants swamped the city and dealing with them qualified as the more pressing task.

Sorry, Mr. Covey, it was going to have to be urgent stuff only for the next ten hours. I'd have to see if they had a copy of *The Seven Habits of Highly Effective Fae* when I returned the library book Sir Raleigh had snitched for me. I smiled and ran up the spiral staircase, tome in hand.

The stairwell dumped me out on my floor, and I grabbed a bag from my room to carry and protect the ancient book. Sure, I felt guilty, and I didn't even want to think about the potential fine, but I knew it would prove important. Otherwise, my wise grimalkin companion wouldn't have taken it.

Desdemona met me in the receiving lounge. "Come on," she urged. "I've got the carriage waiting outside. Have you gotten your petition approved by the director yet?"

I followed her into the hall. "Not exactly. He's dead."

She spun on her heel, and I almost barreled into her. "What? How?'

"Protection charm backfire."

Her mouth twisted when she said, "That has Maeve written all over it."

"Yep."

"Then you're going to need to figure out a different way out of the asylum. You can't walk out the front. The gate will skewer you."

"You're right. There's a mirror in the basement that I've used for transport to the Earth realm. I'll take that."

"It won't work." We both turned to see Jane, who carried herself with an air of authority. For a second, her glamour shifted, and I gasped when I recognized the librarian. She held out her hand. "My book, please?"

"I need it for now. I'll bring it back unharmed, I promise."

"The Librarian," Desdemona breathed. "Sheeeeit. You did find it. There were wagers that you would, but I didn't believe it."

"What wagers? Never mind. We're running out of time. How do I get out of here without using the front gate, Librarian?"

She smiled, but it wasn't a nice one. "There is one other portal that will bring you to either palace. But you've already experienced the perils inherent in it."

My stomach sank to the floor and plopped somewhere around my boots. "The pond. I was afraid of that."

"If you face it and make it through unscathed, you can have the book, Your Highness. Meanwhile, tell me, where is Healer Wilfrin?"

"He—his body—is on the hidden roof. Charm explosion. It went too fast for me to do anything for him except say the final blessing."

"At least you did him that kindness. Very well. Go on."

I turned to Desdemona. "I'll see you at the palace." Then, I faced Jane/Librarian again. "Where does the portal emerge in the palace here?"

"In the Bone Garden."

"And is it the same in the palace in Lorien?"

"Yes."

"And where in the archives do I find the answers I need?"

She smirked. "For that, you'll need an archivist."

"Great," I sighed. Things were about to get creepy.

DESDEMONA AGREED to meet me in their crypt so she could show me the way out. I'd read that water symbolized a transition or passage in dreams. I hadn't thought I'd need to use it that way literally.

When I walked on to the dark lawn, I found Larry Leafmore standing outside looking at the stars.

"I decided to spend my last night alive appreciating the vastness of the universe. Legend used to say that each of them was the soul of a Fae who wouldn't reincarnate. That gives me hope for those of us who are about to be devoured by the revenants."

"I'm working on the problem, Professor. Do you happen to know where I'd look for a book of spells that only the Queen of All Fae could speak in the archives in Lorien? Or here, for that matter?"

He turned to me with a strangely sad expression. "Ah, Your Highness, I wish you hadn't asked me that."

"Why?"

"Because the answer comes with more heartache. There is a hidden room off each of the archive libraries, but it requires a sacrifice to open. Legend has it that when the time comes, the rooms will reveal themselves."

"What sort of sacrifice?"

"A life sacrifice."

"Why? That's ridiculous."

He laughed. "It means that they can only be opened in dire circumstances." He turned back to the sky. "I suppose these count."

"Thank you. I'm sure I'll figure it out."

"Oh, and one more thing... Stop thinking about your sentence here as a human. You have the blood of goddesses in your veins. Remember your favorite myth."

"I don't remember what that was."

He smiled, and for a second, he resembled the young professor who had done his best to guide our rebellious Fae brains. "You will. When it's time."

"Thank you."

I ran down the lawn to the pond. The surface of the water dimpled, and then the circles spread like raindrops fell on it although the sky was clear. I shivered, and my experiences of critters in the waters of Faerie flashed through my mind. The water wolves that had attacked the boat that carried John and Kestrel across the lake outside of Cruaidh. The kraken that had reached out and grabbed Ellerin. The nymph that had guarded the stream that divided the Gray Zone from the lands of the Light Fae. All right, she hadn't been terrifying, but I knew what could happen to nymphs, how their purity could be sullied. That's what had occurred with Astrid in The Aerie when Grylja had stolen her identity and had almost kept her soul.

Did something await in the pond to claim my soul?

"What do you think, Sir Raleigh?"

He placed his paw on my leg, looked up at me with what appeared to be regret in his eyes, and said in a voice that sounded like Ellerin's, "*I cannot go with you through that portal. I will meet you in the crypt.*"

"Of the dark Fae?"

He didn't answer, so I said, "Wait, take this." I pulled my

satchel over my head and wrapped the strap around his neck. "The Librarian wouldn't want her book to get wet, I'm sure."

He nodded.

"Thank you, and be care—"

But he'd already disappeared. I scrunched my eyes against the tears that wanted to emerge, then took a deep breath and faced the pond again. My pad of paper popped to the surface and floated over to me, and I picked it up. The picture I'd drawn of Sir Raleigh looked up at me, whole and un-blurred.

Was that a sign that the pond, or whatever was in it, wouldn't try to hurt me? Or had the magic given me a different signal, one I hadn't interpreted correctly?

"Dammit, why don't these things come with instruction manuals?"

But they had. In dreams, water symbolized places of transition or rebirth. In fairy tales, bodies of water hid secrets both good and bad, and often it depended on the intention of those who entered what they'd find.

I placed the pad on the shore and whispered, "Thank you," to the spirit of the pond. I chose to imagine it as a good spirit like my friend the water nymph. Then I jumped in.

THE WATER SWALLOWED ME, and I almost coughed in surprise that my feet hadn't met the bottom of the pond. But I found I could breathe underwater. A light appeared, and I swam toward it but bumped up against a clear barrier.

I floated back and rubbed my nose. "Ow," I bubbled.

A laugh gurgled in my ears. "You must know the password to be allowed through."

Hades, no one had told me a password. I really shouldn't have been so careless as to allow Wilfrin to be killed, but he hadn't exactly been forthcoming with information.

"I am the Queen of the Light Fae. Allow me through to the crypts."

A diaphanous spirit undulated through the water. Its garments hung around it and moved like fins or rags—I couldn't decide which. Its large orb eyes regarded me with unblinking curiosity, and its face, while not exactly fish-like, didn't look humanoid, either, with its slits for nostrils and mouth and blue-gray scaly skin.

I cast through my memories for the kind of creature it must be. Not selkie. Not kelpie. And definitely not nymph.

I bowed to it. "I apologize, noble one, but I cannot identify you, and so I fear I may be disrespectful due to not knowing the protocol to address you."

It laughed again. "I keep myself hidden in these waters, and few have seen me."

"Then I am privileged and grateful." And terrified, although I didn't say that out loud or even dare to fully think it. What sort of creature had kept itself so hidden it hadn't made it into legend, human or Fae? And what would it do to keep its secrets?

It swam around me with graceful quicksilver movements, and I twisted in the water attempting to keep it in front of me.

"You do not accept who and what you are, Your Highness."

"I'm afraid I don't know what you mean. I'm Reine, Queen of the Light Fae."

"And yet you have dark and gray in you as well." It hovered in front of me and stroked its almost nonexistent chin with one webbed hand.

"So I've been told."

"Gray by blood, dark by choice."

I swallowed the fear that rose in burning bubbles through my gut to my heart, then my throat. My grandmother had healed my scars, but the remnants of my encounter with Ashlee Wyatt remained, as I'd found when I'd subdued Desdemona. "I prefer not to impose my will on others, and I want to create rather than destroy."

"Then you have the spirit of the light Fae, or so you've been taught. But you must accept all your shades before you can pass and embrace your destiny."

"All my shades..." Then it hit me—I spoke with a water shade! They supposedly didn't exist, but I'd heard of them, read of them somewhere. They guarded the oldest of passages, and the passcode was the traveler's deepest, darkest secret.

Oh, Hades.

"You have just found the key. What is the passcode?"

I closed my eyes, but a gentle touch on my arm made me open them.

"This isn't the time for hiding, not even from yourself. Especially not from yourself."

"I don't want to be queen," I whispered.

"Say it. Own it."

"I don't want to be queen! Not of the light Fae, not of the dark Fae, not of all Fae. I want..."

"Yes, yes..." It glowed, and blue and green lights raced through its body and down its many-layered fins.

"I want to settle down with Lawrence. To have our own little cottage somewhere away from all our responsibilities, where we can be a couple and really be together." I covered my face with my hands and sobbed into them. "I just want to be normal. But I've never wanted to be normal."

I looked up, but the shade had disappeared. So had the barrier. I swam through it and emerged into the dark Fae crypt, where Desdemona waited for me with Sir Raleigh, who sat away from her and glared at her. Desdemona was leafing through the book that I'd given Sir Raleigh.

"Well, well, Reine, you did it." Lilith's voice made me turn around in their version of the crypt pool. "Perhaps you can tell me what my useless granddaughter found and how it can help me to be Queen of All Fae."

"Desdemona," I hissed. "You promised."

Her left eyelid flickered so fast I couldn't tell if it was a wink or something else like a tic. "That's what you get for trusting a dark Fae. Haven't you learned by now?"

She reached over and pushed my head under the water. This time I couldn't breathe.

28

LAWRENCE

If I slept that night, I couldn't tell. Did my nightmare visions of Reine as the Dark Queen of All Fae, wielding her impressive power to destroy all she holds dear, count as dreams? Or had my brain tortured me with images of my deepest fears for what would happen to her if we couldn't get her out of the asylum?

Finally, when dawn broke over The Aerie, I greeted it with an early morning flight. The urge to change, to take on my monstrous gargoyle form, had gotten stronger. Had Uncle Augie felt that, too? Was that why he'd given into the temptation to turn to stone?

A question popped into my brain—had Uncle Augie been a Prince Consort? He'd been a legend my mother had told me when I was a lad several hundred years before, which meant he preceded her as well. Did something about mating with a Fae draw the beast forth? Or was that something that happened to all gargoyles as they aged? I'd have to ask Mother, but I didn't want to pry. And I hadn't seen many other older gargoyles in The Aerie. Where had they all gone? Or had they died off?

Or was there a field of statues somewhere waiting to be

discovered?

My path through the air took me to the other side of the river, and I landed beside the Uncle Augie statue. Standing, he'd be taller than I, an impressive creature. Was this even the original Uncle Augie statue? Or had copies been made to proliferate the cautionary tale?

"Why don't you ask him?"

I turned to find Astrid watching me with a bemused quirk to her lips.

"Let me guess, I was thinking loudly again."

She shrugged. "You were looking at him so intently I surmised your question. I've heard there were others at one time, a master race of gargoyles who gave into their bestial side and were punished by being turned forever into stone." She walked around him and trailed a hand over one of the sharp wing tips. "From what I've read, I suspect that the legend between the gargoyles and the trolls who turned to stone because they got caught in the sunlight got confused, but I don't know." She frowned. "I feel...something."

"What?"

She cocked her head. "It's almost impossible to tell this close to the river, but there's a rushing sound in him, almost like the water, but different. Like blood and vessels still exist under his stone exterior, and a heart still pumps so he will be able to help when he's needed. When all gargoyle-kind is in trouble."

With that perspective, the Uncle Augie statue took on a creepy aspect, as if he'd been trapped in his body like a human or animal suffering from a degenerative dementia process. Did he scream, but no one heard him? Or did he sleep in there, waiting to be awakened?

Astrid stood beside me. "What do you think would awaken him?"

"I don't know. But I've heard there are many who feel the

shift because of what happened last night."

"You claiming your queen, or her claiming you as her consort?" Astrid shot me a sly glance through her lashes. "Oh, don't blush. There's nothing to be ashamed of. And I, for one, am thrilled for it. It's time for a new order in Faerie, for someone to really take charge and unite the stubborn Fae."

"And keep witches and other magic wielders like the one who trapped you under control?"

Astrid's beautiful face took on the stiffness of a scorned nymph, and I reminded myself that although she didn't show it or have the same connection with the river, she had power in her own right as well as whatever she might have absorbed from the ice witch. "Give them something to be scared of, more likely."

"I see. I don't blame you. If someone had taken over my body and tried to quench my soul, I'd want to keep it from happening again."

Another sideways look. "You don't think it already has? You didn't have to claim the Crown Prince role. And you didn't have to go on that victory flight to claim your queen. What made you?"

A shiver slid down my spine, a cold droplet of doubt. "I chose it. I followed my instincts."

"And where did those come from? You're a veterinarian. You know how animals follow their urges even though they don't know where they come from."

And I had fought my inner gargoyle because I hadn't wanted to give myself over to the animal urges. I always told myself I needed to rise above them, to be civilized. But where had that landed me? In the hospital the first time.

"So what you're saying is that I'm acting according to some old instinct or script."

"We all are, gargoyle. We all are. So now that I've done my duty as the wild force that sows doubt in your mind, I'll be on my way. But don't forget to say goodbye to Uncle Augie. He'll remember who was rude to him when he awakens."

She left me there, staring at Augie, pondering what he represented—the failure to pull out of the downward spiral that tugged us all toward our gargoyle sides and away from what made us human. But where did the line exist, and how was anyone supposed to know when they crossed it until it was too late to go back?

I shuddered even though the sunlight warmed my dark gray skin. I had certainly acted from instinct when Reine had appeared in front of me, glowing and regal. We would have better spent the time talking, trading knowledge.

"Oh, for Fae's sake," a male voice said, and I jumped. I turned to find Barton standing on the path behind me.

"I didn't realize I wasn't alone. Well, except for him." I inclined my head toward the statue.

"You like to keep quiet company, I see. And who got you all tied up in knots? The water nymph?"

"She asked some interesting questions."

Desmond Eath picked his way down the path as well. He carried a duffel bag full of gear.

"Are you ready for our heist?" Desmond asked. He grinned. "It's been too long since I've had any real adventure."

"You're sure about this?" Barton asked.

"Yes, I have to find the evidence to release Reine. We can't let her go down a dark path." Even though I sensed I already had.

HALF AN HOUR LATER, Barton and Desmond joined me, Minerva, Kestrel, and Lily at the house. My mother had left earlier to go do Regent things, and Micah had gone to start his shift. We had opted not to include him because we'd determined that his diffident nature would create more danger for himself and us more than his strength and grace would help.

Grand-Pied made his entrance, stepping through into the kitchen. "Is there any pie left?"

I served him a piece. "Thank you for coming."

He looked at the map spread over the table. "This is highly inaccurate. I can show you where the Order's headquarters are."

"How are we going to get there?" Kestrel asked. "Can you take us?"

"I'm limited to sharing knowledge only."

"You're going to do it, Kestrel. You're a Trickster. You can fold space." Lily moved her hands together.

"You mean...me? But what if I hadn't come?"

"We would've had to use the Truth Seeker portals," Barton said. "And that meant I would have had to sneak everyone in and out, which would be a feat. Folding space is harder, but more subtle."

Kestrel's freckles stood out against her pale cheeks. "But I don't know where I'm going."

Lily put her hands on Kestrel's trembling shoulders. "I know where the Order's headquarters are. They've been dealing with the dark Fae for centuries. Maeve didn't exactly have an original idea when she allied with them."

"All right."

"And I know how to get in undetected." Grand-Pied outlined how to enter unseen, by landing in the archives room, where no one went. "They're more interested in causing trouble currently than in the past."

"And that's where we'll likely find the letters?" Barton asked.

"Possibly. Whatever you do, don't use your magic beyond your initial arrival. Or use it sparingly. Wolfsheim left spells all over the structure to alert those inside to potential magical attacks."

"And then what?" Lily asked. "Where do we go from there?"

"To Faerie," I said. "To plead Reine's case. Do you have the device, Desmond?"

"Yes." He handed it to me. It resembled the full face mask of a CPAP machine with head straps. Instead of a hose coming out of the mask, a piece like a charcoal filter had been attached.

"This is it?" I tried it on, and it fit perfectly. The filter smelled metallic.

Desmond appeared pleased with himself, and rightly so. "The makeup of the atmosphere in Faerie has changed with less of the harmful element, so I could make a lighter design."

I removed the device and stuck it in my satchel. "Thank you. That's much better. Is everyone ready?"

The chorus of "yeses" wouldn't have made any choir director proud, but my heart swelled with gratitude. These people were helping me, helping Reine. We'd figure this out together.

Minerva's cell phone buzzed, and she checked the screen. "Stones," she cursed.

"What?"

"It's Hazel. Your interview is in two hours, and she wants to know when you can be there for makeup."

"We're going to have to make this a quick heist," I said at the same time Lily insisted, "We can't waste any more time."

"I'll tell her you're tied up. All right, ready!"

"Godspeed," Grand-Pied intoned.

We held hands in a circle around Kestrel, who stood with hands clasped and eyes closed. Her fingers twitched, and I suspected she was reaching for the electric eel-like creature that symbolized her powers for her. She'd described them to me as a school running under her skin.

"There!"

The kitchen melted away.

29

REINE

I attempted to sink out of Desdemona's grasp, but she had the hair on top of my head in her iron grip. Spots appeared and spread in front of my eyes, the blooming fungus of impending unconsciousness. I attempted to access my water elemental powers, but the neutral liquid in the crypt pools didn't respond to magic. With my last reserve of strength, I grabbed her wrist, then kicked off from the side of the pool and flipped her in. She let go, and I grasped the pool's lip and hoisted myself into the air.

I coughed the water from my lungs in a few searing bubbles, then laid my head against the side of the pool. Strong hands grasped mine and lifted me so I could flop out of the pool and on to the stone floor.

"You weren't supposed to almost drown her," a familiar voice said from above me.

"You were supposed to take care of Lilith more efficiently."

I opened my eyes to see Rhys and a dripping Desdemona standing over me. Desdemona's dark hair always lay close to her head, and her unintentional dip in the pool had plastered it to her skull in a dark helmet.

"Rhys?" I coughed again and rolled to my side to let the rest of the water loose on Desdemona's shoes. Not that it made her black boots any more wet, but I felt better. "What in Hades is going on?"

Desdemona spat, "Your brother has been playing a deadly game of Fae chess and is lucky he hasn't gotten hurt."

Rhys preened. Obviously, he didn't find anything regrettable in his actions.

"And why do you care about what happens to him—oh!"

As my physical and magical visions both cleared, I caught on to how they glanced at each other, the proximity of their hands, and the metaphysical connection between them.

"Rhys, she's old enough to be our mother!"

"Reine, she's a Fae. And you're old enough to be Lawrence's grandmother, so don't even try to judge me."

He had a point. And he was an adult even if he didn't always like acting as one.

"Explain, please?"

The contact with the stone of the crypt gave me strength, as connection with a dense Earth element typically did. I moved to sitting with my back against the wall of the pool, and the gentle vibration of the water on the other side further soothed and bolstered me.

"I was undercover with Maeve, and after you made your second bargain—not your smartest moment, Sis—she changed her strategy. Being acting Queen of the Light Fae wasn't enough for her. She'd learned from researching how to defeat you that there used to be one Fae queen, and she decided to become Queen of All Fae."

I laid my head against the stone behind me. "Doesn't surprise me."

"She sent spies to see what you were up to and if you'd found the old library at the asylum yet because she knew she'd need the knowledge from before the Light/Dark Battle and Rift."

"That was all news to me, too. And I did, but not until very recently."

"Good timing, that. I attempted to bring the knowledge to Lilith, but she had no use for 'the scarred Fae prince' even though Grandmother healed me before she died. That's when I met Desdemona."

"But then Lilith heard what Maeve was up to, and that's when she visited you. I had to go see, too, and noticed that you were already showing signs of developing balanced powers." She rubbed her neck and winked. "That's why I challenged you. I knew if you could defend yourself, you were meant to hold the Throne of Crystal."

I groaned. "I am truly sorry. I didn't mean to hurt you. And the Throne of What?"

"Part of the legend." She pointed to the book that thankfully hadn't gone in the water with her. "According to the history, the Queen of All Fae sat on a throne made of crystal, and when the realm split, it fractured into the thrones of onyx and diamond that are in our respective throne rooms. It also released the gas that settled in the realm between the light and dark Fae lands and turned it into the Gray Zone, which is where the revenants are supposed to be until they transition from all spirit to spirit plus flesh and find their way back to their homelands."

"How did I not know all of this?"

"Only the actual queens had access to the knowledge," Desdemona told me. "And they weren't supposed to tell their successors until the very last moment before death."

"And my grandmother's last moments were spent watching her daughter and granddaughter battle." I put my head in my hands. "So how do you know?"

Rhys handed something to Desdemona, and she smiled when she grasped it.

I gasped, and icy dread over what my brother had done to "take care" of the dark Fae queen slid through my chest. "The onyx crown! What happened to Lilith?"

"Yes, sadly Queen Lilith is no more."

"Rhys, did you...?"

"I cannot confirm or deny, Sis. That's why we needed you under the water. You didn't see anything. You don't know what happened."

I wanted to argue, but the lump in my throat kept me from speaking. Although Lilith hadn't been a nice Fae, and she'd tried to have me killed, she was still from the era of my grandmother, and they had been friendly.

Desdemona placed the crown on her head, and warm air whipped around us. It dried both of us, and I stood. Desdemona kneeled on one knee and presented the crown to me.

"I swore my fealty to you, and I renew my vow. You now hold the crowns of the light and dark Fae."

The crypt rumbled around us.

Rhys jumped out of the way of a wave that splashed out of the pool. "Uh, Des, I don't think your ancestors are happy with this arrangement."

Indeed, the crypt doors around us rattled. Sir Raleigh rubbed against my leg and disappeared.

"We can't transport out of here like that, can we?" I whispered.

"No, run!"

WE DASHED THROUGH THE CRYPT, and I kept my attention on the path ahead so I could leap over obstacles that tried to trip me up. I found the smaller stones and bones that flew at us from the walls harder to dodge. The roaring sound and crashing behind me told me that either a lot more Fae had risen and assumed revenant form or that the structure of the crypt had melted at the heresy of Desdemona offering her crown to me.

And the question beat at my brain—what was happening in Lorien, the light Fae capital? Were they seeing a similar revenant surge?

I leaped over a sarcophagus that slid into my path and nearly took Rhys down with my landing. We stumbled, linked hands, and kept going.

Desdemona led us up the stairs into the palace courtyard, where many of the dark Fae courtiers and palace staff had gathered.

I could only imagine how we must have looked. Dust and ash covered all three of us, and gray and black smudges and bruises from small flying projectiles marked our skin.

"Princess?" a young woman asked. She wore long robes in jewel tones, and I guessed she must have been one of Lilith's ladies-in-waiting.

"Go to your chambers, bolt yourselves in, and put up the strongest magical wards you can." She pointed to a tall Fae in long, dark robes. "Felric, seal the door here. Do you know whether there's another way out?"

"Yes, Princess. No, Princess."

Desdemona rubbed her eyes, and I stifled a hysterical giggle.

"Elaborate," she snapped.

"Yes, I'll seal the doors. No, there's not another way out. At least there shouldn't be."

"Good. And you lot, get out of here."

All the assembled hesitated and looked at each other in confusion.

Desdemona plopped the crown on her head. "You heard me. Lilith is no more, and the dead are rising. The danger isn't just outside the city walls anymore. Go!"

They scattered, and we dashed into the palace and up two

flights of stairs to the archive room.

30

LAWRENCE

"Well, fuck." Barton had lost his usual confident composure in the face of the mess that passed as the archives of the Order of the Silver Arrow. We hadn't found the letters, not even with Lily and Kestrel's magical assistance, which we'd become desperate enough to use. At this point, both of them were slumped on the floor eating the protein bars that Barton had brought. I thumbed through a file drawer without much hope of finding anything, and Desmond sat behind the computer in the corner and cursed under his breath. Even if he'd been able to find a list or catalog, there was no guarantee that the room matched the map.

And boy, was the room a mess. Minerva had immediately posted herself by the door "in case someone comes," but I'd seen the look in her eyes. Chaos and mess had always short-circuited my mother's brain, and I suspected Minerva had inherited those genes. The place looked like it had been organized by a tornado, but nothing had been damaged and everything was on shelves or tables, so I suspected that the Order wasn't good about cleaning up after themselves.

Still, we should have found something...

I said the thing I knew the others didn't want to hear... "I don't think the letters are here."

"You're right," Desmond sighed. "I finally got through. There's a vault in the director's office, where they keep their important documents."

We all groaned.

"And where's that?" Kestrel asked.

"Upstairs. Top of the east tower."

I closed my eyes and felt for the stone castle's layout. The stone whispered to me about where it was. "It's about opposite across the castle from where we are now."

Lily moaned. "How do we get up there? Kestrel and I can't manage anything more right now."

"And this place is immune to Truth Seeker magic," Barton added. "Even if we could use it."

The fact that one of them would even admit to willingness to bend the rules made me smile, as did the other secret the stones had told me.

"Luckily for us, this is an old castle, which means there are plenty of secret passages. I can get us up there."

"Great!" Minerva gave me a thumbs-up. "Where do we start?"

"Unfortunately, in the dungeon."

We crept out of the archives and down one level to the dungeons. Because of course there were dungeons. They smelled of must, dust, and a hint of iron from long-ago bloodshed, but all the organic matter had decayed a century before.

And no lights, not even a torch of any persuasion, relieved the darkness pressing on our eyeballs.

"Uh, Lawrence?" Minerva's question echoed into the fog. "What now?"

"I can't make a Fae light," Lily added.

"Nothing here, either," Kestrel agreed.

"All right, everyone, hold hands." I closed my eyes so the ultra-blackness wouldn't distract me and felt around with my gargoyle senses. The stones down here whispered as well, but in a frantic warning instead of encouragement. Had we gone into a trap?

"Here, Uncle Lawrence." Kestrel's hand found mine and squeezed. I reached out in front of me and found nothing, just space, but like an antenna, my arm gave me a fuller sense of the layout. The entrance to the secret passage lay all the way at the end of the hall.

We passed the first cells, one on either side, and they illuminated. I kept my eyes closed, but Kestrel gasped.

"Mother!"

"It's an illusion, don't pay attention to it," Lily encouraged.

"And father! They're here. They're not dead." She sighed. "No, they are. I saw them. I buried them."

"Kestrel..." The hiss came from both sides. It resonated like it held more than one tone, and I could almost hear John and Beverly calling together, "Save us... You failed before, but you can now..."

"You're not real, you're not real..." Kestrel's tears came through her voice, so I squeezed her fingers and pulled her along.

"No, they're not real."

The light went out when we reached the next cells, and I almost sighed in relief. The illumination had revealed our presence, so I hurried us along.

"Lily," a male voice said. "Daughter of Desdemona, Granddaughter of Lilith, why are you betraying your people like this?"

"Father?"

What was this, parent day in the dungeons? I almost smiled at the thought that Reine would have said something similar, but I had to steel myself for what I suspected would come next.

I focused ahead, and the voice I hadn't heard in over a century didn't surprise me.

My father chided me, "Lawrence, what are you doing? Rescuing a Fae? Are you out of your mind?"

Having prepared for the possibility, I didn't think I'd react, but...

That part of me that I'd locked away, the small boy who had cried at night in sorrow at his family being torn apart, his father gone, he and his mother on the run from the Fae, who might come back... That crack tore open and ripped apart the defensive layers I'd built.

The sting, then throb in my knees told me I'd buckled, but Kestrel still held on. With the attacks increasing in intensity, what would come next? What unresolved grief could Barton, Minerva, and Desmond hold?

"Enough!" Desmond's resonant voice bounced off the walls of the space. The light vanished, and someone pulled me to my feet, but my ears still rang.

Barton's voice sounded like it came from the bottom of a cotton well. "Desmond, you don't have to."

"No, this is a travesty of disrespect to the dead, and I refuse to allow it to pass."

A softer light that I knew wouldn't hurt illuminated the backs of my eyelids soft red instead of the bright orange, and I opened my eyes.

Desmond stood in front of me, his arms open. He glowed a soft purple, more indigo than the lavender of the black lightning bugs, with white shot through it. The shadows of large black wings flickered behind him.

"Oh, great goddess, help us," Lily murmured. "A death god."

Desmond executed a slight bow from his waist and inclined his head. "Princess, forgive me for not saying, 'At your service,' but you probably aren't ready for that yet."

Lily's delighted laugh sounded out of place. "A death god with a sense of humor. Who would have thought?"

Desmond winked, then spread his arms. Lightning flashed from his hands and arced through the cells. When it moved through the spaces inside the cells, it outlined the spirits as they'd appeared to us, then melted them into gape-jawed wraiths, which disappeared in a puff of smoke.

The huddled form in the final cell didn't. I assumed it had been a true prisoner who had died.

The outline of a door appeared behind Desmond, who closed his fists. The lightning and purple glow disappeared, and he fell to his knees, then collapsed into his raven form.

Barton gathered the limp bird to his chest. "We won't leave you, friend." When he raised his gaze to me, his expression had hardened into anger. "If he discorporates and goes into his long sleep, I'm holding you responsible."

"He chose to do what he did. I do not accept responsibility for others' choices or their consequences."

"Yet you compelled us to help you."

Stones, he was right.

"Gentlemen, we don't have time to argue," Minerva reminded us. "Is that the door, Lawrence?"

"Yes. And I release anyone who doesn't want to come from following us." I shot Barton a pointed look.

"I'm doing this for Reine," he said.

I walked toward the door, which took me by the inhabited cell. I nearly jumped into gargoyle form when it lifted its head and asked in a shaky tenor voice, "Who's there?"

We all exchanged startled glances.

"Who's there?" I asked. "Show yourself."

The male creature unfolded himself from the fetal position, and Lily gasped. "It's Fae. He's Fae."

He bowed. "I am light Fae council member Roshal. Can you get me out, Princess Liliana?" He collapsed into a coughing fit.

She reached toward him, then drew her hand back with a hiss. "Iron. Don't try to talk. You're suffering from prolonged iron exposure. Lawrence, can you do something?"

I walked to the cell and pulled at the door. It didn't move, but its structure revealed itself, and I tried to figure out if I had anything in my satchel I could use to dismantle it. Then a calm sense washed through my brain—I could do this. I called upon my enhanced power to manipulate Earth element-based materials to weaken the hinges, and the door fell off in my hands.

Roshal stumbled out, and Lily caught him.

"Who put you in here?" she asked.

"Maeve's man. Water?"

I handed him my canteen, and he took a long gulp. "I'm sorry, we don't have time to spare. Can you manage to come with us?"

"Walk or talk."

"Meaning he can either answer our questions or move," Lily translated.

"Thanks, I figured. Walk...for now."

He nodded. He also regarded me with undisguised curiosity to the point I thought I might have a cut or something on my face I couldn't see. Or could he sense the Crown Prince aura? I didn't want to waste time on finding out.

Had being Crown Prince magnified my elemental powers and allowed me to release him?

I opened the metal door at the end of the dungeon, and we stepped into the stone spiral staircase. For a second, I saw it overlaid on another one and the shadow of a gray cat-like creature ascending in front of me.

31

REINE

"Here we are," Desdemona said and snapped her finger. A series of Fae lights illuminated around the walls and showed a relatively clean and tidy space.

"Do dark Fae not do much research?" Rhys asked.

Desdemona shot him a look. "We know how to clean up after ourselves, unlike some princes I know."

"All right, I don't want the details, messy or otherwise, of your relationship." I tapped my lips with my right index finger. "Where do we find the information we need? Where are the old or rare manuscripts?"

A *thunk* sounded from behind the far wall, and we clustered together, hands spread in magic defense posture. But no revenant came through the stones. Rhys lowered his hands first and approached it.

"Oh, it looks like these shelves are newer than the rest."

A rare and tender smile curved Desdemona's mouth. "Yes, when Lily was working up here, she and the archivist replaced some of the shelves that had become rotted and worn. She was very proud of helping to preserve our history. I'm not sure how

I produced such a little bookworm. Well, I am. I fucked the president of the Archivist Guild."

"TMI, Desdemona," Rhys muttered. "Would you queens like to help me move the stuff off these shelves, or are you too dainty to get your hands dirty?"

"I should have your head for that," Desdemona grumbled, but we complied. We didn't use magic to move the books and scrolls —it would have been faster, but we didn't want to risk damaging anything. It might hold the information we needed. Maybe the sound had been a friendly spirit telling us to look over there.

We stepped back, and Rhys curved his fingers around the back of the bookcase and swung it outward. The vaguest whiff of decay from a spent defensive death spell floated out and dissipated.

"Someone's already been in there." Rhys poked his head in. "It's safe."

Desdemona had pressed her lips into a tight line.

"What happened here?" I asked. "Does this have something to do with why Lily ran away?"

"Silly girl was too sentimental. Got attached to the archivist. Lilith sacrificed him to the spell so she could see what was in there."

"Did she know?"

"She told Lily to figure it out and tell her if she found anything important."

Rhys and I made eye contact. "It's quite possible she did," I said. "But something in there still wanted to be found."

We walked in, and a Fae light in the ceiling flickered on. A wooden box lay on the ground, but it hadn't spilled its contents or even seem to have fallen in spite of an empty spot of about the same size above it on a ledge. But it didn't appear sealed shut and should have lain partially open on its side.

All three of us looked down at it.

"Someone should pick it up?" Rhys suggested.

"Go ahead, my brave prince," Desdemona teased.

He bent down, but when he went to touch it, he snatched his hands back with a hiss. "It's burning. It doesn't want me to touch it."

A pattern emerged on the top, that of two sceptres crossed with a crown above them. Underneath it, lettering in Old Fae spelled out, "Queens Only."

Except in Old Fae, Queen was a word closer to the French translation for it—*reine*.

"Looks like it's for you, then," Desdemona told me. "We'll just step out so I can heal Rhys' hands."

"Go ahead." Something told me I wanted privacy. They walked back into the main archive, and I knelt in front of the box and reached for it, centimeter by centimeter, waiting for another defensive spell to activate. But none did.

I caressed the wood, smooth and soft from centuries of being passed from hand to hand. I could almost see its history, the journeys it had made. It had once resided in the secret magical library I'd visited. The Librarian would be excited to hear about it if I saw her again.

I lifted the lid to find a scepter and a crown, the ones I'd seen in the mirror, and a set of three glass jars, each of which held a rolled-up piece of paper in them. The first I pulled out was blank. The second one unrolled itself and stuck to my fingers until I whispered,

"I am the night and the day
I am the wave and the shore
I am the Queen of All Fae
Ruling with justice forevermore"

. . .

A wind stirred my hair, and tingles spread over my skin. The paper rolled itself back into a little scroll with a snap and fell into its jar.

"Uh, Sis, what did you do?" Rhys called.

"I just said another verse of the Queen Spell."

Desdemona poked her head in, and on her face I saw...relief?

"I should have told you, but it compelled me."

She waved her hands. "Oh, no, honey, that honor and all its attendant responsibilities and pains in the ass are yours. What are the other two?"

"The first one is blank. The third one..."

I opened it to find the first four lines of a spell. As I read through it, my heart thudded. The wording suggested that it could be the Breath Spell. However, the structure, as I recalled from my Spells and Potions classes during my young Fae-hood, was for an eight-line spell. That meant half was missing.

I must have groaned aloud because Rhys poked his head in. "What is it?"

"I think this is what we need, but half of it is missing."

"And I bet I know where the other half is," Desdemona said.

I nodded with a sigh. "In the archives in the palace of the light Fae."

I pulled the obsidian mirror from my pocket. "Basil," I said. "I need to talk to you."

His picture appeared, and my heart landed somewhere around my large intestine when his face filled the mirror. He looked as dirty and harried as the rest of us.

"What in Hades have you been up to, Reine? We have a full revenant Rising happening, and the palace is in chaos."

32

———

LAWRENCE

"Worst death god ever," someone, probably Lily, muttered. I motioned for them to shush. Although we crept through the walls and had a good six inches of solid stone between us and anyone who might hear us, I didn't want to take any chances. Who would have guessed that they'd have that level of security in the dungeon? As far as I could tell, there was nothing to guard except the entrance to the secret passages and one lone Fae prisoner.

Yes, I wanted to find out how Roshal had ended up down there—Fae council members tended to be a protected bunch— but I respected his need to conserve his strength, especially if he'd been tormented by the spirits of his past. Had the ghouls in the cells been put there to torture prisoners, driving them mad with incessant whispering until they took their own lives or died from the stress of it all?

The leader of the Order must be a diabolical ass if that was the case. Or had the dungeon inhabitants been left there from the time of Wolfsheim?

And who had taken over? I had lost touch with news of the Order of the Silver Arrow since moving to the States, where I hoped to be safe from them and their anti-shifter prejudices. Not that the US had turned out to be much better, especially after the eugenics movement had swept through the country, leaving in its wake more entrenched attitudes about genetic and racial superiority.

I reminded myself to focus. Something about being in old castles made me connect with history. In truth, gargoyles had once been the guardians of places such as this. According to legends, that's how we'd satisfied our protective instincts after being booted out of Faerie—we'd protected old buildings from erosion due to water, hence why gargoyle statues had served as water gutters for cathedrals.

The passage took a turn and led to an iron-studded door. The stones whispered, *up, up!*

Kestrel's whisper floated to my left ear. "What are they telling you, Uncle Lawrence?"

I pointed at the door, then to the ceiling. Out and up.

"I'll go first," Minerva mouthed. "I can tell if anyone's coming."

I nodded. She'd honed her stone communication skills as part of my mother's security force, and I appreciated her abilities more each moment. She crept through the door and returned, gesturing for us to follow. Lily ducked as she walked under the frame and helped Roshal to do so as well. When I passed under it, I sensed that iron nails had been used in the construction.

We crept up the narrow staircase, Minerva in the lead and me in the rear. Barton still carried Desmond, who looked at me over Barton's shoulder with glittering eyes. I couldn't tell if he was conveying his displeasure or watching for anyone coming up behind me.

Kestrel stumbled up one of the stairs, and Lily caught her before she fell backward. Kestrel smiled and nodded thanks to her friend, and I had to rein in my protectiveness. Had Kestrel used too much of her energy in the archive, and how much had been depleted in her struggles against the dungeon ghouls? And what about Lily? She hadn't shown any issue with the iron in the dungeon, but she might have been shielding herself magically. What if someone caught us or attacked us again? We had four depleted magic users, two gargoyles, and a Truth Seeker whose powers I didn't have a good scope of.

We emerged onto a landing in front of another iron-studded door. Minerva pushed it open, and we all cringed at the creak that echoed down the stairs behind us.

"Quickly, then," Minerva whispered. We piled into the office, and Barton traced the outline of the now-closed door. It flared orange.

"That will keep anyone from sensing we're in here," he explained in a low tone. "Where do we start?"

The office of the Order's leader had bookshelves lining the non-window and door walls of the octagonal space, a large desk, and a fireplace in the center open on four sides. The embers glowed like it had been left for some time.

"I'll take the desk," Barton said. "I know how to break into magically warded ones."

Desmond squawked, and Barton chuckled.

"It's too late to pretend I don't have a shadowy past, my friend. We'll face the consequences of this adventure later."

I tried to smile at him, but he wouldn't meet my gaze. I shrugged and moved to one of the bookshelves to see if it had any hidden compartments behind the books that could hold the letters. Why couldn't these types clearly file and label their evidence of wrongdoing? It would make snooping so much easier.

Kestrel and Lily also searched, and Minerva stood at the door, her ear to the wood. She kept an index finger poised on one of the iron studs. Roshal collapsed on the floor in a state of such stillness I half-expected him to start turning to dirt.

"Aha," Barton breathed, and Desmond hopped over to see what he'd found. The latch clicked with gunshot intensity, and events unfolded too fast to track. The fire flared to life with a roar. The sudden light blinded me, and I fell back against the bookshelf I'd been feeling through.

Shadows grew along the walls and herded us to the center of the room. Not all of us. Lily darted to Roshal, murmured something to him, and he nodded and disappeared. She moved to me and helped me stand.

"What did you do?" I whispered.

"Loaned him enough power to get back to Faerie. He'll gather Reine's allies there."

"But why send him back now and not before?"

"I needed time to build my strength. But he had to go. He's in no shape to fight and could slow us down if we have to."

All right, she had a point. We gathered in a clump between the desk and the fireplace, which scorched my backside. I couldn't see if Barton held anything or not, and I dared not ask.

He'd said he knew how to deal with warded desks. What had happened? Had he failed to take something into account?

Or had he tripped the alarm intentionally? But why?

Or had this been a trap all along?

"You're too clever for a gargoyle," a familiar voice told me. "And if you were to live longer, you might learn to not think so loudly. How many times do you need to be warned?"

I turned toward the voice. "Hello, Maeve. It's been a while."

~

THE LAST TIME I'd seen Reine's mother, she had been all blonde and light, and she still was, but now I saw beneath the veneer to the greedy heart beneath.

"Who told you?" I asked. "You've obviously been waiting for us."

"We knew you'd come." She grinned, and I looked away from her blue gaze.

"Oh, don't worry about it, Doctor Gordon," another familiar voice told me. I whirled to see Basil, formerly known as Troubadour, standing on the other side of the room. He shook his head. "You look so disappointed."

Terror and betrayal clawed and twined from my gut to my throat. I choked out, "You were supposed to be helping Reine."

"And I was. From afar and at my own pace." He walked to the desk and reached underneath it. A blue light flared, and he pulled out a manila envelope. "Couldn't let you find these too soon."

Barton stood with clenched fists. "You wanted us to try to find them. You wanted us to come here."

"And so you did. It's much easier to capture you here than in The Aerie, after all. So much more secure there, especially with its head of security and new Crown Prince."

"You deceived us." I struggled to keep my gargoyle form from emerging. I couldn't risk the few seconds of vulnerability the change would give me.

"I'm a dark Fae." He shrugged. "What did you expect?"

Kestrel shuddered. "You possessed me at one point. What were you thinking?"

"Fae play the long game," I told her. "And his is...what, Basil? Get close to Reine so you can take her throne?"

He laughed. "I'm already part of her Council of Three. I've demonstrated that I can rule the light Fae. No, Crown Prince of the Gargoyles, my game has been to show her I can be counted on to rule *with* her. Just the two of us. Once Maeve steps down, of course."

"So you helped trap her in the asylum for what, captive wooing?"

"I knew she would end up somewhere helpless and alone. Who better to get close to her than a friend she already trusted?"

This time, my gargoyle tore through me and my clothing with a roar. I lunged toward him, but he flicked his wrist, and I tumbled back against the fireplace tower. My right wingtip met flame, and a hiss and the acrid smells of burning flesh and cartilage filled the room. The searing sensation all but knocked me to my knees.

A tremor shook the tower, and we each grabbed on to whatever was closest. A lightening, a flare of hope, swept through me, and for a brief second, I saw Reine standing in a small room lined with parchment books, scrolls, and wooden boxes. Cool healing energy poured through me, but I continued to hold my repaired wingtip. Let them think I was still injured. I invoked all the shielding techniques Reine and later Grand-Pied had taught me.

"A worthwhile endeavor," Maeve mocked, "except you didn't count on her resourcefulness in getting herself out of the asylum first. And her sentence will still stand no matter what those letters say. Speaking of which..." She held out her hand, and Basil gave her the envelope. She threw it in the fire, and the six of us who had risked everything to retrieve them cried out. A golden glow flared through Kestrel, and I could tell she'd tried to do something, but her pursed lips indicated she hadn't quite succeeded.

Barton recovered first, and his dark eyes flickered with reflected flames and...hatred. Although Truth Seekers were known to be intense, he'd never shown that side of himself. But he spoke calmly. "That's not true. I'm familiar with the law of both realms, and you don't have a case."

"Oh, my dear Truth Seeker, you don't know the nuances of the laws of the realm of Faerie. And I'm not going to tell you how you're wrong. That would be a mistake almost as stupid as you bunch appearing here." The air grew thick, and heaviness seeped through my limbs. Maeve walked around and touched us each on the forehead. "Let's see, we have..." Desmond snapped at her. "A death god who hasn't been good about charging his magical batteries. A Truth Seeker with his own agenda...as you all have. A trickster. A missing Fae princess. The gargoyle Regent's daughter and head of security. And the Crown Prince."

I jerked back before she could touch me.

She smirked. "Who is stronger than he looks, even in his big, scary gargoyle form. Does love for my daughter keep you going?"

I wouldn't answer her.

"Very well, we'll see how you fare back in Faerie. What did good doctor say, one more time would kill you?"

Barton and I exchanged worried glances.

"And guess who will hold her and comfort her in her grief?" Basil crowed. I refused to give into his desire to bait me, and Maeve's spell had taken hold of me again. He or Maeve wouldn't hesitate to kill me if given the provocation. Or were they waiting so Reine could watch me die in Faerie and know all hope was lost? Still, I had to protect the others as much as I could even if I wouldn't leave the situation alive.

When Maeve and Basil had us all line up, our limbs moving in response to their desire, not our own, Barton slipped the new breathing filter into my hand. The device, which I'd formerly been impressed with the small size of, now looked puny in the face of the imminent challenge.

The fire rose in the central chimney again, and the room

faded to bright. Basil's voice came to me through the roaring echo of slipping consciousness. "What in Hades have you been up to, Reine? We have a full revenant Rising happening, and the palace is in chaos." Then, "Stop her! She's getting away."

I slipped the breathing apparatus on just before I passed out, but I smiled when the question came to my mind. Which *her* had escaped?

33

AUGUSTUS GRAVEL IRONKEYS III

"You need to wake up now. Your people are in trouble."

I'd heard the voice of the witch before. She'd told my many times-great nephew that I still lived, still existed in this shell of stone. I hadn't minded. He seemed a good sort, that Lawrence. Not like that blighted offspring of the other branch of my family, Harold Ironkeys. How had he kept my surname and Lawrence not?

Harold had ignored me, even laughed at me when passing by. Lawrence had sometimes come talk to me, and the stories he told me of him and his Fae princess had quickened my blood, made my heart beat again, first with painful, plodding beats and now with readiness. I'd come alive again, slowly, from my heart outward. Now I waited and rested under a thin layer of stone, moss, and the constant mist from the river.

The time drew near. They couldn't sense it, but I felt Faerie approach. Its metaphysical boundaries almost touched our own. I would be called to duty again.

They all knew part of the legend, of course, how poor old "Uncle Augie" had stayed in gargoyle form too long. But no one knew why. They only assumed the worst, that I had succumbed to temptation and not wanted to return to my human form.

If only they knew the truth.

The witch drew her thumbs over my eyelids and brushed the minerals from my flesh. I blinked my eyes open. My grimace at the burning of the sun, albeit shaded, cracked the stone on my face.

"Yes, yes, that's it." The redhead stood back. "Claim your right. Claim your identity, Augustus."

I didn't ask how she knew my name. Fissures raced through the final layer of my rocky prison with pops, crackles, and hisses. I stretched and moved whenever I felt the mineral carapace loosen.

With a roar, I stood and stretched my wings.

Then I collapsed.

My voice grated through my throat. "What have you done to me, witch?"

"I've helped you awaken. Now you need to remember what you are, gargoyle. Draw the energy from the earth, then swim in the river and fly through the air. Replenish your elemental connections, and your strength will return."

I did as she suggested. Earth energy poured through me with the strength of a hundred Viking raiders, and the plunge in the cold river rejuvenated me. I took off straight from the water and did somersaults in the air. The wind dried my skin and welcomed me back to its realm.

Then I saw the opalescent oval of a Fae portal.

Without questioning, I flew through and found myself hovering outside the window of a castle tower. Inside, a light Fae held court. No, a prison.

A dark-haired Fae by the window turned, and her eyes widened. She had the purple irises of one of the Fae queen lines.

Duty called. I crashed through the window and grabbed the dark Fae, then turned and leaped through to outside.

"Stop her! She's getting away!"

I laughed and dodged their spells. Didn't they know who I was?

"Who are you?" the young woman in my arms asked.

Huh, I guess they didn't.

She held on to my neck and frowned at me. I gave her my best attempt at a reassuring smile.

"I am Augustus Gravel Ironkeys the Third, leader of the Fae guard. And you are?"

She sighed. "Princess Liliana, but everyone calls me Lily. I've never heard of you. Dark Fae or light Fae guard?"

I growled. "Neither. I am from a time before such artificial divisions."

"Ohhh... I have so many questions, and you have a lot of catching up to do." She shook her head. "But that doesn't matter. Faerie is in trouble."

"Then I am at your command, Princess."

34

REINE

I turned to Desdemona. "Is there a way to get to the palace in Lorien quickly? We have to finish this."

"As in, did the queens have portals to each other's palaces? I don't think so. You would have found it when you became queen of the light Fae."

She had a point, but... "Tatiana didn't give me nearly as many secrets as you seem to have access to."

Rhys snorted. "They probably went to Maeve. You're going to have to do the Gray Fae thing and fold the path again."

I swallowed and attempted to dredge up the courage to do so. The last time had taken a lot out of me, and I didn't know what awaited me when I reached the palace. But then, the last time, I hadn't been Queen of All Fae. And it seemed appropriate to use my gray Fae powers to bridge my path from the dark Fae capital of Cruaidh to the light Fae capital of Lorien. Perhaps I'd even land us in the throne room again.

"Very well. Hold my hands."

They did as I commanded and held each other's as well. We made a circle of three, and I drew from the stability of the number and the place inside me that craved neither creation nor destruction, but merely a way forward. For a second, I saw a balance of light, dark, and gray, three wedges in a circle, and then the long, gray ribbon of energy connecting us from where we were to the throne room of Lorien. The path undulated like a satin ribbon being shaken at one end, and I struggled to grasp it, to fold it. I tried to release Rhys' hand, which I held in my right one, and he squeezed instead of letting go.

"You can do this, Sis."

"Thanks." With the renewed confidence of his faith in me—faith I'd never had from my mother—I managed to hold both ends of the ribbon in my mental grasp and fold them.

The sensation of falling flooded out all else, and I braced myself for the landing. But no bump jarred my body, only an awareness of cold stone pressed against my right hip, elbow, and foot. I opened my eyes to see that we'd landed in the throne room. A dirty and battered Basil waited for us, and he rushed to take my hands.

"Thank the gods, you're all right."

I looked around. Rhys was coming to, and Desdemona lay motionless on the floor.

"Desdemona!" I tried to move to help her, but Basil held me.

"Give her a minute. We dark Fae don't travel well by path folding. That was an impressive feat. Did you come castle to castle?"

"Yes. Wait... How did you know where I was?"

Rhys rolled to his feet with a moan. "He's been spying on you the whole time, Sis. I told you not to trust him."

This time I pulled myself from Basil's grasp.

"You told me not to... Oh, the mirror. It cut off your message. Why didn't you say anything later?"

"Because I thought you'd heard it."

"Hades. I trusted you, Basil." The prickly heat of shame exploded in my chest. I'd been a fool. "I trusted you with my realm. With my family. With my mate."

Basil smiled, and with a whirl of white sparks, his appearance turned to his normal, handsome self. His normal, deceptive self.

"I never claimed to be anything I'm not, and I am a dark Fae. But I haven't hurt anyone...yet."

"Yet?" I almost dared not whisper the question. I'd been so concerned about Maeve's long game I'd been blind to the one he played.

"Yes. Your mother allowed me to meet you here so I could offer you a bargain."

Now the roiling ball of emotion in my chest turned to sharp-edged ice. "Not another bargain," I whispered.

"Yes, another bargain. But it's the final one you'll need to make. Give Maeve the Crown of All Fae, and she'll allow your lover to live. Yes, he's gotten himself trapped yet again along with some of your friends."

He waved a hand at an obsidian mirror that sat against the wall, and a scene appeared. I recognized the room as the light Fae palace archives, and five prisoners sat chained to the tables. Well, four and a raven in a cage.

"Is that Desmond Eath?"

"Yes, he found and disabled my traps in the dungeon of Wolfsheim's secondary palace, but that used up his strength. Good thing, too. Otherwise, he would have introduced an unpleasant loose end."

"And Lawrence, Kestrel, Barton, and Minerva." I leaned closer and touched the mirror over Lawrence's image. He had taken on his gargoyle form, and he wore some sort of apparatus over his nose, but he still drooped.

"Yes. Alas, Princess Liliana escaped before we could force her to return to her rightful place in Faerie."

"Liliana!" Desdemona turned to Basil. "Tell me where she is, Cousin. I command you as Queen of the dark Fae."

"And you handed that crown to Reine. Tsk, tsk." He shook

his head. "How did you get rid of Lilith? I thought she'd never die."

Desdemona pressed her lips together, and to her credit, she didn't look at Rhys. He was already in enough trouble, and indeed, I questioned what else he had hidden in his dark sleeve. Something good, I hoped.

I kept myself from grinding my teeth in frustration. It was time to think rationally, not emotionally. "What if I offer you a counter-bargain?"

"Oh, this is getting interesting." Basil leaned against the throne in a deceptively casual posture. "Do say. I'm all pointy ears."

I closed my eyes and took a deep breath. I had to get to the archives, and if I didn't, it wouldn't matter who lived or died as the result of Maeve's ambition. But I couldn't give her the Crown of All Fae. I hated to do what I was about to. It felt like a big step backward, but I reminded myself that we didn't live life in a straight line. It spiraled upward, and while we came back to similar points, it was with increased wisdom, clarity, and resilience. At least I hoped so.

I looked at Basil and tried to see him as the handsome Fae I'd once trusted. One who wasn't as selfish as he'd made himself out to be. The Troubadour who had helped and guided me. And even if he'd done it for his selfish reasons, he'd still done it and defied Maeve during our last throne room confrontation. Yes, he had his dark Fae moments, and I had no doubt that he worked for himself primarily. He had ambition to spare, and I had to admire that even though I detested how he'd put me in this position. I had to trust my gut in my conclusion, my observation of the bulk of his actions over his last few words. There had to be some light in that dark Fae I could appeal to. It might take centuries, but I'd find it.

"I propose that you ally with me in this situation. Help me get to the archives. Let Lawrence and the others go."

"In exchange for...?"

"Sis, no," Rhys breathed.

"In exchange for being allowed to be my primary Prince Consort."

He grinned. "Why, my dear Reine, are you proposing to me?"

"Yes, I suppose I am. I'm afraid I didn't have time to shop for a ring or anything."

Basil crossed his arms. "I don't know... I'm more of a monogamous Fae, and you have a mate already."

"Yes, and I'm not getting rid of him. I can't." I found myself rubbing the spot on my chest over where the anchor still connected us. Indeed, it thrummed with Lawrence's closeness, and it took everything I had to not go join him.

"We'll see."

"Basil..." *Some light in the dark, some light in the dark...*

A tremor shook the castle. Basil's expression flickered with fear, then hardened into the opposite of what I'd come to expect from the jovial Fae. In fact, I had no doubt that he had come from the dark Fae realm and would be ruthless in seeking his aims.

But there had been that microsecond of fear...

"I didn't lie about the revenants, Reine. What are you going to do, delay here quibbling while your people are eaten alive by hungry risen Fae?"

And every soul they consumed would corrupt them that much more when they fleshed out... I battled not only for my current citizens but those yet to come.

"Spell it out exactly. What do you want, Basil Troubadour Emerald Gloriag the Fourth?"

The compulsion took hold of him before I realized what I'd done. "I want to rule by your side as more than your consort. I want to share your life and your bed. I want to be the only male you think about morning, noon, and night."

"I can't give you that."

"Not yet. But you may. Someday. All I ask is that you give us a chance. Release the bond to that gargoyle. See if you still feel this way about him. If you do, I'll leave you be."

"Do you promise?"

Golden sparkles emerged from his mouth and swirled above his head with the words, "If you release the bond and find it impossible to continue living without him, I solemnly swear I will release you from any promises you have made to me. However, if you, on the other hand, can move forward without him, I will claim you as my queen, and Faerie will have its first king."

I wanted to examine the trickery in his words. I didn't want to test my and Lawrence's love, but the shaking continued, and the terror of the Fae within the castle and the hunger of the souls without wafted through the air. And I had seen the bleak future that would materialize if I delayed any longer.

"Very well. I accept your vow." I almost added my own, but I kept the words inside lest I inadvertently give him more of a loophole than I was sure he'd already provided himself, if I could only figure it out.

The golden sparkles swirled around his head, and then they zoomed toward me too fast to block. They entered my nose and chest, and I choked but didn't expel them. Sharp-clawed fingers rooted out the mate bond, unhooked it from my heart and ripped it out. I clutched my chest and collapsed into the darkness.

35

LAWRENCE

I awoke still in my gargoyle form, but I had been chained to a table in yet another archive, this one in a room with luminous golden stone walls. The décor struck me as familiar, that of the palace in Lorien, the capital of the light Fae. Kestrel, whose hands were also chained, sat across from me. Indeed, we all wore shackles, and poor Desmond Eath huddled in an iron cage on one end of the table.

No, not all of us. Lily had disappeared. Had she been the one to escape? But would she make it out of the Order's headquarters? And how would she get word back to Mother and The Aerie?

I had to trust her resourcefulness. As much as I wanted to control circumstances and be okay with not having all the answers, I found myself squirming. Anxiety crawled through my nerves like ants wearing steel-toed boots, and the sensation converged in my chest, a thousand tiny, dancing prickles doing their own diabolical tarantella. Something was happening. Something I didn't want to happen but that I couldn't prevent. The shackles around my wrists kept me from clawing my own chest open to ease the torture, give it an outlet, although I knew it wouldn't help. Whatever happened was occurring on a meta-physical level, and it searched for something I had protected without realizing.

But I couldn't protect it forever. I hunched over in a vain attempt to shield the anchor of the mate bond Reine and I had forged unintentionally, but which I had come to cherish in spite of the impossibility of our eventual full union. But the clever ants in their clever boots swarmed too many and too fast for me to fight them.

"Uncle Lawrence?" Kestrel's whisper floated through the fog of pain. "Are you okay? What's happening?"

Maeve snickered. "Oh, Basil, you clever boy."

Her words made me recognize the dark Fae energy in the thousands of little fingers that dug through my heart and found the anchor of the bond, the little prying, levering, crevice-digging bastards. I could have held on against even a hundred, but the internal tug-of-war overwhelmed me, and the bond loosed, then pulled free with the agony of a thousand fishhooks dragging through my soul.

With a snap, I threw my head back and howled in grief. In rage. In loss. In betrayal. How had she allowed this to happen? How could she have not protected us, our bond, our future?

I shrank in on myself. No, I returned to my human form. Unfortunately, my wrist shackles shrank to fit before I could get my hands out of them, but I jerked my feet back before the ankle rings adjusted.

Emptiness filled me. Colors muted. Sounds muffled. Despair poured through me, through the hole in my heart to my aching throat and my solar plexus, which would only allow me short sips of air. I managed to adjust the breathing appa-ratus so it covered my nose and mouth, but had I already breathed in too much of Faerie's poisonous air?

Did it matter?

I focused on Kestrel. Staying alive for her, even as a gargoyle with a mortally wounded spirit, a broken heart beyond repair, would have to be enough.

I had promised her parents. And unlike some Fae, I didn't break my promises.

36

REINE

"Well, this is a mess, isn't it?"

My grandmother's voice floated through the liquid that encased me, but she didn't sound like she was underwater.

I opened my eyes to the ceiling of a grotto. Luminescent green vines twined overhead and dripped with thick leaves and glowing blue, purple, and pink flowers. I reached out my arms to find the edges of a basin...or something.

Then my brain recalled the legend of what happened to the Queens of Faerie when they went into their long sleep. Rather than being in some sort of stasis, their spirits went to The Grotto of the Dead to wait until it was time for them to be born again.

"Am I dead?" I asked. It seemed a logical question. I could feel my surroundings, but I couldn't feel, well, me. No internal sensations. No feelings. Blessed numbness at the thought of what I'd allowed Basil to do to me, to Lawrence. Barton Lucia had offered to break the mate bond. I suspected he had a gentler way to do it.

The only good thing about losing the bond was that if I was dead, it didn't mean that Lawrence would be, too.

Another female voice cracked with age and resonant with wisdom replied, "No, you're just in spirit shock. That boy barely knew what he was doing. You'll have a scar, as will your gargoyle lover."

"In my heart?"

"In your soul."

I raised my head. Every time I tried to grasp the walls of the pool to push myself up, my hands slipped. "Why can't I get out?"

My grandmother leaned over the pool and held out a hand, but another Fae, this one with a shadow of the dark Fae crown on her glossy dark locks, held her back. "No, Tatiana. She cannot emerge. Otherwise, she will start her time here, and she has much left to do."

I groaned and laid my head back, allowing the water to cradle me. "Why am I here, then?"

My grandmother laughed. "Always with the questions. That, my dear, is why I chose you for this task."

"We had been waiting," the others murmured. I couldn't tell how many they were since my vision was so limited. Maybe ten? Twenty?

"Waiting for...?"

My grandmother responded. "One who would be strong enough to defeat a soul-eating assassin with heart rather than magic. One who would forge her own path when all others were denied to her. One who would ally with the gargoyles and be clever enough but also have enough heart to win over the Regent. One who would go beyond the Fae compulsion of self-justification and acknowledge and make amends for her past sins."

"Yeah, great. And look where that's landed me."

Tatiana leaned over and brushed my hair away from my face like she had when I was little. "I am so proud of you, Reine.

You can never know just how much hope I placed in you. How much hope Faerie placed in you, all its queens and the powerful ancestors who are watching yet."

"And yet there are those who will be destroyed." That was Lilith's voice, and I raised my head again, trying to see, but my grandmother frowned at someone outside of my field of vision.

"It was time for you to step aside, Lilith. You refused and tried to take the Crown of All Fae for yourself. And you were punished."

I closed my eyes. "Tell me why I'm here. What I'm supposed to do."

"I cannot tell you exactly. All I can say is to remember that you are a creature of light, gray, and dark."

"A creature, huh?" I opened my eyes a crack to see if she smiled at me. She maintained her serious expression, but the corner of her mouth quirked.

"Yes, a creature. As are the gargoyles and humans and other Fae. None are above or below any others. Remember that. There's something to the expression of pride going before a fall. All advantages can be lost in a moment of carelessness."

I nodded. It was good to remember that the universe sought balance. That in the end, Fae needed it, too.

"*Statera*," I whispered. "That's Latin for balance. I'd forgotten."

"Yes." This voice had the weight of centuries of weariness. "That was our capital before the Great Rift. Before the expulsion of the gargoyles and The Aerie."

"And I'm the one to bring balance, somehow." Now I did feel the sting of grief in my heart. Did that mean I would eventually fall for Basil? I couldn't imagine.

"Somehow. Remember your journey. Your spiral."

The water sucked me under, and I reached up to my grandmother, but she was gone. I opened my eyes to see Basil, Desdemona, and Rhys bent over me.

"Welcome back," Basil said. "Where did you go? Your lips were moving."

"I'm..." The details faded like a dream, and I hoped they would return when I needed them. "I'm not sure."

"Right, then." Rhys stood and wiped his hands on his black pants. Had he been nervous for me? "Let's go. I'm not eager to be revenant food."

A constant vibration now thrummed through the palace. I couldn't tell if it constituted an improvement over the large tremors or meant something worse.

Basil helped me to my feet, and I released his hands as soon as I stood. "Yes, let's get this over with."

BASIL LED the way down to the archives so it would look like I'd agreed to Maeve's bargain. Had I made a better one with Basil? Hard to tell. I followed with Rhys behind me and Desdemona in the rear. Dark-light-light-dark, like a Fae sandwich cookie. The thought made me sad. What had Fae been before the Rift? What colors had we lost in our division? And after we reunited, would we be more than gray, or would the deeds of our past rob us of the hues we could perceive?

We arrived at the door to the archives, and Basil asked, "Ready?"

I wished I could hate him, but all I could feel was apathy and pity. My emotions had gone gray. I could feel the energies of all in the archives including Maeve and her two guards. How had I not recognized Desmond Eath as a death god? It was in his name, for goddess' sake. He'd masked his energy well.

That reminded me...

"Basil, don't let our agreement show in your aura."

"Good idea."

I opened my Fae senses further and checked to make sure

his violet aura showed no trace of my gold. It would be a pretty combination—gold and purple—a regal combo.

A pretty combo for a royally ugly agreement. I hoped Lawrence would understand, but I'd felt the backlash of betrayal before the bond disconnected.

"We'll go help outside," Rhys said. "C'mon, Desdemona."

She hesitated. I motioned for her to go. "The more people Maeve has in there as hostages, the more power she'll have. Go."

She pressed her lips together, but she nodded.

Basil and I walked in, and I didn't have to pretend to be concerned about Lawrence. He had returned to human, and his clothes hung on him in limp tatters. His breathing apparatus appeared intact, and it covered his human nose and mouth. He looked up with glassy eyes, then blinked and focused on me. The dilating of his pupils and hitch in his breath struck me like an arrow through my gut.

I forced myself not to give anything away. We couldn't signal to Maeve that we'd changed the bargain.

"We have reached acceptable terms," Basil, ever the honey-tongued Troubadour, told her.

"Under the circumstances," I grumbled with genuine unhappiness.

"Reine, I'm sorry." Lawrence's voice came out oddly distorted, but I attributed the flatness to the same emotional emptiness that filled me. "I didn't mean to trap you. Again."

"I forgive you," I blurted before I could argue with him and beg his forgiveness. Of course he would be the gentleman gargoyle and take responsibility for our predicament on himself.

"Excellent." Maeve looked me up and down, and her grin faded. "Where are the crowns? I want the crowns."

The rustling of a paper to my left tickled my awareness. Someone had found the hidden chamber, disarmed the spell, and reconstructed it as an alcove. The other half of the Breath Spell was in there! A previous archivist had probably seen it and not realized what it was but kept it because it was old.

But would changing the atmosphere of Faerie matter if I never saw Lawrence again? If he could never join me in Faerie because he knew I'd dissolved our mate bond?

Yes, because Fae after me might take gargoyle consorts. I could make their lives better by sparing them my heartbreak.

"I'll give you the crown, but I have a loose end to tie up. I know how much you hate those, and I wouldn't want to leave you with any."

Maeve shrugged. "You're right, and you did need to fulfill the last of that original bargain. Fine, tie up that last loose end."

I moved to the alcove, and a box slid a couple of inches forward on its shelf above me. I pulled it down. It opened easily, and I brought out the other half of the rolled-up spell. I removed the first half from my pocket and fit the second piece to the first. The tear in the paper healed.

If only the tear in my heart would do the same.

I opened my mouth to speak the spell, but a sudden gust of wind tore the paper from my hands.

"Oh, no you don't." Maeve held out her hand to grasp it, and I cast my own wind spell to bring it back to me. I looked at Basil, but he stood with arms crossed and a smirk on his face. I couldn't count on help from him.

Maeve and I battled with wind, and I tried to be gentle so as not to damage the paper, but she didn't take the same care. The ancient parchment flaked in midair.

"No!" I physically reached for it and jumped, but it was too late. The spell had disintegrated into dust.

A white-hot flood of anger erupted from my solar plexus, and I shouted, "Why did you do that? You didn't know what it was!"

"Oh, didn't I? What else could you have been so interested in invoking but a spell to defeat me?"

"It wasn't that at all." Frustrated tears swelled in my throat and pricked the backs of my eyes. "It wasn't that."

Kestrel let out a little moan. "It was the spell to change the air, wasn't it?"

I nodded. I couldn't even try to pretend it wasn't. If anything, Lawrence appeared even more despondent.

Maeve and Basil exchanged glances, and my heart whooshed from my chest to my feet. I rushed to block Lawrence, but one of the guards grabbed me. I tried to swipe at Basil, but without effect, and my spell bounced off the shield Maeve popped in front of him.

Basil ripped the breathing apparatus from Lawrence's face.

37

REINE

ever reveal what you can do. What we can do.

The old warning played in my head. Lawrence gasped for air and pulled back against the rings holding his wrists to the table. His skin turned gray, but not gargoyle gray. A dark mottled purple crept from his neck to his face, and his eyes bugged out.

"Uncle Lawrence!" Kestrel's cry brought me out of panic mode, and I took a deep breath.

Never reveal that Fae can manipulate all the elements, not just the ones we've been associated with.

If I did what I considered, only Lawrence would know. But that would be enough to betray the core meaning of being a Fae. And he might hate me now. What would he do? Who would he tell?

But I couldn't let him die. I couldn't be the one responsible for killing him. Basil took the first step—and that was the loophole in our bargain because if Lawrence was dead, I would have to go on without him—but me not doing anything would complete the act.

And I might be a Fae, but I'm not a killer.

I took a deep breath, and yes, I could tell that the transformation of the air in Faerie was almost complete. I could change the air in the room, but what if it made all the difference elsewhere? What if it stopped the revenants? Or at least slowed them down enough to capture them?

In that moment, I didn't care. Soul-bond or not, I loved Lawrence, and I would. Not. Let. Him. Die.

I broke free from the guard and stretched out my arms. I turned translucent, became pure spirit, expanded beyond my physical boundaries. The walls of the palace and wooden ceiling, then floor, didn't hold me. I grew through them, connecting to all the elements to my entire realm, not just the lush, fertile lands of the light Fae. I found the silly borders we'd erected, the murky fog of the Gray Zone, the stark beauty of the lands of the dark Fae. I even saw the asylum as a mirage overlaid on the former school and the library.

With a wriggle of my fingers, I found the underlying substance of Faerie. The quantum wiggle that made it different from the Earth realm, the Nightmare Realm, and the other dimensions it laid next and orthogonal to. I saw the very pattern of its matter, the fabric that had been woven and the flaw introduced to make the atmosphere impossible for gargoyles to breathe there. And that had kept the revenants trapped in their forms long enough for them to become ravenous monsters before turning back into Fae.

I pulled at that thread, the one that had been woven into the fabric with the Rift, not by any creative force, but by the one that sought to destroy, to bring everything from the largest world down to the smallest creature to its lowest level. It resisted, of course. It had been there a long, long time. Millennia. But nothing was impossible for the Queen of All Fae.

"This is my land," I told it.

It writhed like a snake, but I held it.

"These are my people."

It lashed at me, and to do so, it had to extract some of itself from the fabric. It turned gray.

"The gargoyles belong here. They are our guardians."

It pulled itself free and tried to wrap itself around my neck. I made it disintegrate into the base particles that had formed it, and the entire realm breathed a sigh of relief.

I collapsed back into myself and pulled myself up to see Lawrence take a full breath. Then another. And another.

But the chaos thread hadn't disappeared. I turned to see Maeve holding it like a snake, which she wrapped around her neck like a fuzzy gray feather boa.

"I'm not giving up, Reine. You may have healed your realm and your lover, but you still have to face me."

I stood straight and tried not to betray my trembling limbs. "Bring it, bitch."

A FLASH FILLED THE ROOM, and I found that Maeve and I had been transported to the room in the light Fae crypt with the pool in the middle. Ellerin and Sir Raleigh stood there. The grimalkin dashed to me and twined around my legs, then turned into his full, bat-winged panther form.

"That's enough, Maeve," Ellerin said.

"Nice trick, Ellerin." She crossed her arms, but the chaos energy flowed through and around her and made my skin prickle. "But I have an issue to settle with our daughter."

"Our daughter is Queen of All Fae. You tangle with her at your peril."

"Oh, do I? Or does she challenge me at hers? I know the signature of her magic, remember?" She made a "come get me" motion with her hands.

I lobbed a fireball at her to see what she would do. She didn't bother with a shield. Instead, she twisted my magic such that the fireball turned into a snake and came back at me. I had to shield myself against my own magic. Sir Raleigh hissed at her, then trilled a warning at me.

Hades, he was right. Between her knowledge of what I could do, what she'd learned from our previous battle, and the chaos magic she'd embraced—and I suspected my pulling the thread hadn't been her first exposure to it—she'd take anything I tried, corrupt it, and send it back at me. Pure power and brute force wouldn't win this one for me.

Remember all that you are.

The wise voice returned. Maeve likely expected me to fight like a light Fae, but I now had dark and gray to draw on as well. She stood on the other side of the walled pool. What could I do to surprise her?

I created a wall of water, which would absorb most of her magic since it was neutral crypt fluid. In fact, it startled me that it had responded, but then I saw the faces of Astrid, the water nymph from The Aerie, the one that guarded the border stream between the Gray Zone and light Fae lands, and the water shade from the passageway under Cruaidh. They were helping me, and I smiled.

I had one thing that Maeve lacked—true allies.

Maeve attempted to stop the water with her own magic, but it washed over her, and I used the distraction to dash around the room and behind her. She stood and glanced around, but I used my dark Fae magic to melt into the shadows. Sir Raleigh and Ellerin stood out of the way, watching. Although I had allies, they could only help so much. This was my battle.

"Reine, where are you?" Lightning crackled from her fingers. She sent bolts into random areas of the room, causing Ellerin and Sir Raleigh to duck. I stayed behind her, waiting for her to get close enough. I suspected that she'd head for a corner so I couldn't sneak up on her.

She didn't disappoint. She backed straight into me, and I

grabbed her and pulled her arms behind her back. Her wings emerged, and I had to release her arms but grabbed her neck and wrapped my legs around her waist. Her sour energy pulsed through me like a live wire, but I wouldn't let go.

"Use your. Magic again," she gasped. "I dare you."

I didn't. I pulled the silver knife I always carried from my boot and used it to slash the chaos snake away from her body. It fell into the pool and disintegrated, this time for good. But she still didn't stop.

"You don't have the guts to kill me," she sneered. "It's one thing to use magic to deal an honorable death, but Fae don't use knives. Not like humans."

She backed me into an upper crypt, and I grunted, but I didn't let go. She batted at the knife, and I slashed at her wing. She screamed, and we dropped, landing beside the pool. I tumbled away, and she righted herself and turned to me.

I struggled to my knees, but I couldn't get up yet. I'd absorbed too much chaos energy, and it tried to do to my nerves what it had done to Faerie—split them. She picked up my knife and held it to my throat.

"Thankfully one of us has the courage to finish this."

I blinked, then smiled. "Yes, one of us does." I gathered the remnants of the energy that coursed through me and chan-neled it into a repel spell. The knife spun and plunged into her chest. Blood spread across the front of her light blue frock, and dark lines spread over her skin. She staggered backward and caught herself on the edge of the pool. She didn't bother to remove the knife—my hit had been true, and she already showed signs of going into the Fae rot cycle.

"That was for Wilfrin and everyone else you've killed in your foolish quest," I told her.

She gasped, but then her lips twisted into a grimace. "And yet you will still be banished to the asylum when all is said and done. Enjoy your rule from prison."

Her words didn't affect me this time. "Better a physical prison than one around my heart. Did you even love me and Rhys? Ellerin? Or was power your one true love?"

The crypt had gone silent except for my labored breathing and the lung-rattle of her impending demise. She didn't answer, but she raised her eyes from my face to gaze beyond me. Her sneer melted for the barest of moments.

Then she disintegrated before I could turn and see what had captured her attention. For all I knew, it could have been a vision of the Crystal Throne. Or perhaps she remembered a time when she'd been happy as Crown Princess. If she ever had.

Maeve's soul hovered over the pile of dirt she had become.

Ellerin helped me stand. "I couldn't help you in your battle, but together we can banish her spirit so it will not return to cause trouble in ten thousand years."

Had she been looking at him? Had he still harbored feelings toward her? Was that why he'd mostly stayed in the background instead of coming to my aid?

It didn't matter now. I accepted his help.

"Thank you."

Her spirit held out its ethereal hands palms-up, then pressed them together. Her words floated to us. "Forgive me."

"I do," I told her although I didn't know which one of us she asked.

Ellerin added, "As do I. But I don't trust you."

"Me, neither." I turned to Ellerin. "Ready?"

We held hands, and I called upon my gray Fae power. Together, we sent her soul to an orthogonal dimension, where it would be trapped forever.

38

LAWRENCE

I thought I was dead. As it turns out, I was, but not for very long.

After Basil ripped off my breathing apparatus, my lungs filled with cement. I couldn't get part of a breath. The world went truly gray, then black.

I saw two mighty beings battling, and one ripped the other from the thread of existence, but instead of disappearing, the thread fell out of the sky and joined its ally. I don't know what happened after that, only that Maeve and Reine disappeared, and I could breathe again.

"Don't just stand there like idiots, release them!" Basil spoke to the guards, and after a moment of confusion they obeyed. I still didn't have the strength to open my eyes, but the shackles around my wrists snapped open, and I fell backward.

"Easy now..." Barton caught me and guided me to a lying position on the bench. I finally opened my eyes to see Barton, and Kestrel standing over me. Desmond, still a raven, flapped over and joined them. He squawked.

"No, you don't have to escort this one to the other side as you thought," Barton replied.

"Is that why the death god came?" My question came out as a croak.

Barton shrugged. "He thought he might be needed."

"Are you all right, Uncle Lawrence?" Kestrel blinked, and her eyes shimmered.

My tears almost came in response. "I think I will be."

"What happened?"

I rubbed my chest. As when Reine had been locked in the asylum, the point of connection felt numb, but this time, it was more. I felt its absence.

Another face joined the ones surrounding me, and with a growl, I clamped my hand around Basil's neck. Gargoyle strength surged through me, and although I didn't change, I stood and held him above me.

"Explain yourself, Fae."

He waved his hands at mine, so I dropped him. He landed on the table, and the antique wood shattered into a million dusty shards. I hoped he ended up with splinters in his ass.

"You know what?" I asked. "Never mind. You've never made your feelings for her a secret. Whatever happened, however you tricked her, I hold you responsible if something happens to her."

He staggered to his feet. I hoped he wouldn't heal his bruised neck. He deserved for other Fae to mock him. "It wasn't supposed to go like that."

"And how was it *supposed* to go?"

At least he appeared ashamed, although I couldn't tell if the shame came from getting caught or true remorse. "She made a bargain that I would be her ally against Maeve if she would give me a chance. But she needed to be over you first. I meant to give you a noble death."

"Gasping like a fish?"

"Dying as her guardian. It's not my fault you couldn't do it with style."

I reached to grab him again, but Barton and Kestrel held me back. The two guards had disappeared.

Barton explained, "You're a guardian of the Fae again. You can't kill him. It would be against your nature."

I closed my eyes and took a couple of deep breaths. "You're right. And not because I'm a guardian of the Fae, whatever that means now. I'm not a killer." I gazed straight into Basil's eyes. "I'm better than you."

"And that's why you're the one who's better suited to be her mate." Basil bowed. "I concede to your nobility. And I hope you won't hold this against me when you're her Prince Consort."

I wanted to argue with him that she might not want me, but some deep instinct, told me to wait. I knew what I'd seen. I'd witnessed a Fae battling a dark force, and the Fae had changed something fundamental about the atomic makeup of Faerie so I could breathe. Fae could do that, work beyond an elemental level? If so, they were more powerful than anyone had given them credit for.

I thought back to the times Reine had done something unexplained. She'd saved me in the halls of the CPDC, somehow pulling earth energy through dead stone and concrete. She'd saved herself from an iron chain, although she hadn't said how. Had she changed it to something not metal?

And if she'd trusted me enough to reveal that power to me... A little flame of hope ignited in my chest.

WE MADE our way out of the archives to the castle courtyard, where we expected to find the palace guards engaged in a battle against the revenants. Instead, we found the head of the guards, Darien, organizing a rescue operation. Guards handed out blankets and cups of water to confused and naked Fae.

"What happened?" Basil asked.

"The revenants turned into Fae. We're trying to figure out what to do with them," one of the ladies-in-waiting explained. "Oh!" She curtsied to Rhys and Basil. "What do you want us to do, Councilors?"

"This is going to be fun," Rhys muttered. He stood with a dark Fae I recognized as well as Lily and the Fae from the dungeon, Roshal. Desdemona and Lily didn't speak, but they kept glancing at each other. Could a reconciliation be in the works?

A rumbling preceded a paver moving aside, and Reine emerged with Ellerin and Sir Raleigh. The grimalkin had taken on his full battle shape, and he nearly knocked me over when he rubbed against me.

"Hey, big kitty," I said and rubbed him behind his ears. He poofed into his smaller form, then ran back to Reine.

She lifted her head and smiled, and I didn't need a mate bond for joy to stab me straight through my heart when her green eyes met mine.

"Hey," she said.

"Hey, yourself."

I walked to her and took her hands, and a green shimmer appeared around us.

"Are you all right?" I asked. "Did Maeve...?"

"She tried. And now she's gone. Forever. Are you okay?"

"I am. Thanks to you, I think?"

She smiled, and wistfulness tinged her tone. "I have a lot to explain."

"I'm ready to listen when you're ready to talk."

She leaned up, and our lips met. Our hunger for each other hadn't abated with the loss of the mate bond. Not for the first time, I questioned what it had meant.

Maybe it was time for a different kind of bond.

When we came up for air, I told her, "I have a question for you."

"Oh?"

She had a gray smudge across her forehead and another on one cheek. The circles under her eyes showed the strain she'd been under. And there was still that damn asylum bargain to worry about. But she'd never looked more beautiful.

I knelt on one knee in front of her. "Reine, Renee River, Queen of All Fae, would you do me the honor of becoming my wife?"

39

REINE

The clearing of a throat kept me from saying what I'd imagined I would in the tiny chance that Lawrence would be able to ask me that question. We both turned to see the head of the Fae Council, the judge who had accepted my plea bargain to serve thirty years in the asylum.

"Yes, Councilor?" I asked.

"I'm sad to interrupt such a joyous moment, especially as you've saved the realm and apparently made it safe for your Prince Consort to join you here, but there is the matter of your sentence. There's no precedent for you to be able to marry and serve your time."

Kestrel stepped forward. "I have evidence to the contrary that may help to mitigate her sentence." She reached up her shirt and pulled out a manila envelope that showed signs of being singed. She handed it to the dour Fae.

Lawrence gaped at her before stammering, "Kestrel, how did you get those?"

"One of my fishies happened to be a salamander. He rescued them before they burned, and another one hid them."

The Fae judge rifled through them and read segments. They looked like old handwritten documents.

I finally clued into what they were and what Kestrel and Lawrence were talking about. "Are those Brigadine's letters?"

"Yes," Kestrel said. "Now you won't have to go back to the asylum."

Judge Stuffypants—that's how my mind identified him—frowned. "Not so fast, young lady. While these letters do help to establish a certain element of wrongdoing on Sir Gerald Brigadine's part, there are still incidents that Queen Reine needs to atone for. These will help mitigate her sentence to, oh, ten Fae years."

Roshal stepped forward. I'd almost forgotten about him, and he looked rough. What had happened? Whatever it was, it made him appear more determined, and he'd lost the last traces of his youthful uncertainty. "With all due respect, Councilor, I would like to remind you that had Queen Reine's mother not convinced our beloved late queen Tatiana to exile her grandchildren, Queen Reine would not have engaged in the actions she did to secure her brother's healing. Consequently, I would like to argue that the fault lies with High Princess Maeve, who should be punished."

Basil joined our growing circle. "I concur with Councilor Roshal's assessment and can attest to the actions and intentions of High Princess Maeve."

The judge didn't appear to be impressed. "Very well, five Fae years."

Still too long for Lawrence to wait for me in the Earth realm, and I cursed, "Hades...wait."

Larry had told me to remember my favorite myth, which had at one point been that of Hades and Persephone. I'd always considered him to be an ass for kidnapping her, hence why I took his name in vain. I'd later met him, and he'd turned out to be a decent god, but he didn't mind. He thought my taking his name in vain was funny.

"Yes, Your Highness?"

"As I am Queen of All Fae now and have government duties that I need to be free to move around to conduct, I would like to propose a compromise, for which there *is* a precedent. I will serve my sentence one week per Fae year at the asylum, which I will revert to its original form as a school and library with a wing for Fae who need healing. Otherwise, I am free to serve my people and to marry my Prince Consort."

He paused for so long I thought he was going to say no, but finally he nodded. "That is an acceptable compromise, and you're right. King Hades and Queen Persephone have established the precedent."

"Good." The rest of the tension left my body and I leaned into Lawrence's strong embrace. "The answer to your question is yes."

He picked me up and twirled me around, and we kissed. Our embrace held the promise of more, and I couldn't wait to get somewhere private where we could enjoy each other's company without restriction and worry about being separated. Plus, we'd have the fun of re-establishing our mate bond. This time when it kicked in, it would come with full knowledge, permission, and welcome.

Because even a Fae could end her own fairy tale with her own version of...

And they lived happily ever after.

EPILOGUE

Lawrence

The director shouted, "Three, two..." He mouthed, "one," and the light on top of the center camera turned red.

Hazel Archwork smiled straight into it and said, "Welcome back. I'm thrilled to have that long awaited interview with Fae Queen Reine and King Consort Lawrence Gordon." She turned to us, and Reine squeezed my hand. I hadn't wanted to do the interview, but Minerva had convinced me I'd promised and I couldn't go back on it, even though it had taken months.

"Thank you. We're happy to be here," I replied.

"Well, it's been quite a ride, you two, and we have a lot to talk about. But first, the question that everyone in The Aerie is asking—how is Uncle Augie settling in at the palace in Lorien?"

Reine laughed. "He's doing well and is a comfort to many of our risen Fae, who remember him from his service during their era."

Uncle Augie had taken the change in stride when The Aerie had been transported back into Faerie. There had been some confusion about how to manage commerce and the integration of gargoyles back into the Fae realm, but overall, it had gone as smoothly as possible with Augie's help. His centuries of listening to other paranormal creatures had paid off in surprising ways, and he'd stepped up and served as an ambassador and cultural translator for other gargoyles who had taken a while to catch on.

Hazel asked a few more questions, but she kept them neutral and not too gossipy. Minerva had told me that our appearance needed to comfort the gargoyles who were still adjusting from being ripped from the Earth realm into Faerie and remind them that we—and my mother—were remaking our lives, too.

The Aerie's location transfer and the Great Rising had kept me and Reine busy, but we always found time to spend the evenings together. There was just one loose end...

We arrived back at our Aerie house, which I'd built near Minerva and Karen's place. It gave us privacy and some distance from the guards stationed around it. We walked into the kitchen to find a letter on the island addressed to me.

Dear Uncle Lawrence,

You and Reine offered me any reward for saving the letters, and I've made my decision. After talking with Lily and Professor Grand-Pied, I've decided not to join the Normals, but to try to live like one, at least until I finish college. I'm in therapy with a paranormal-friendly psychologist, and I need time to figure out who I am and who I truly want to be. I feel I would best do that if I could be left alone for a while. I'll be in touch occasionally, but please don't reach out unless there's an emergency.

Thank you for understanding.

Sincerely,
Kestrel Graves

I HANDED the letter to Reine to read. I couldn't speak. It was too hard for me to imagine not being part of Kestrel's life, but after all the trauma she'd been through, I could also understand. She'd told me she wanted time to figure things out when she moved to Athens, and then she'd gotten dragged into this adventure.

Reine looked up when she finished reading. "Don't worry. I can still make sure we know what's happening with her."

"I don't want to spy on her."

Reine kissed me on the cheek. "It's not spying. It's occasional checks. You can decide how often."

"I'd rather respect her wishes. As hard as that will be."

"Very well."

Reine walked into my arms, and I closed my eyes and inhaled her scent, of fresh air and earth and water and fire... All the elements plus her own indescribable spirited Fae aroma. She'd told me about Fae being able to change elements from one to the other, and I'd sworn to keep her secret without her asking me to. I was honored by her trust, and I returned it.

Sir Raleigh, meanwhile, had decided which side of himself to embrace. He trotted in from the back yard and deposited a pixie on the kitchen floor.

"Raleigh!" Reine went to check on the little winged humanoid creature. It gave her a dazed look. "How many times do I have to tell you to leave the poor pixies alone?" She scooped it up and brought it outside.

I shook my head and chuckled. My heart ached for Kestrel, but I knew she could take care of herself. Plus, Lily and Grand-Pied would look after her. As for me and Reine, we had our domestic life and our royal life and our friendship life and our sex life...

The look Reine gave me upon returning from outside told me which I'd be experiencing next.

"Well, Doctor Gordon, how should we kill time before Ellerin and your mom come for dinner?"

"I don't know, Queen of All Fae Reine, did you have anything in mind?"

She leaned up, nipped my ear lobe, and whispered, "Let me show you." Then she took me by the hand.

I gladly followed. Who says a gargoyle can't have a happily ever after, too?

FROM THE AUTHOR

Thank you for reading *Risen Shadows*! I hope you enjoyed it.

While this is the final book in Reine and Lawrence's story, there will be other books in this universe with these characters including Kestrel, Lily, Rhys, and others.

Do you want to know when new Fae Files books are underway and get access to special behind-the scenes info and previews? Join the Fae Team VIP newsletter (https://www.subscribepage.com/faefilesnews), and I'll send you the story of Reine and Rhys' exile from Faerie.

Also, reviews help me know what you liked about my books and help other readers find them. Please help me write more of what you love by leaving a review at the site where you bought the book. Thank you!

WHAT TO READ NEXT…

Oh, no! You've reached the end of the series. Thank you so much, and I hope you enjoyed reading it as much as I loved writing it.

IF YOU WANT the background on Gabriel, Lonna, Max, and Selene and to see where Reine originally waltzed into my brain and my books, check out the Lycanthropy Files. They start with Book One, The Wolf's Shadow. Snag your copy from your favorite retailer or read on to find out more.

IF YOU'RE curious about the Truth Seekers, which were mentioned a few times, read the Dream Weavers & Truth Seekers series. That one starts with book one, Tangled Dreams. Grab it from your favorite retailer or read on for more info.

. . .

NOTE: You can find all my books, help me out, and support your local bookstores by purchasing paperback books from my Bookshop.org store:

https://bookshop.org/shop/ABCDbooks

ABOUT THE WOLF'S SHADOW

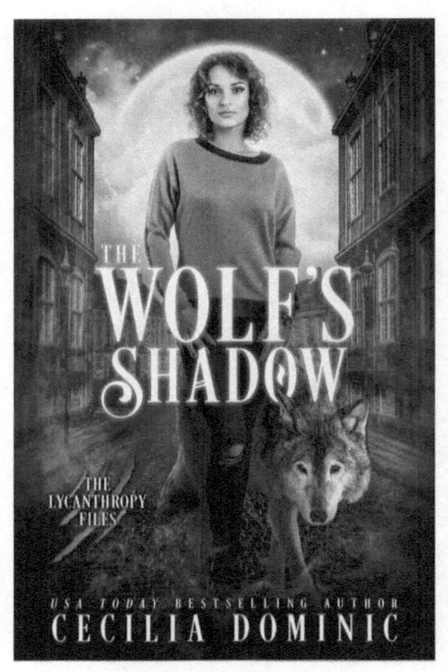

L*ife as she knew it is over. At the next full moon, the real trouble begins...*

. . .

EPIDEMIOLOGIST JOANIE FISHER can't catch a break. After her lab burns to the ground, her boss simultaneously fires her and ends their affair. And though she's inherited her grandfather's multimillion-dollar estate, Joanie's shocked to discover the property comes infested with werewolves.

Confronted by a ruggedly handsome shifter who begs her to continue her cutting edge research into the wolves' physical changes, Joanie unearths a sinister conspiracy that puts her own life in danger. And as she pushes hard to find the cure, shadowy figures will do anything to make sure she never develops a treatment... including resorting to murder.

Can Joanie end the wolfish disease before she's next on a killer's list?

THE WOLF'S Shadow is the first book in the pulse-pounding Lycanthropy Files urban fantasy series. If you like strong female characters, insidious cabals, and medical thriller-style storytelling, then you'll love Cecilia Dominic's hair-raising genre mashup.

Buy *The Wolf's Shadow* to claw your way to the truth today.

DON'T FORGET, you can find all my books, help me out, and support your local bookstores by purchasing paperback books from my Bookshop.org store. Go to:

https://bookshop.org/shop/ABCDbooks

ABOUT TANGLED DREAMS

S leeping magic awakened. Ancient deities shattering myths. Can one independent woman survive the games of gods?

. . .

Audrey Sonoma is bored out of her skull. And though she relishes the autonomy of her freelance career reviewing restaurants, she craves a spicier existence. But when the crazy purple dragon in her dreams spills into reality, she's stunned to discover she's endowed with supernatural power... and tasked with saving a goddess.

Teaming up with a cute cop, Audrey struggles to fend off the beasts and demons spewing out from a paranormal disaster. And as nightmares threaten to consume the world, she's desperate to control her abilities before the deadly whims of Greek immortals claim her life and her only shot at love.

Can she master her mythical gifts and stop the mischievous creatures from destroying the waking realm?

Tangled Dreams is the exhilarating first tale in the Dream Weavers & Truth Seekers urban fantasy series. If you like fiery heroines, explosive chemistry, and revamped legends, then you'll adore Cecilia Dominic's otherworldly adventure.

Buy *Tangled Dreams* to banish the night terrors today!

Don't forget, you can find all my books, help me out, and support your local bookstores by purchasing paperback books from my Bookshop.org store. Just go to:

https://bookshop.org/shop/ABCDbooks

ABOUT THE AUTHOR

By day, clinical psychologist Cecilia Dominic helps people cure their insomnia. By night, this USA Today bestselling urban fantasy and steampunk author writes fiction that keeps her readers turning pages past bedtime. She prefers the term "versatile" to "conflicted" and has published both short story and novel-length fiction. She lives in Atlanta, Georgia, with her husband and the world's cutest cat.

ceciliadominic.com

Sign up for Cecilia's newsletter and get your copy of Perchance to Dream, a story that's only available to newsletter subscribers, at the following link:
https://www.subscribepage.com/CeciliaDominicbackofbook

If you'd like to get exclusive bonus scenes for The Fae Files, sign up for the Fae Team, the VIP list specifically for lovers of Reine and her world(s). Go to:
https://www.subscribepage.com/faefilesnews

I hate spam and promise to keep your email safe!

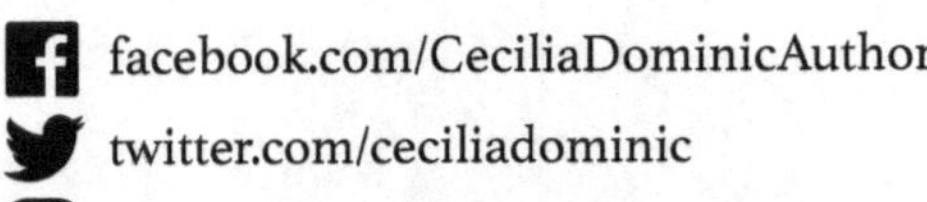

facebook.com/CeciliaDominicAuthor
twitter.com/ceciliadominic
instagram.com/randomoenophile

LOOK FOR THESE TITLES BY CECILIA DOMINIC:

Urban Fantasy Series:

The Lycanthropy Files
The Wolf's Shadow
Long Shadows
Blood's Shadow
A Million Shadows

The Fae Files
The Shadow Project
Shadows of the Heart
The Shadowed Path
Shadows of the Sky
Shadows of the Past
Risen Shadows

Dream Weavers & Truth Seekers
Perchance to Dream
Truth Seeker
Tangled Dreams